Dear Readers,

I hate saying goodbye.

My college boyfriend and I stayed together for ten years; he's now the godfather to my children. In a perfect world, all the people whom I have loved would have a permanent place in my life. Since I generally adore my characters, I feel the same about them. After finishing *The Ugly Duchess*, I couldn't bear the idea that Griffin, my hero's closest friend, didn't have a happy ending of his own.

So I wrote "Seduced by a Pirate," bringing Sir Griffin Barry home after fourteen years to meet the wife whom he scarcely knew. I do hope you love the story of how Griffin falls in love, not only with Poppy, but with the three children he finds in his household when he walks through the door!

When I finished "Seduced by a Pirate," I still wasn't ready to say goodbye. Griffin and James were such great friends, spending every Christmas together . . . surely their children would fall in love? I began writing "With This Kiss," thinking that it would be a brief novella, but I fell in love with these two characters and couldn't let them go.

The twinned stories before you bring closure to the world of pirates that sprang to life when James Ryburn, Earl of Islay and heir to the Duke of Ashbrook, ran away to sea. I hope my characters become as dear to you as they are to me.

With all best wishes,

By Eloisa James

Eloisa James

As You Wish

**Includes WITH THIS KISS and
SEDUCED BY A PIRATE**

AVON
An Imprint of HarperCollinsPublishers

"With This Kiss: Part One" was originally published as an e-book novella in March 2013 by Avon Impulse, an Imprint of HarperCollins Publishers.

"With This Kiss: Part Two" was originally published as an e-book novella in March 2013 by Avon Impulse, an Imprint of HarperCollins Publishers.

"With This Kiss: Part Three" was originally published as an e-book novella in April 2013 by Avon Impulse, an Imprint of HarperCollins Publishers.

"Seduced by a Pirate" was originally published as an e-book novella in November 2012 by Avon Impulse, an Imprint of HarperCollins Publishers.

Excerpt from *Once Upon a Tower* copyright © 2013 by Eloisa James.

AVON BOOKS
An Imprint of HarperCollins*Publishers*
10 East 53rd Street
New York, New York 10022–5299

ISBN 978-0-06-227696-4
www.avonromance.com

First Avon Books mass market printing: April 2013

Avon Trademark Reg. U.S. Pat. Off. and in Other Countries, Marca Registrada, Hecho en U.S.A.
HarperCollins® is a registered trademark of HarperCollins Publishers.

Printed in the U.S.A.

10 9 8 7 6 5 4 3 2 1

Contents

Seduced by a Pirate

One

May 30, 1816
45 Berkeley Square
The London residence of the Duke of Ashbrook

As a boy, Sir Griffin Barry, sole heir to Viscount Moncrieff, had no interest in the history of civilized England. He had dreamed of Britain's past, when men were warriors and Vikings ruled the shores, fancying himself at the helm of a longboat, ferociously tattooed like an ancient Scottish warrior.

At eighteen he was a pirate, and at twenty-two he captained his own ship, the *Flying Poppy*. By a few years later, just a glimpse of a black flag emblazoned with a blood-red flower would make a hardened seaman quiver with fear.

No one knew that Griffin's ship was named for his wife, whose name was Poppy. He had even tattooed a small blue poppy high on one cheekbone in her honor, although he had known her for only one day—and never consummated the marriage.

Yet he always felt a certain satisfaction in that trifling sign of respect. Over the years, Griffin had forged his own code of honor. He never shot a man in the back, never walked anyone down the plank, and never offered violence to a woman. What's more, he sacked any of his crew who thought that the *Flying Poppy*'s fearsome reputation gave them the liberty to indulge their worst inclinations.

Though to be sure, the royal pardon recently issued for himself and his cousin James, the Duke of Ashbrook, described them as privateers, not pirates.

Griffin knew the distinction was slight. It was true that in the last seven years he and James had limited themselves to attacking only pirate and slave ships, never legitimate merchant vessels.

But it was equally true that he was, and had been, a pirate. And now that he was back in England he wasn't going to pretend that he'd been fiddling around the globe in a powdered wig, dancing reels in foreign ballrooms.

On the other hand, he was damn sure that the wife he scarcely remembered wouldn't be happy to find out that she was married to a pirate. Or even to a privateer.

However you looked at it, he was a sorry excuse for a gentleman, with a limp and a tattoo and fourteen hard years at sea under his belt. Not exactly the respectable baronet to whom her father had betrothed her.

He didn't relish the idea of strolling into a house somewhere around Bath—he wasn't even sure where—and announcing that he was Lady Barry's long-lost husband. An involuntary stream of curses came from his lips at the very thought. He even felt something akin to fear, an emotion he managed to avoid in the fiercest of sea battles.

Of course, he and James had entered those battles together, shoulder to shoulder. That was undoubtedly why he blurted out an unconscionably ungentlemanly offer, one that would horrify his father.

"Want a bet on which of us gets his wife to bed faster?"

James didn't look particularly shocked, but he pointed out the obvious: "*Not* the action of gentlemen."

Griffin's response was, perhaps, a little sharp for that very reason. "It's too late to claim that particular status," he said to James. "You can play the duke all you like, but a gentleman? No. You're no gentleman."

From the grin playing around James's mouth, it seemed likely he was going to accept the bet. It was hard to say which of them faced the biggest battle. Griffin couldn't remember his wife's face, but at least he'd supported her financially in his absence. James's wife had been on the verge of declaring him seven years missing, and therefore dead.

"If I accept your bet, you'll have to take yourself off to Bath and actually talk to your wife," James observed.

Talk to her? Griffin didn't have much interest in talking to Poppy.

He had left a lovely young woman behind. Due to various circumstances beyond his control—which he didn't like thinking about to this day—he had left her a virgin. Unsatisfied.

Untouched.

No, he didn't want to *talk* to his wife.

It was time to go home, obviously. It would be easier if he hadn't taken a knife wound to the leg. But to come home a cripple . . .

After James left, Griffin walked around the bedchamber once more, trying to stretch his leg, then paused at a window looking over the small garden behind James's town house. The alley was full of gawking men, journalists who had caught wind of the news that the returned duke was a pirate. They'd probably be out there for the next week, baying like hounds at a glimpse of James or his poor wife.

Griffin's man, Shark, entered the room as he turned from the window. "Pack our bags, Shark. We need to escape the menagerie surrounding this house. Has rabble congregated at the front as well?"

"Yes," Shark replied, moving over to the wardrobe. "The butler says it's a fair mob out there. We should bolt before they break down the door."

"They won't do that."

"You never know," Shark said, a huge grin making the tattoo under his right eye crinkle. "Apparently London is riveted by the idea of a pirate duke. Hasn't been such excitement since the czar paid a visit to the king, according to the butler."

Griffin's response was heartfelt, and blasphemous.

"The household's all in a frenzy because they don't know whether the duchess will leave the duke or not." Shark shook his head. "Powerful shock for a lady, to find herself married to a pirate. By all accounts, she thought he was five fathoms deep and gone forever. She fainted dead away at the sight of him, that's what they're saying downstairs. I wouldn't be surprised if your wife does the same. Or maybe she'll just bar the door. After all, you've been gone longer than the duke has."

"Shut your trap," Griffin growled. "Get someone to help you with the bags and we'll be out the door in five minutes." He grabbed his cane and started for the hallway, only to pause and deal his thigh a resounding whack. For some reason, slamming the muscles with a fist seemed to loosen them, so that walking was easier.

Not easy, but easier.

"Yer doing the right thing," Shark said irrepressibly. "Run off to yer missus and tell her yerself before she finds out the worst in the papers."

"Summon the carriage," Griffin said, ignoring Shark's nonsense. That was the trouble with turning a sailor into a manservant. Shark didn't have the proper attitude.

A moment later, he was pausing on the threshold of the library. Over the years, he and James had been entertained several times by no less than the King of Sicily, but even so, Griffin was impressed by the room's grandeur. It resembled rooms at Versailles, painted with delicate blue and white designs, heavy silk hanging at every window.

Unfortunately, James didn't suit the decor. He sat at his desk, sleeves rolled up, no coat or neck cloth in evidence. Like Griffin, he was bronzed from the sun, his body powerful and large, his face tattooed.

"This is remarkably elegant," Griffin observed, wandering into the room. "I've ruined you, that's clear. I never saw a man who looked less like a nobleman. You're not living up to all this ducal elegance."

James snorted, not glancing up from the page he was writing. "I've just had word that the pardons will be delivered tomorrow."

"Send mine after me," Griffin said, leaning on his cane. "I have to find my wife before she reads about my occupation in the papers. In order to win our bet, you understand," he went on to say. He truly felt a bit ashamed of the wager he and James had placed; one ought not place bets regarding one's wife.

James rose and came around from behind his desk. Griffin hadn't paid attention to his cousin's appearance in years, but there was no getting around the fact that the tight pantaloons he wore now weren't the same as the rough breeches they had worn aboard ship. You could make out every muscle on James's leg, and he had the limbs of a dockworker.

"Remember the first time I saw you?" Griffin asked, pointing his cane in James's direction. "You had a wig plopped sideways on your head, and an embroidered coat thrown on any which way. You were skinny as a reed, barely out of your nappies. Most ship captains looked terrified when my men poured over the rail, but you looked eager."

James laughed. "I was so bloody grateful when I realized the pirate ship following us was manned by my own flesh and blood."

"How in the hell are you ever going to fit in among the *ton*?"

"What, you don't think they'll like my tattoo?" James laughed again, as fearless now as when he first faced Griffin and his horde of pirates. "I'll just point to Viscount Moncrieff if anyone looks at me askance. Maybe between the two of us we'll start a fashion."

"My father's still alive," Griffin said, wondering whether he should go through the trouble of collapsing into a chair. It was damnably hard to get upright again. "I'm no viscount," he added.

"His lordship won't live forever. Someday we'll find ourselves old, gray, and tattooed, battling it out in the House of Lords over a corn bill."

Griffin uttered a blasphemy and turned toward the door. If his cousin wanted to pretend that it was going to be easy to return to civilization, let him revel. The days of being each other's right hand, boon companion, blood brother, were over.

"Coz." James spoke from just behind him, having moved with that uncanny silent grace that served him so well during skirmishes at sea. "When will I see you again?"

Griffin shrugged. "Could be next week. I'm not sure my wife will let me in the front door. Yours has already declared she's leaving. We might both be busy finding new housing, not to mention new spouses."

James grinned. "Feeling daunted, are you? The captain of the *Flying Poppy*, the scourge of the seven seas, fearful of a wife he barely knows?"

"Funny how *I* was the captain on the seas," Griffin said, ignoring him, "but now you're the duke and I'm a mere baronet."

"Rubbish. I was the captain of the *Poppy Two*, by far the better vessel. You were always my subordinate."

Griffin gave him a thump on the back, and a little silence fell. Male friendship was such an odd thing. They followed each other into danger because bravado doubled with company: side by side, recklessness squared. Now . . .

"Her Grace will presumably be coming down for dinner soon," Griffin said, looking his cousin up and down. "You should dress like a duke. Put on that coat you had made in Paris. Surprise her. You look like a savage."

"I hate—"

Griffin cut him off. "Doesn't matter. Ladies don't like the unkempt look. Shark has been chatting with the household. Did you know that your wife is famous throughout London and Paris for her elegance?"

"That doesn't surprise me. She always had a mania for that sort of thing."

"Stands to reason Her Grace won't want to see you looking like a shiftless gardener at the dining table. Though why I'm giving you advice, I don't know. I stand to lose—what do I stand to lose? We made the bet, but we never established the forfeit."

James's jaw set. "We shouldn't have done it." Their eyes met, acknowledging the fact that they were easing from blood brothers to something else. From men whose deepest allegiance was to each other to men who owed their wives something. Not everything, perhaps, given the years that had passed, but dignity, at least. A modicum of loyalty.

"Too late now," Griffin said, feeling a bit more cheerful now that he knew James felt the same twinge of shame. "Frankly, I doubt either of us will win. English ladies don't want anything to do with pirates. We'll never get them in bed."

"I shouldn't have agreed to it."

"Damned if you don't look a proper duke with your mouth all pursed up like that. Well, there it stands. The last huzzah of our piratical, vulgar selves. You can't back out of it now."

James growled.

Shark poked his head in the library door. "We're all packed, milord."

"I'm off," Griffin said. "Good luck and all that."

For a moment they just looked at each other: two men who'd come home to a place where they didn't belong and likely would never fit in.

"Christmas?" James asked, his eyebrow cocked. "In the country."

Griffin thought that over. Spending Christmas at the seat of the duchy would mean acknowledging that James was like a brother. They'd find themselves telling stories about times they had nearly died protecting each other, rather than putting it all behind them and pretending the last years were some sort of dream.

James moved his shoulder, a twitch more eloquent than a shrug. "I'd like to know there's something pleasant in my future."

The duke didn't want to be a duke. Griffin didn't want to be a baronet, let alone a viscount, so they were paired in that.

"It's as if Jason—or the Minotaur, for that matter—returned home," Griffin remarked. "I've got this bum leg, you sound like gravel on the bottom of a wheel, and no one will know what to make of us."

James snorted. "Actually, that makes us Odysseus: didn't Homer have it that no one recognized Odysseus but the family dog? I don't give a damn what anyone makes of us. Christmas?" he repeated.

If Griffin said yes, he would be declaring himself a duke's intimate friend, going to a house party for the holiday, acknowledging a closeness to power that his father had always lusted after.

He had thought becoming a pirate was the ultimate way to thwart his father's ambitions.

It seemed fate had something else in mind.

"I wish you weren't a duke," he said, to fill the silence as much as anything.

"So do I." James's eyes were clear. Honest.

"Very well, Christmas," Griffin said, giving in to the inevitable. "Likely you'll still be trying to bed your wife, so I can give you a hint or two."

A rough embrace, and he walked out without another word, because there wasn't need for one.

Now he merely had to face his family: His father. His wife.

Wife.

Two

June 2, 1816
Arbor House
Near Bath

"You're married to a *pirate*?"

Phoebe Eleanor Barry, wife to Sir Griffin Barry, pirate, nearly smiled at the shocked expression on her friend Amelia Howell-Barth's face. But not quite. Not given the sharp pinch she felt in the general area of her chest. "His lordship has been engaged in that occupation for years, as I understand it."

"A pirate. A real, live pirate?" Amelia's teacup froze halfway to her mouth. "That's so romantic!"

Phoebe had rejected that notion long ago. "Pirates walk people down the plank." She put her own teacup down so sharply that it clattered against the saucer.

Her friend's eyes rounded, and tea sloshed on the tablecloth as she set her cup down. "The *plank*? Your husband really—"

"By all accounts, pirates regularly send people to the briny deep, not to mention plundering jewels and the like."

Amelia swallowed, and Phoebe could tell that she was rapidly rethinking the romantic aspects of having a pirate within the immediate family. Amelia was a dear little matron, with a rosebud mouth and brown fly-away curls. Mr. Howell-Barth was an eminent goldsmith in Bath and likely wouldn't permit Amelia to pay any more visits once he learned how Sir Griffin was amusing himself abroad.

"Mind you," Phoebe added, "we haven't spoken in years, but that is my understanding. His man of business offers me patent untruths."

"Such as?"

"The last time I saw him, he told me that Sir Griffin was exporting timber from the Americas."

Amelia brightened. "Perhaps he is! Mr. Howell-Barth told me just this morning that men shipping lumber from Canada are making a fortune. Why on earth do you think your husband is a pirate, if he hasn't told you so himself?"

"Several years ago he wrote his father, who took it on himself to inform me. I gather Sir Griffin is considered quite fearsome on the high seas."

"Goodness me, Phoebe. I thought your husband simply chose to live abroad."

"Well, he does choose it. Can you imagine the scandal if I had informed people that I was married to a pirate? I think the viscount rather expected that his son would die at sea."

"I suppose it could be worse," Amelia offered.

"How could it possibly be worse?"

"You could be married to a highwayman."

"Is there a significant difference?" Phoebe shrugged inelegantly. "Either way, I am married to a criminal who stands to be hanged. Hanged, Amelia. Or thrown into prison."

"His father will never allow that. You know how powerful the viscount is, Phoebe. There's talk that Lord Moncrieff might be awarded an earldom."

"Not after it is revealed that his son is a pirate."

"But Sir Griffin is a baronet in his own right! They don't hang people with titles."

"Yes, they do."

"Actually, I think they behead them."

Phoebe shuddered. "That's a terrible fate."

"Why is your husband a baronet if his father is a viscount and still living?" Amelia asked, knitting her brow. Being a goldsmith's wife, she had never been schooled in the intricacies of this sort of thing.

"It's a courtesy title," Phoebe explained. "Viscount Moncrieff inherited the title of baronet as well as that of viscount, so his heir claims the title of baronet during the current viscount's life."

Amelia digested that. Then, "Mrs. Crimp would be mad with glee if she found out."

"She *will* be mad with glee," Phoebe said, nausea returning.

"What do you mean?"

"He's back," Phoebe said helplessly. "Oh, Amelia, he's back in England." She handed over the *Morning Chronicle*, pointing to a notice at the bottom of the page.

"In England? Without informing you? And you've had no contact with him since—"

"Since the night we married, in '02," Phoebe said. "Fourteen years ago. And now he's back in England, without a word of warning."

"I know you've been living apart for years, but surely he will pay you a visit immediately," Amelia said, reading the short piece.

"Quite likely they'll throw him in prison before he has the chance," Phoebe replied. Her daughter Margaret ran by them, curls dancing about her shoulders. She'd lost her ribbon again.

"Did you tell him about the children?" Amelia asked, looking up from the paper.

"What was I supposed to do? Write him a letter addressed 'in care of the South Seas'? I suppose I could have informed his man of business, but to be quite honest, I never thought he'd come home! Amelia, *what am I going to do?*"

"He can hardly complain about the children. He's a pirate, for goodness' sake. He hasn't a leg to stand on. — Oh! Do you suppose that he has a peg leg? I've heard of that. Or an eye patch?"

"What a revolting idea." A shudder went straight through to Phoebe's toes at the thought.

Amelia bit her lip and put down the newspaper. "Seriously, Phoebe, you're facing a terrible predicament."

"I know it."

"So your husband left England the night of your wedding . . ."

Phoebe nodded.

"And now he's coming home to three children!"

Three

June 3
Arbor House

Phoebe's youngest, Alastair, ran past her, his shriek coming in a long stream like shrill bird-song.

"Behave yourself, Master Alastair," Nanny McGillycuddy shouted. "He's losing his nappy again. Where is that dratted girl? I swear she spends the better part of her time daydreaming. Lyddie!" she bellowed, waving across the lawn to where a young nursemaid lounged in the shade of a willow.

Satisfied that the girl was rising, albeit reluctantly, to her feet, Nanny turned back to Phoebe. "What will you tell people about this muddle?" Since the death of Phoebe's mother, her old nanny had become her only real confidante.

"I don't want to tell anyone anything."

"You'll have to. And you'll have to deal with him as well." Nanny put down her teacup and surged to her feet. "Drat that child; Alastair is in the lake again." She turned back to Phoebe. "Whatever happened on your wedding night, you'll have to put it out of your mind, child. If he seeks you out, that is. He's your husband, more's the pity."

Phoebe hesitated, the truth trembling on her tongue. But she bit it back, and besides, Nanny was already trundling toward the lake.

Griffin had been so horrified when . . . when *that* had happened. She had been braced for the searing pain her mother had described, ready to get it over with and count herself a properly married woman.

Then, when there had been nothing whatsoever to get over . . .

She had never blamed him for jumping out the window. At first, she had thought he would return in the morning. But he hadn't. It wasn't until the end of the week that she'd finally confessed the truth to her family: her husband had deserted her.

It was beyond humiliating, especially when they'd concluded that he must have boarded a ship and left England altogether. Her father hadn't made things any better. "I paid for that churlish blue blood fair and square," he had said between clenched teeth. "Paid up front for the privilege of making my daughter into Lady Barry."

"I am still Lady Barry whether Sir Griffin is at my side or not," Phoebe had hastened to say.

Her mother had taken a much more cheerful attitude. "She's better off without that young sprig," she had said. "He's too young by half, and I told you so at the time. He'll be off to see a bit of the world and then find his way back home again. You'll see."

As for the wedding night fiasco, her mother was of the opinion that Phoebe was lucky, and that was that.

The problem was that Griffin never did make his way home again.

For a long time—years!—Phoebe fretted about the possibility, especially after a man named Mr. Pettigrew paid her a visit, announced that he was her husband's agent, and deposited a large sum of money in a household account for her.

Then, after the fire in which she had lost both her parents and one of her sisters . . . well, after that she stopped thinking about Griffin altogether. It was hard enough just to get through the day.

When the mourning period was finally over, the children came along.

Her husband had been just about her height, she thought, with no sign that he would grow much taller. They had snuffed all but two candles on her wedding night, but even so she had realized that he was nervy, and then horrified when his tool wouldn't do its business.

Over the years since, she'd heard quite a few stories of men in the same situation. In fact, just last week Mrs. Crimp had told her of the baker. His wife had driven all the way to Pensford in order to ask the apothecary a private question, but she'd had the bad luck to be overheard by Mrs. Crimp's oldest granddaughter.

Phoebe had just shrugged. She didn't care about *that*, especially now she had children of her own. She would welcome an incapable husband. At least he wouldn't be bothering her when she was tired or out of sorts.

Mrs. Crimp had said the problem was near to an epidemic. And if that was the case, well then, Griffin probably felt better by now, knowing that his friends were in the same boat.

But it was one thing to be thinking all these thoughts over the years, and it was quite another to imagine her husband walking through the front door.

She had forged such a comfortable life, with friends like Amelia, whom he would probably look down on. No one in her close circle was from the gentry, let alone the aristocracy.

What if Sir Griffin wanted to rub shoulders with Bath's polite society? Or worse, pay a visit to London for the season? The very idea gave her a feeling of profound disquiet.

Yet surely she was worrying in vain. How could a nobleman-turned-pirate possibly reenter polite society?

Just as it had throughout the sleepless night, her mind bounced back and forth between terrifying possibilities.

Nanny had plucked Alastair from the lake and was wringing out his little nankeen coat. It was so peaceful at Arbor House. Beyond the river she could see men mowing grass and, in the far distance, a faint haze that suggested it might rain later on.

A man of violence had no place here. Griffin would likely recognize that in one glance.

She was worrying about nothing.

Four

Griffin kept telling himself that he wouldn't recognize his own wife. There was something swashbuckling about that notion, he thought, something that took the edge off the way he felt.

Not that he could put into words precisely how he felt, other than that his stomach got this rocky only in the most choppy of seas.

By the time his hired carriage trundled up the rather long road that led to his house—a house he'd never seen but had apparently acquired eight years ago—and finally stopped, he would have described himself as irritable.

Pirates didn't have nerves, damn it.

Out of the carriage, he adjusted the ruffled linen at his wrists. He had dressed particularly magnificently, in a coat of Prussian blue with silver buttons. His breeches fit like a glove, and his boots were made by Hoby.

Inasmuch as he had to limp in the door, he reckoned he might as well look as good as possible doing it.

It seemed he owned a comfortable, sprawling mansion, which stood on a small hill looking over Somerset countryside. Its mellow brick had weathered to a rosy orange. In the distance he could see fruit orchards and fields spreading out to the sides. It was a working farm, then, not a nobleman's estate. It was large and imposing, but not extravagantly so.

As unlike the house he'd grown up in—the country estate of a viscount fiercely aware of his place in the hierarchy of the peerage—as could be imagined.

This was a house designed for a family, though of course that was not the case.

Maybe Poppy had brought her family to live with her? He vaguely recollected that she had a great number of siblings. Merchants generally had many children.

Shark came around the carriage, holding Griffin's cane. "Would you like me to summon the butler so he can have you carried in on a litter?"

Griffin glanced at him. "Stuff it, Shark."

Didn't it say it all that Griffin couldn't make it to his own bloody front door without a cane? For all his was mahogany topped with a dull ruby, and hid in its innards a vicious blade, in the end it was an old man's stick.

Pride goeth before a fall, he thought, hobbling toward the front door. And damn it, he *had* been proud. He'd racketed around the world, collecting pirate's booty and investing it. Rather surprisingly, money made money. It turned out that timber made money, as did spice, and birdcages, and whatever else he and James felt like picking up and shipping to a different part of the world.

But then a pirate had slit his cousin's throat and almost killed him, and the same man had slashed Griffin's thigh. And James had realized he was still in love with his wife, and decided to return to England. There was no such realization in store for Griffin, since he had known his wife for precisely one day. But he did know that a pirate with a game leg is a soon-to-be-dead pirate, which was just as important an insight.

He'd come home because he couldn't think of another bloody thing to do. He had travelled the world. He had made a fortune eight or nine times over. Nothing left but waiting for the grave, he thought grimly.

As he stumped his way to the bottom of the steps, the front door swung open. Griffin straightened, expecting a butler to materialize, but the shadowy entryway appeared to be empty.

He glanced at Shark with a raised eyebrow. Shark fit into the sleepy green landscape around them about as well as a mastiff at a tea party.

"Best not go in," he said now. "Might be an ambush."

Griffin snorted and hauled himself up the steps. If his leg didn't improve, he'd probably find him-

self killing people just to relieve his own irrita-
tion.

The entryway was deserted. It was large and
gracious, with a marble staircase that curved
gently up and then to the left. Not bad, he thought.
But where on earth were the servants?

A noise came from somewhere behind them,
just a scrabble. They hadn't been retired from the
sea long enough to dull their reflexes; Shark drew
his dagger in one smooth movement, swinging
about to put his back against the wall. Griffin
flung the door shut, poised to unsheathe the blade
concealed in his cane.

A small boy had been crouching behind that
door. A boy clutching a wooden sword and wearing an eye patch.

After fourteen years at sea, Griffin knew a pirate
when he saw one. This one's visible eye was wide,
and his chest rose and fell with gusty breaths.

Griffin hadn't been around children much
. . . ever. He stood staring down at the boy for
a moment before he snapped, "For God's sake,
Shark, put your blade away."

The boy couldn't be more than five or six, and
he was clearly scared out of his wits. But his lips
firmed and he pushed himself to his feet. His
knees were scabbed and smeared with dirt, but
he was obviously well-born.

"Mama won't want you here," he said, just as
Griffin was trying to figure out whether he should
say *Ahoy, mate*.

"But we're pirates," Griffin said, suppressing a grin. "She must like them, since she has you."

Cautiously, the boy slid an inch or two to his right, obviously planning to make a run for it.

Griffin jerked his head at Shark, who stepped back. But the child didn't move any further. He was a brave little thing.

"Where's your butler?" Griffin asked.

"We haven't got one," the boy replied. "We don't need one, because no one comes to call except our friends." His eyes narrowed a bit. "You aren't friends, so you shouldn't be here."

There must be some mistake, Griffin thought. Was the address his agent had given him incorrect? Though that was hard to understand; he could see the card in his mind's eye: *Arbor House, Somerset*.

"Is this Arbor House?" he asked.

"No, it isn't!" the boy shouted, and then he ran full tilt, disappearing through a door at the back of the entry.

"We've made a mistake with the address," Griffin said, somewhat relieved. "The child's mother can give us proper direction so we can find—"

He broke off. Shark was regarding him with a distinct trace of pity in his eyes.

Griffin's next words were unrepeatable.

"I was sitting on the box, you see," Shark said. "I seen the sign, clear as can be. It said Arbor House."

Griffin felt as if someone had given him a kick in the stomach. It seemed . . .

"It's not as if you kept yourself pure as a lily," Shark said, interrupting that thought.

"Keep to your place, for God's sake," Griffin said with a scowl.

Shark shook his head. "You was having a fine time; she's got the same right."

"I don't see it that way," Griffin said tightly.

"Yer title doesn't give you the right to be an ass."

Griffin shot him a look, and Shark finally shut up. Griffin had allowed his men wide latitude—but in the end he, and he alone, was captain.

He limped across the entry and pushed open the nearest door, discovering an empty sitting room. It was rather lovely, hung with watered silk and a painting of the Thames that was as beautiful as any he'd seen.

But there were also piles of books, and a group of soft chairs before the fireplace where a chessboard lay waiting to be used. Someone had tossed embroidery to the side, and a piece of knitting had fallen to the floor.

Even more telling, a toy ship lay on its side, surrounded by a scatter of tin soldiers. The ship was flying a tiny Jolly Roger.

His wife had moved on.

"She can't have married someone else," he muttered, half to himself. "I would know. Pettigrew would have told me. She'd have to have declared me dead."

"No sign of a man," Shark said from his right shoulder. "The little one and herself, I'd guess.

No pipe. No brandy." He nodded toward the side table. "That's sherry."

"Don't spit," Griffin said. "Spitting is not allowed in a gentleman's house."

"I wasn't going to spit," Shark said, offended. He'd spent the last two months soaking up all the information he could from a sailor who had once worked in a noble residence. "I'm just saying that yer missus has got a child, but she don't—doesn't—have a man."

"Or she hasn't brought him into the house," Griffin said, through clenched teeth.

He backed into the hall again. The next two doors opened, respectively, into a dining room and a small, very feminine sitting room.

The fourth door—the one the boy had fled through—opened, unexpectedly, into a courtyard shaped by two backward-extending wings of the house. It was charming, paved in uneven bricks, with a couple of trees providing shade. On the far side he could see a broad lawn spreading down to a lake.

"There he goes," Shark said, laughter rolling in his voice.

A small figure was tearing down the hill, his legs pumping. At the water's edge, there was a flutter of white skirts and a parasol.

Griffin stepped forward into the courtyard but immediately realized he couldn't walk to the lake. By the time he reached the bottom of that hill, he'd be sweating and shaking. His leg was already throbbing, thanks to the steps leading to the front door.

"You can sit over there," Shark said, jerking his head toward a table with a crowd of serviceable chairs. It stood to the side of the courtyard under the shade of a spreading oak tree. Griffin sank into a chair with a sigh of relief.

For some time, nothing happened.

They sat and listened to birds singing. At sea, the ship was accompanied by seagulls' wild shrieks. By comparison, these birds sang Mozart arias, speaking to each other in trills and tremolos, performing elaborate courtship dances on the branches over their heads.

Minutes passed. Apparently, Poppy had paid no heed to the boy, who by now must have told her that pirates had taken over the house. You could hardly blame her for ignoring his nonsense. Yet it wasn't safe to have a house open like this, a house without, as far as he could see, any male servants. What if robbers stopped by? Marauders?

After a while he couldn't take it any longer. "See if she's coming," he growled at Shark. "And if she isn't, step down the hill and ask her if she would be so kind as to greet her husband."

Shark walked over and looked toward the lake. "She's coming up the hill," he said. Then: "You never mentioned your missus was such an eyeful."

Griffin narrowed his eyes, and Shark shut his mouth, retreating to a chair.

He should probably send the man off to the servants' quarters, except there didn't seem to be any servants. And Shark would undoubtedly send the cook into hysterics if he strolled in without introduction. The saber scar on his chin lent him a particularly ferocious air.

Griffin sighed and pounded his aching thigh again. Shark had no need to remind him that Poppy was beautiful. Her face was pretty much the only thing he remembered about their wedding night. There he had been, all of seventeen years old and skinny as a twig, whereas she had been an older woman of twenty: exquisite, shapely, utterly beautiful. Terrifying.

The outcome was hardly unexpected.

He'd left a virgin wife behind, though it appeared she hadn't stayed that way. The wave of anger he felt was unfair to her, and he knew it. A man couldn't leave for fourteen years and expect his wife to remain faithful.

Though wasn't Penelope faithful to Odysseus?

Odysseus probably satisfied his wife before he took off for war. Likely gave her some children. Griffin had read Homer's tale so long ago that he couldn't quite remember.

Still, he had never imagined that his wife might take those unconsummated wedding vows as lightly as he himself had. That she might have a child. A son. A boy who would inherit his title and be viscount someday.

He'd stayed at sea for years precisely because he loathed his father's obsession with titles, nobility, standing, et cetera. He couldn't start caring about that claptrap now.

Where the hell was the boy's father? The pirate was a smart, scrappy little fellow who likely hadn't been told he was a bastard. He would learn that later, in school.

Actually, he wouldn't, because the pirate wasn't illegitimate. He was born within the bounds of marriage; in fact, he stood to inherit a viscountcy. Griffin's mouth tightened.

A smaller version of himself in more ways than one.

"You'd better not swear like that in front of yer wife," Shark observed. "She won't like it."

Five

$\mathcal{L}$yddie brightened up, screamed, and very nearly fainted when Colin ran down the hill and gasped out the news that there were two men in the front entry, and one of them had skin with pictures drawn on it. Actually, he thought they both did. And one had a cane.

"A cane!" Margaret cried, jumping up and down. "It's a pirate with a peg leg! Let's go!" She and Colin were obsessed by pirates, which Phoebe, who had never breathed a word to her children about Sir Griffin's profession, had thought a rather humorous coincidence. It didn't seem so amusing now.

Nanny McGillycuddy grabbed Margaret's arm just in time. "No, you will not," she said, in the tone of voice that none of the children—nor indeed Phoebe—ever disobeyed. "Your mother shall speak to the gentlemen by herself."

"You'd better get up there, Mama," Colin cried. "These men are big. Big! So big."

"How big?" Margaret asked, sounding cheerfully interested rather than dismayed. That was Margaret. She would ask questions of a highwayman demanding her money.

Phoebe rose and collected her parasol. She didn't want to go up to the house. With every particle of her being, she didn't want to climb that hill.

"Huge!" Colin answered. "They could have eaten me up. Though I had my sword, of course. They would have eaten *you*," he said to his little brother. Alastair gave a shriek and hid behind Phoebe's skirts.

"Colin," Phoebe said sharply, "you are not being helpful. There are no cannibals in England."

"These men aren't like everybody else! What's more, they can't be from England, because no one has drawings on their skin here. So they might be cannibals."

Phoebe knew that she was white as chalk. But as her mother used to say, what could not be avoided must be faced. She had made it through her parents' and sister's funeral, and she could make it through this.

"Children, stay with Nanny."

"Mama, you shouldn't go," Alastair whispered, hanging onto her skirts. "They might be bad. Bad men."

"I told you that we needed a butler," Nanny put in unhelpfully. "I'd best come along."

The words of the *Morning Chronicle* were seared

in Phoebe's memory, and she knew precisely who was waiting for her at the house. "Absolutely not, Nanny. Please remain here and make sure Alastair doesn't wade back into the lake. You may join us in . . ." How long did it take to greet a husband one didn't know? Ten minutes?

And after that greeting was dispensed with, how long should one wait before informing him that he had three children?

"Fifteen minutes," she decided. "Please bring the children to the house in a quarter of an hour." With that instruction, she headed reluctantly toward the house.

Her temples were throbbing.

What if he rejected her children?

She would leave him, of course. Thanks to her father's careful stewardship, the estate was thriving, her jointure along with it. She could more than afford to scoop up the children and buy a house. Her mind reeled. What was she thinking?

This was *her* house. If he rejected the children, she would order him to leave.

She paused at the top of the hill to allow her breathing to return to normal before she walked through the courtyard and into the house. She was making too much of it. After all, she remembered Griffin clearly. He had been thin, small, and rather shy. Even in the scant light of just two candles, she remembered how red his face had turned.

Men didn't change. Everyone knew that. She merely had to be polite but firm. He would leave again. A criminal would not be allowed to stay in the British Isles, no matter how powerful his father.

Thankfully, the resulting scandal would have no effect on her life. The thought was steadying. There was a time, just after her marriage, when her father-in-law had urged her to become part of his circle. Humiliated by her husband's desertion, she had declined.

Now, years later, she was deeply grateful not to be involved in the petty meanness that engaged so-called "polite society."

She shook out her skirts, took a final deep breath, and moved toward the house. Halfway through the courtyard something made her stop. She pivoted on her heel.

They were seated under the tree. Two of them. *Pirates.*

One of them wore an earring, and both had strange designs on their faces. They were huge, just as Colin had claimed. Big, muscled men who sprawled in her chairs like . . . like nothing she'd seen before. One of them rose at the sight of her. He was immense, his shoulders broad as an ox, and his face bronzed. He looked at her with unnervingly steady eyes as she walked closer; something about his gaze sent an errant wave of heat up into her cheeks.

But at the same time, she realized, with a sense of relief that made her feel positively dizzy, that neither man was her husband. Neither resembled him in the least. It stood to reason that Griffin would have grown a bit more, since he was only seventeen when he bolted, but he would still have brown hair and a wiry build. These men must be his emissaries.

"Gentlemen," she said, summoning a smile as she came to a halt before them. "I am so sorry that no one was here to greet you. I expect that you are acquaintances of my husband, Sir Griffin Barry."

They were both on their feet now, but a moment of silence ensued while they stared at her. Despite herself, her smile slipped. They were so large, and in appearance so non-English. Perhaps they didn't speak the language?

"*Bonjour*," she said tentatively, silently cursing the fact that she had always been too bored to pay attention during French lessons.

"Poppy?" the big one asked. He had dark blond hair, cut very short, and skin the color of honey. Not to mention the decoration under his eye. He was terrifying.

Poppy? She didn't quite know what to make of that. "I'm afraid we haven't any poppies here, but that can't be what you mean?" She tried to look at him again, but her eyes skittered away.

He was so *male*. She wasn't used to being near people like him. In fact, she couldn't think of a single Englishman, other than the blacksmith, who had that air of fierce masculinity.

They continued to stare at her silently. It was really quite irritating. Then Phoebe noticed that the man who had spoken was wearing a coat that was far too elegant for a mere servant.

She folded her hands in front of her and summoned the patience she'd developed raising three small children. "Gentlemen? Do you work for my husband, Sir Griffin Barry?"

The blond man cleared his throat. "We are—we do know your husband." He shifted his weight, and she saw he was leaning on a cane. It was hard to reconcile this infirmity with the muscled brute he appeared to be, but of course there was no way that strength could compensate for a partially missing limb.

"Please," she said quickly, "do sit down. I know it must be very difficult to manage your balance."

He looked at her through absurdly long lashes. Really, if he weren't so monstrously large, he would be attractive, the way laborers sometimes were.

For a moment she thought he hadn't understood her, but at last he sank back into his seat.

His associate backed against the wall and remained there. One hardly noticed a footman standing at the ready, but this fellow had a distinct air of menace, evoked by the fearsome scar across his chin. The hairs on the back of her neck prickled at the very idea of such a man under her roof.

Once Sir Griffin arrived, she would have words with him about sending such a pair of reprobates to greet her, even though it was considerate of him to send advance notice. She truly appreciated that.

"Please tell me what I can do for you," she said, spacing the words slowly. "I understand that Sir

Griffin Barry has returned to the country." She hesitated and then plunged in. "Are you here to inform me of his imminent arrival?"

"Something like that," he replied. His voice was deep and lovely, like water on stones. "Do you suppose the boy would like to join us?" He nodded behind her.

She turned and saw the tip of Colin's sword poking out from behind the bricks. "Colin Barry, I told you to stay with Nanny," she scolded.

The blond man stared at Colin with his brows furrowed. She did not allow people to scowl at her children, and she gave him a look that told him to stop it, *this minute.*

Really, the man seemed a bit thick. Naturally, Colin hadn't paid her the slightest mind; he was edging toward them for all the world as if she might not notice his disobedience.

"Is this your son?" the man asked. 'Twas an impertinent question from a total stranger, unless perhaps he was a foreigner—yet he sounded English.

"He is indeed," she said, putting some severity into her tone. "I am disappointed to say that he is quite naughty."

"Ah, but he's a pirate," the man said. "Pirates *are* naughty."

Phoebe took another deep breath. "Should I assume, sir, that you speak from experience?"

"Retired," he said solemnly.

Colin was at her side now. "I'm not retired," he said, his voice coming out in a near bellow. "I'm going to spend my life sailing the seven seas."

"How old are you?" the man asked.

Colin pushed out his chest. "Five and a half. Almost six, really."

Phoebe wrapped an arm around him and kissed his hair. "He turned five a couple of weeks ago."

"I should like to speak to your mother alone for a few minutes," the man said.

Colin obeyed him instantly and moved to the far end of the courtyard; given his usual disinclination to listen to whatever *she* had to say, this was profoundly vexing.

Still, it probably showed an instinct for self-preservation that she was glad to see in her child.

The servant stepped away from the wall. "Perhaps the young master and I could stroll down to the lake," he suggested.

Phoebe gave him a searching look. His nose had been broken at some point, and his face was marred by a flower design near his eye, not to mention the scar. A single sentence was all she had to hear to know he'd grown up in the East End of London.

But she'd made it her business to stop judging people by superficialities like accent and appearance. There was kindness in his eyes, almost as if he were laughing inside. "What is your name?" she asked.

The blond man planted his cane to stand, but she touched his sleeve lightly. "Please, sir, do not bestir yourself."

She turned back to the servant and held out her hand as her mother had taught her to do. "Ladies curtsy," her mother had said. "Women of worth and value shake hands. Without gloves. And even with servants, upon meeting them for the first time."

The pirate's hand enveloped hers, and his eyes crinkled as he smiled at her. "Lady Barry," he said, "my name is Sharkton, though I am usually called Shark."

"Shark!" Colin cried with delight from across the courtyard.

Shark grinned over at him. "Aye, it's a pirate's name, my lad."

The other man had risen, despite what she said. "Take Colin down to the lake, Shark," he said. Although his voice was mild, a strand of tension shot through Phoebe: she was suddenly edgily aware that she was about to be left alone with him.

She walked across to her son, bent down, and tapped his nose. "Now remember, you're the host. What would your guest like to see?"

"Not Lyddie," Colin said. "She might faint." He trotted over, reached up for Shark's hand, and led him away.

Phoebe turned back, feeling strangely unsettled. The blond man was still standing; she gave him a cool smile and held out her hand. "I am Lady Barry," she said, pulling out of thin air the title that she never used. But there were times when it was wise to stand on precedence, and this was one of them.

"Lady Barry," he said. He leaned his cane against the table and took her hand in his, but he did not shake it. Or kiss it. He wasn't of the gentry, then, for all the magnificence of his coat.

His hand was even bigger than Shark's. She could feel calluses on his fingertips, and saw a white scar that snaked across the back of his hand.

In that instant, she was struck by a realization so unnerving that she felt quite unsteady.

She withdrew her hand and sank into a chair, her eyes fixed on his. Blue eyes. Terribly blue. She remembered those eyes, but they had belonged to a different man.

"You were *short*," she whispered, disbelief paralyzing her.

"Not any longer."

There was a moment of silence as they stared at each other.

Then: "Sir Griffin Barry at your service. — Your husband," he added, when she didn't say a single word.

She couldn't.

Six

Griffin was in the grip of a feeling so overwhelming that he didn't have a name for it. He was looking at his *wife*.

The word hadn't meant anything to him for years. Nor had it meant anything to her, apparently, given that he had just met his heir.

Anger burned in his chest at the idea that another man had touched his wife. Still, during all those long years abroad, he hadn't sired any children because he knew the ins and outs of a French letter. Poppy almost certainly didn't. And he couldn't say that he left her satisfied. So . . .

"Colin's father," he began, and despite himself his voice emerged from his chest like the slam of a hammer on metal. "Where is he?"

For the last decade men had jumped when he'd raised his voice. But the lovely woman seated before him? She didn't even twitch. "He is dead," she said, after a moment had stretched to an eternity.

"Do you have other children?" He could have choked on the question. He'd been so careful with his seed, and all the time his wife was . . . well.

"Two," she replied, her eyes direct and unafraid.

Damn, but she *was* a pirate's bride. There wasn't even the smallest flare of shame in her eyes. Not even a twinge.

"You must have thought that I was never coming back."

"You gave me no reason to believe otherwise. In the first decade of our marriage I asked your Mr. Pettigrew on occasion, but I must admit that I stopped asking."

That was fair. Logical.

"You were gone. And I gather you were engaged in piracy, a pursuit from which I believe few men return. It appears you were successful, given the large amounts that Mr. Pettigrew deposited into the household account."

There wasn't a shade of blame in her tone. His wife was outrageously pretty, with hair like bright butter. But she had a backbone of steel.

"I've been a privateer for the past seven years," he said. "My ship flew the flag of the Kingdom of Sicily, and we sank pirate ships rather than the other way around."

"I'm afraid I don't know the difference."

"Privateers are sanctioned by a government to attack pirates, thereby keeping the shipping lanes safe. We also made it a practice to attack slave ships and free the captives."

"So you didn't walk people down the plank?"

He shook his head. "Never. Even my first ship, after I was kidnapped, never—"

"You were kidnapped?" He'd finally said something that shook her from that unsettlingly calm demeanor. "Stolen? Forced onto a ship?"

"You didn't think that I *meant* to leave England?"

She had. It was hard to believe that porcelain skin could grow paler, but hers did. A flash of sorrow crossed her eyes. For him?

"I was seventeen," he said. "Short, as you said, and not very good at handling myself. And I was drunk for the first time in my life. I was an easy target for a press gang. We sailed for the West Indies just before dawn on the morning after you and I wed."

"Drunk? You mean, after you left . . ."

Damned if it wasn't still embarrassing all these years later. "After the failure of our wedding night," he said, his voice wry, "I went to a public house and proceeded to drink myself into a stupor. From which I awoke to find myself at sea."

"We never knew that," she whispered. "I thought you deserted me."

He considered accepting her implicit apology, but he had decided long ago that the only way to thrive was by ruthless honesty. "I might have run away if I had thought of it. I got too drunk for anything so coherent."

"We never imagined that you'd been kidnapped, or we surely would have searched further. My father . . . we thought you couldn't bear the shame of marriage to a commoner."

"Is your father still alive?"

She shook her head. "He died seven years ago."

That made sense; she had waited until her father died to take a lover. For some reason, he found that detail gut-wrenching. Perhaps he should have come home sooner.

"Where are the other children?" he asked, forcing the words out.

"Are you angry?" she asked, ignoring his question. "Many men would be furious to come home after a long absence to find three new additions to the family."

"I don't have the right," he said, knowing his voice was tight.

"Did you father children?"

"No!" The word shot out, unexpectedly violent.

But she didn't startle. Instead he saw a disconcerting level of sympathy in her eyes, and she leaned forward and covered his hand with her own. "I want you to know," she said gently, "that your affliction is not unique. You must have realized that during your travels around the world."

Her words were probably characteristic of her, Griffin thought. She was both kind and restrained, with admirable dignity.

Then he caught her meaning. She thought he was incapable. Not merely of fathering a child, but altogether.

"Is that why you had children of your own, Poppy?" Despite himself, the words came out through clenched teeth.

That earned him a steely-eyed glare. "What are you talking about?"

"The fact you have illegitimate children?" he shot back.

"No, no," she said, her hand waving as if her children meant nothing. "Why do you persist in calling me Poppy?"

"Because it's your—it's not your name?"

"Of course it's not my name." She wrinkled her nose. "And I don't like it."

"You don't like it?" He was dumbfounded. He had named his ship after her, after the wife he left behind. The *Flying Poppy* and then the *Poppy Two* were dreaded by pirates all over the world.

"My given name," she stated, chin high, eyes flashing, "is Phoebe."

He cleared his throat. "Lovely." He must have misheard during the wedding ceremony. Bloody hell.

"Exactly what are you doing here, Griffin?" The faintest hint of smugness told him that she was pleased that she knew his name.

"I've come home," he stated simply. For all the complications—that Phoebe believed he was impotent, that she had given birth to three children in his absence, and that he hadn't remembered the name of his own wife—there was something that felt right about her nonetheless. About being here, with her.

"This is *my* home," she said.

"But you are *my* wife." He gave her a smile, enjoying the way her luscious pink lips pursed. She was a bit stiff, this wife of his. He'd have to teach her to take life more easily.

"I'd rather not." She said it as simply as if she were declining a cup of tea.

"Rather not what?"

"Rather not be married to you. I'm sure our marriage can easily be annulled on the grounds of non-consummation. Or we could petition Parliament for a divorce based on your profession."

"Or on the grounds of your three children!"

She blinked. He'd touched a nerve, but how could she be surprised? Surely she was a pariah among the neighbors. "Yes," she said, almost too quickly. "There are the children. If we divorce, you can have children of your own."

" 'Children of my own'? Did you not just offer condolences for my incapability?"

After a moment she said, with dignity, "I gather from your evident amusement that your problem was due to youth rather than constitution."

"Or," he suggested, "the problem might crop up only in your presence."

Her brows drew together. "What do you mean by that?"

"You're too beautiful," he said, starting to enjoy himself. "It may well be that you'll incapacitate me again. There's only one way to find out."

"Such an experiment would be most unwelcome," she flashed back. "If you, sir, have such worries, it would be better not to put yourself in a difficult situation."

He leaned forward, ignoring the pain that shot through his thigh. Up close, her skin was like silk, untouched by the sun, the soft color of new cream. "A man could never turn down a challenge of that sort, darling Phoebe."

"I am *not* your darling Phoebe!"

"My darling, my wife?"

Seven

$\mathcal{P}$hoebe stared at her husband, trying to think of an appropriately mature response, when Nanny McGillycuddy, Mr. Sharkton, and the children topped the little hill, Lyddie drifting behind them like a kite on a string.

Her mind was such a whirl that she said nothing even when they entered the courtyard. Her husband believed the children were illegitimate. He hadn't known her name. He thought she was some sort of lightskirt, a jade who would . . . would . . .

She hated him.

"Please forgive me for not rising to meet you," Griffin said to Alastair. "I've injured my leg. I have met Colin, but what's your name?"

"Alastair." Her three-year-old stood squarely on his spindly legs, gazing at the pirate as if he met men of his cut every day . . . which he did not. They scarcely had a male servant other than two young men who worked in the house when they weren't in the garden. And the bootblack, of course.

"Do you call yourself Dare for short?" Griffin inquired.

Alastair frowned. "That's a silly name. My name is Alastair because that's the name my mama gave me."

"Alastair is an ancient and respected name," Phoebe said, throwing Griffin a cold look.

She'd already figured out that her husband wasn't the sort of man who could be silenced by a glance.

"Alastair sounds a bit silly, isn't it? But Dare sounds like a fellow who can climb into a tree house. Have you?"

"Have I what?" Alastair asked suspiciously.

"Built a house in a tree. Or even climbed up a tree? That's a perfect tree for a house," Griffin said, pointing to an ancient oak on the other side of the courtyard.

"He hasn't," Margaret said, elbowing Alastair aside. "But *I* have."

Her curls were wild and disordered, and she wore only one stocking. The other was wound around her head and tied in the back.

"Oh, Margaret," Phoebe groaned. "Why are you attired in such an outlandish fashion? You were fairly tidy an hour ago."

Margaret fixed her gaze on Griffin and didn't bother to glance at her mother. "I'm a pirate

queen," she said stoutly. "This is what they wear."
There was a moment of silence. "Well, you're a
pirate," she demanded. "You should know. Don't
they wear this? It's called a turban."

Griffin was in the grip of one of the oddest feelings of his life. There the three of them were, lined
up before him: Colin, the stubby but fierce pirate;
Margaret, the pirate queen; and Alastair, the wet
one. They were all rather grubby. But they were
his now. Born under the protection of his name
and title. His children.

"I have been a pirate," he said. "But I'm home
now, and I cannot remember what pirate queens
wear on their heads."

Margaret reached out with a slender finger and
poked his tattoo. "You're not supposed to write on
yourself."

"That's right," he confirmed.

"Did you kill anyone?" Colin asked.

"Yes."

"Good!"

Griffin shook his head. "No, not good."

"Pirates *always* kill people. Walk 'em down the
plank!" Colin clearly had a bloodthirsty side.

"Not the action of a gentleman," Griffin said,
"and that's the most important rule of all. More
important than being a pirate. Kill only in self-
defense, only if a man has taken up a weapon
against you. No innocents, no women, no children."

Colin narrowed his eyes, thinking about it.

"Where's your sword?" Griffin said, turning to

Margaret. "A pirate queen should have a sword, it seems to me."

"We only have one, and Colin has it on Mondays. I don't get it until Wednesday."

"Sir Griffin," Phoebe interjected, "may I introduce you to the children's nannies?" She sounded rather desperate, as well she might. He didn't remember his governess teaching him the rules for introducing one's by-blows to one's long-lost spouse.

He came to his feet, swallowing a curse as his cane slipped and he lost balance for a moment.

"Mrs. McGillycuddy was my own dear nanny," Phoebe said, giving him a narrow-eyed look that suggested she'd overheard the blasphemy he'd swallowed.

At least now he knew where Alastair had inherited his critical gaze.

The nanny had hair that presumably had once been red but was now a faded pink. She had a big bosom and a big behind; all in all, she looked nanny-ish to Griffin's uneducated eyes. His own nanny had been tall as a tree and mean to boot. Nanny McGillycuddy didn't look mean at all.

"And this is our nursemaid, Lyddie," Phoebe added, nodding to a young girl, who dropped into a rather flustered curtsy.

"Well, my lord," Nanny McGillycuddy said in a tone that made it clear she was more than a servant, though not quite the mistress of the house, "should we take your appearance as a sign that you have abandoned a life of crime?"

"Nanny!" Phoebe cried in an anguished voice.

But Griffin liked Nanny. She hadn't challenged him out of impudence, but because she was saying what needed to be said.

He answered in kind. "I have been given a full pardon by the Crown, and I intend to live a life of impeachable sobriety in the bosom of my wife and our family."

There was a Napoleonic air about the way Nanny snorted in response to that statement. Griffin had met Napoleon once, and he'd never forgotten the way the Corsican bared his teeth when he'd spoken. Apparently Nanny didn't think a pirate was suited for the sober English life.

That made two of them.

"Well, now that we've all met," Phoebe chirped, sounding positively feverish, "why don't we have tea?"

"We've had tea," Colin told her. "And so have you, Mama."

Griffin looked at his wife. It was a strange thing to discover that she was still utterly beautiful, like coming across a discarded plate and turning it over to find out that it was made of solid silver. Her cheeks were pink with embarrassment, or perhaps anger, and she had the most exquisite skin he'd seen in his entire life.

In retrospect, he had always minimized the role of her beauty in his disastrous wedding night, blaming his failures on youthful ineptitude and nerves. But damn . . . she was exquisite. Enchanting.

More than any woman he'd seen in all his travels.

"His lordship has not had tea," Phoebe stated, a bit desperately.

He took pity on her. "Nanny McGillycuddy," he said, "take these piratical rapscallions off to the nursery, will you? My wife and I have to catch up on fourteen years' worth of conversation."

The nanny gave him a hard look that said without words that he'd better not make her mistress unhappy, then bustled the children away, the nursemaid trailing after them.

"I'll go to the kitchens and see about tea," Shark said, patently eager to escape a round of marital conversation.

"Why no servants?" Griffin asked after Shark disappeared. "No butler, no footmen? We weren't even greeted by a housekeeper."

"She must have been busy. I do employ a few manservants, but they're occupied in the fields or the gardens at this time of day. I don't keep a butler, because mine isn't that sort of household."

"*That* sort of household?" he repeated, raising an eyebrow.

"A gentry household," she clarified. "I don't use my title, and I don't aspire to re-create that atmosphere."

"Isn't life easier with servants?" he asked, genuinely curious.

"A butler who merely stands about and answers the door for a random visitor? Footmen whose only role is to polish the silver?"

He shrugged. It wasn't something he gave a damn about either way. He himself ran a tight ship, every man assigned to four or five tasks. Noblemen like his father liked to have a passel of servants standing around merely to demonstrate consequence.

Clearly her mind went in the same direction. "Your father will be anxious to see you. Doubtless he saw the same notice in the paper that I did. I am sure that he is waiting on tenterhooks for your arrival."

"I'm not capable of playing the prodigal son. No regret, for one thing."

"You sound as if the subject of piracy amuses you. I do not know your father well, but I assure you that he sees nothing amusing in your occupation."

Griffin shrugged. "We have never shared interests. At sea one soon realizes that titles and precedence don't matter to a dying man."

"I don't suppose they do. But there is a great deal to be said for a fortune that is not built on theft."

"All fortunes are built on theft of one sort or another."

Phoebe didn't seem to be the twitchy sort, but he had clearly made her nervous. She kept clasping and unclasping her hands. "We must talk," she said finally.

"We are talking," he said, just to be contrary.

The anger in her eyes woke her up and made her look less like a saint and more like a flesh-and-blood woman.

"Actually," he drawled, "I think we should be doing more than talking."

Her brows drew together.

"We are married," he prompted.

"I know that."

"Yet our marriage was not consummated."

She rolled her eyes. "I was there. I remember. And the answer is no."

Lord, there was something wildly freeing about being in company with a woman who hadn't the slightest awareness of his fearsome reputation.

"You can't blame a man for the sins of his youth," he said piously.

"That's got nothing to do with it."

"Does your refusal have anything to do with the children's father?"

"No!"

The relief he felt was well out of proportion to the situation. But it would have been damned awkward to return after fourteen years and find one's wife grieving for a dead lover. "Well, then, we'd better get about the business with expedience," he said cheerfully.

"Sir Griffin," his wife said, leaning toward him. Her eyes were dark blue, eyes a man could drown in. "You have not been away from England so long that you've forgotten your English. I do not want to consummate this marriage because I do not want to be *in* this marriage!"

Just in case he didn't understand, she got up and took herself into the house without another word.

After a minute, a capable-looking housekeeper

appeared, introduced herself, and escorted him to the master's bedchamber.

It showed no signs of use. How long had that fellow been dead? Or perhaps she never brought him to the house.

It was all very interesting.

Eight

$\mathcal{P}$hoebe fell into her bedchamber and leaned back against the closed door, her heart galloping. In a wilderness of Sundays, she never would have imagined something like this.

Griffin had changed so much. Not even a shadow of the shy boy she'd married remained. This man had an air of danger about him that made her feel like a rabbit in sight of a wolf: frozen, enticed.

When her father had first suggested the match with the future Viscount Moncrieff, Phoebe hadn't demurred. She had always known that her father would find husbands from the nobility for herself and her sisters. He had the money, and he wanted the bloodlines.

Her primary feeling had been gratitude that he had chosen someone who wasn't sixty, even though she would have preferred someone a bit older than herself, or at least her age. By the time the young baronet was finally old enough to marry, she had just celebrated her twentieth birthday, and felt sophisticated and worldly in comparison. She had been taller than her fiancé, and certainly weighed more.

But now, fourteen years later, their positions were reversed. He had become a man of the world, a man whose shoulders were twice the size of hers. And she was a country partridge who lived at home with her three children.

This was a disaster.

There had to be some way out of the marriage. There just had to be. He thought she was a loose woman. The idea sickened her. But what if she let him continue in that misapprehension? Surely he would not allow a love child to become the future viscount.

A sob rose in her chest. Her life, her sweet life with her darling children . . . That man did not fit in here. Whatever would her friends think? Her neighbors? Even if they didn't discover that he had been a privateer, he was marked under the eye like a New World savage.

Common sense told her that someone would inform him that she had adopted the children, so infidelity would never work as a reason to dissolve the marriage.

Tears caused by pure frustration fell onto her hands and slipped between her fingers.

In a way, it was worse that he was so handsome, with such a male appeal. Even his tattoo wasn't entirely uninviting. And there was something sensual and possessive in the way he looked at her. An unwilling flicker of heat lit in her stomach, followed by a churn of nausea.

The door burst open. "Shark says he will take us to the sea," Colin cried, running into the room. "The sea, the sea, the sea!"

Phoebe surged to her feet, her maternal instinct sweeping all her other feelings to the side. How *dare* Mr. Sharkton say something of that nature to her child? Lure him into a dangerous, bloody career—indeed, if it could even be dignified with that title?

"Colin Barry," she said in a voice that he had rarely heard, "return to the nursery."

Colin gaped up at her.

"Now!"

He turned around and trotted away as fast as his legs would carry him.

She had instructed Mrs. Hastie, her housekeeper, to put Griffin in the largest bedchamber. Luckily, she had never occupied it herself, but had taken the airy bedchamber closest to the nursery.

Now she marched straight toward Griffin's room, her tears dried by pure rage.

She would fall dead before she allowed her son to be lured by a couple of felons to death at sea. She threw open the door without knocking. "I must speak with you."

Her husband was at the window, staring down at the lake and the fields beyond. He turned around slowly, leaning on his cane.

For a second she just stared, as if seeing him

for the first time. Griffin was so much bigger, so much more *manly* than she could have imagined. Paradoxically, the fact that he was wounded didn't diminish his ferocity; instead she had the feeling that she was looking at a wounded lion nursing his paw, but ready to spring at any moment.

As dangerous as he ever was.

Even his dark blond hair lent itself to that vision. Although it was cut short, it sprang from his scalp like a shorn mane. She was stricken by an edgy awareness that sent a flush of heat to her face, but she straightened her backbone.

She had to protect her children.

"Hello, Phoebe," Griffin said, as if she barged into his bedchamber every day. "May I offer you a seat?" He took two steps toward the fireplace, leading with his stick, and pulled forward one of the armchairs.

Phoebe sat, since it would be impolite not to. "I came to inform you that my son will *never* go to sea, and it is reprehensible and irresponsible of Mr. Sharkton to discuss the possibility with him."

Griffin leaned against the back of the chair opposite her and raised an eyebrow. "Mothers make rules, but children don't always agree."

"Colin may be entranced by the idea of piracy now—and I regret to say that your arrival will only exacerbate that—but in time he will outgrow it."

"What would you like him to do with his life?"

"Something safe," she flashed. "Something in England, perhaps in Bath."

"So you see him as a merchant?"

Of course she saw Colin as a member of her own class, rather than one of the gentry or above, whom she privately considered to be ne'er-do-wells. "Yes," she said, keeping her gaze steady. "I would much prefer that Colin earn an honest wage, whether he owns a business or works in one."

To her surprise, Griffin nodded. He must have seen a flicker of disbelief on her face, because he added, quite reasonably, "You may not like the way I have earned a living, Phoebe, but I assure you that I worked very hard for it. I know the value of money."

She didn't want to think of him in a positive light. "We must discuss how we will dissolve this marriage," she said, setting aside the topic of child-rearing for the larger one. "I think it will be a relatively simple matter, since it was never consummated. I know there are provisions for that sort of thing."

His eyes darkened, and Phoebe instinctively straightened. Griffin's blue eyes were like a summer sky: they told her a storm was coming. "You truly want to dissolve our marriage?" Not a trace of anger colored his voice, and his expression hadn't changed. But . . .

"You needn't be angry about it," she said, meeting his eyes squarely.

"I am not angry."

"You are lying to me, and I most dislike false-hoods. I would judge you furious, and without merit, I might add. I am not the one who absented myself from the country for years."

"I apologize. You are correct. I do not wish to dissolve our marriage, and I find the idea . . . annoying."

If that look in his eye was annoyance, she'd hate to be in the vicinity if he lost his temper.

Griffin was also thinking that he might have understated his reaction to her suggestion. "We could not dissolve the marriage on the grounds of non-consummation," he said, keeping his voice even only with effort.

"Why not?"

"Because it would label the children as bastards." Really, he felt he was behaving in a remarkably enlightened fashion. It was all very well for Shark to talk about a woman's right to dally with other men, but Griffin himself was finding the whole concept quite difficult to come to terms with.

"Further, annulling the marriage would mean that I swore to being impotent," he added. "And I've been impotent only once in my life."

The moment Phoebe had lifted her veil in the church and he had seen her for the first time, panic struck. At twenty years old, she had been wildly sensual and far beyond a boy's ken. Her hair was golden and her lips were rose, and she looked like the princess every man dreamed about. Worse, she was *older* than he. Unquestionably older.

He had felt a paralyzing wave of embarrassment. Naturally, that had been the beginning of the end.

"You're even more beautiful than when we married," he said abruptly.

She frowned. "What has that to do with anything? We are in an untenable situation. Mr. Sharkton just promised to take Colin to sea. I would rather die than see my children follow in the footsteps of a bloodthirsty pirate."

He couldn't help the grin that spread across his face. She was adorable. Formidable, but adorable.

"Why are you smiling?" she asked in a threatening tone. "Do you find the idea of injury to my children *amusing*?"

"No!" he said quickly. "Not at all. Never."

"Right." She paused, but he was happy to let her carry the conversation. "Why haven't you seated yourself, Sir Griffin?"

"You called me Griffin earlier." With a silent groan, he dropped himself into a chair. He missed the young body he'd had when they last saw each other, for all he had been skinny as a finger bone.

Sunshine was pouring through the window behind her. It slid over her hair like warm honey, making every strand glow as if lit from within. Still, the bright light also revealed small lines at the corners of her eyes.

Phoebe had changed as well. There was something a bit sad about her now. Subdued. She hadn't been subdued at their wedding; he would have remembered that.

"Griffin it is, then," she said, nodding sharply. "Let's return to the question of our marriage."

"I shall not be arrested," he said, "so that won't

work as an excuse for divorce. I've received a full pardon from the Crown."

She snorted. "My father used to say that everything has its price."

"It is true that a ruby may have helped." She was so delicate, perched on the edge of the chair. Her features were delicate, and her bones were delicate. . . . She looked like the ideal of English womanhood.

She also looked skeptical, so he added, "The stone was approximately the size of the Prince Regent's big toe."

"I suppose it was stolen from someone?"

"We had it off a pirate's ship, so it likely was stolen from somewhere, yes. But not by us."

Her back became even more rigid. "While I am relieved to learn that my husband is not in imminent danger of imprisonment, it doesn't solve our current problem."

"Right." Griffin sprawled out in his chair, trying to make it look as if he were comfortable, whereas in fact his leg was in flames.

"If you're in that much pain," she said, "perhaps you should stand up again."

"Standing doesn't help." How the devil had she known when he was angry, and known again when he was in pain?

He pounded his thigh to get the muscles to relax. "I don't see what makes our marriage so problematic. If we dissolve the union on the grounds of non-consummation, it would label your children bastards."

The word fell sharply from his lips, although he didn't mean it so. Somehow in the last few minutes he had made up his mind. It had been her right to have children, given his long absence. Which meant they were now *his* children. It didn't hurt that Colin was just the sort of plucky, brave boy he liked.

Phoebe seemed frozen in her chair. Naturally, it would be difficult for her to discuss her infidelity.

"I won't say that I wouldn't have preferred that you waited to have children until I returned," he continued. "But you had no idea that I might ever come back, and frankly, had I not received this injury, I might have continued aboard ship until I lost my life at sea. If I remember correctly, you are now thirty-four."

"Yes. Rather old to have children," she said, her voice wooden.

"Given your age, I suppose that you and I might never have children. Therefore, I should thank you for taking the precaution to provide me with heirs."

"Does it not bother you?" The words came out like something of a croak.

"Yes," he said frankly. "Of course it bothers me that my wife slept with another man during my absence." Even saying the words made a feeling of near madness rise up his spine. "But how can I blame you? We were married for less than a day. I didn't even remember your name correctly. I named my ship after you, you know: the *Flying Poppy*."

"It's unfortunate that was not my name," she said dryly. "Or perhaps fortunate; the *Flying Phoebe* sounds absurd."

Exhibiting a remarkable stubbornness, she added, "But surely you want children of your own, Griffin. My advanced age precludes that, and combined with non-consummation, I am certain that the courts will agree to an annulment."

"Do you see me telling a court that I am impotent?"

Her eyes drifted uneasily over his body. There was a powerful surge of attraction between them, whether she wanted to acknowledge it or not. For whatever reason—probably some long-delayed response to their disastrous wedding night—the only thing he wanted to do was sweep her off to bed.

He wanted to kiss her until those pink lips were dark rose, leave bites all over her creamy skin, tease and stroke and lick her until she was writhing under him, gasping his name.

The way she was blushing, he might as well have spoken aloud every lusty idea that had run through his mind the moment he saw her.

"May I assume that you came straight here from London?" she asked.

Griffin nodded. He was trying to decide how Phoebe would react if he simply picked her up and took her to bed. Enough conversation. She was no virgin, after all. That made it easier.

"I think we will all be more comfortable if you removed to your father's manor while we work out this mess."

"No." The word came out like a bullet.

He wanted this wife of his. In fact, it came to him with an incandescent clarity that he wanted Phoebe more than he'd ever wanted any other woman. She was *his,* from the top of her buttery hair to the bottom of her no doubt dainty toes. "I see no grounds to dissolve the marriage."

"Because—"

He interrupted her. "You have supplied the children that we lack. We will simply pick up where we left off."

She stared at him, apparently dumbfounded.

Once again the feeling of rightness swept over him in a flood. Phoebe was his wife, and she would stay that way.

"I don't care who you slept with. I will accept Colin and the other children as my own and treat them with the same love as if they had been. We bought this house about eight years ago, am I right?"

She nodded.

"It's not entailed, and I have several fortunes—none entailed, for obvious reasons. Money will not be a problem. We can establish all three children in the world." He narrowed his eyes. "Acceptance into the gentry might be more difficult. What has your experience been?"

"What experience?" she asked, knitting her brow.

"In polite society," he clarified.

Her mouth curled in something like disdain. "I never bothered with that. I have friends. Family."

"You never bothered with society," he echoed,

stunned. "But that's—that's what you married me for."

"You are mistaken," she replied, chin held high. "That's what my father bought you for. I disappointed him in that respect. I would never fit into that world, and I wouldn't want to."

"Phoebe," he said, schooling his voice to gentleness, "you *are* Lady Barry, for all you wish to deny it."

She shrugged. "No one I care about is interested in that sort of thing. And please, don't address me by the title. I don't consider myself your wife, not after a fourteen-year separation."

Griffin shifted his weight to the other hip. He'd stopped trying to disguise the pain.

"What happened to you?" she asked. "Was part of your leg eaten by a shark? Or did you lose it in a battle? I can see that it gives you quite a bit of pain. Will that improve, over time?"

"I still have the whole leg, though it took a slash from a rapier and the wound became infected. But it's getting stronger every day."

She shifted too, as if in sympathetic pain. "I am grateful for your forbearance in the matter of my children. But I do not wish to be married to you."

She said it quietly, but emphatically. As if the outcome of their marital debacle were her decision, and her decision alone.

"You did not buy this house," she added. "I did. My father left me a great deal of property. You will find that I have never touched the money that Mr. Pettigrew deposited for my allowance."

For at least the third time that day, he was struck by the poverty of his vocabulary. What was a man to say upon learning that his wife had taken nothing from him over the years? That she had not only rejected his support but indeed hadn't needed him at all? Whatever the feeling was, it ran through him like molten steel, taking his breath away. "Why?" he managed.

She met his eyes with no apology. "I refuse to live on the spoils of piracy."

"Then you will be happy to know that the spoils of piracy, such as they were, are long gone. The fortune I bring home with me derives partly from privateering—which is not piracy—but primarily from the proceeds of imports and exports."

"I do not wish to be married to a pirate."

He started up from his chair. "It's too late for that, Poppy."

"My name is Phoebe!" she hissed.

He loomed over her. "I forgot." Her head tipped back, yet there wasn't a trace of fear in her eyes. For the past decade, grown men had trembled in his presence. They had caught a glimpse of his tattoo and pissed in their breeches.

Not Phoebe.

Not his wife.

"Move aside," she said. "You cannot bully me!"

"I see that." Joy was sweeping up through his veins. With one swift movement he picked her up and dropped her on the bed before the sound of her gasp had left the air.

She put her hands against his chest and shoved. "Stop it!"

She smelled like rose blossoms after a rain, an quintessentially British smell that he hadn't even remembered until now. He braced his arms on either side of her head, gazed down at her furious face, and declared, "I want to stay married."

"Not even a pirate gets everything he wants!"

"Why not?" He bent down and nuzzled her neck. He felt the shock of his touch reverberate down her body. "I like you. And you're damn beautiful. Why not stay married?"

"Because I *don't want to*!" she said in a near shriek.

"How can you know until you try it?"

"I don't want to try it. You don't understand. I have a *life* here. I have children; I have friends. There's no place for—for you."

Her words punctured the sensual haze that had his hands hovering just below her breasts. No place for him?

There was a faint, hollow ring within his chest every time he heard the word *home*. He didn't belong in the world of his father, that of titles, and noblesse oblige.

Nor did he belong on board ship, not anymore. That life was over.

Poppy—no, Phoebe—was his home, his new home. Even if she didn't want to acknowledge that.

He straightened. Tousled hair spread around her face. She looked vulnerable and unbearably desirable. His fingers trembled to pet and caress her until she was as aroused as he was.

So much for the impotence of their wedding night. He'd had an erection from the moment she entered the room.

"Very well," he said, falling back a step.

She sat up, stark relief on her face. "You'll be happier in London, Griffin. People there are more sophisticated than they are here. Why, they probably won't turn a hair at that mark on your cheek."

He burst into laughter. She sounded like someone reassuring a merchant awaiting his imports that pirates are far and few between.

"You would be terribly bored here," she insisted.

There was no doubt in his mind but that he would spend the rest of his days in this precise place. Unless Arbor House became too small for all the children he hoped they'd have. "Perhaps I will pay my father a visit now, as we are not far from Walford Court."

He watched her eyes lighten and added, "But I will return home for dinner, if you wouldn't mind holding the meal for me. Would it bother you if my father disowned me? I think there's a reasonable chance that he will."

"Not at all," she said, before adding, "but it doesn't matter what I think."

"You are my wife. What you think matters." Their eyes caught for a moment and he put everything in that look, telling her silently that there was no chance he would leave the marriage. Under any circumstances.

She swallowed, and he thought she probably understood.

"I am your husband, Phoebe," he stated. "The marriage may not be a legal one yet, but it will become one tonight."

"Why would you want me?" she whispered. "You . . . the children . . . I'm not a *lady*, Griffin. I'd make a wretched viscountess."

He couldn't help grinning. "Do you imagine I'll be a suitable viscount? We can cause our scandals together. I would like children of my own blood, but I don't mind that Colin will inherit my title. Frankly, inasmuch as your dowry brought my father's estate back out of debt, you should have the right to choose its successor. And you did."

"About the children—"

He put a finger over her lips before she could make whatever apology she had in mind. He didn't want to hear about the children's father, not now. The man was dead.

"I want you, Phoebe." His voice had dropped to a husky key that spoke for itself.

She responded with a look of panic. Yet the ripple in her slender throat as she swallowed sent another slash of lust through him. He was in bad shape.

"My mother . . . I am . . ." A moment of silence. "All right."

It felt as if she had accepted his marriage proposal again, not that there'd been a first one. Their marriage had been a business matter settled between their fathers, with talk of jointures and dowries and settlements.

This was a simple matter between a man and a woman.

"It's a bad bargain for you," he said, voicing what he was thinking. "I spent years on the wrong side of the law, I'm lame in one leg, and ferocious to boot. Scarred and tattooed."

She looked him over. "I don't care about your scars, but there is one thing that concerns me. I have no doubt but that you had something of a harem, Griffin. I will not tolerate it here. You'll need to stay on the right side of the law, and out of other women's beds."

His smile threatened to burst out, but he reined it in. Damn, but she was a tough woman. It was thrilling. "There will never be another woman for me, Phoebe. Not even if I finally meet a woman named Poppy. And I don't find theft interesting in itself."

She nodded, and he held out his hand to bring her to her feet. It wasn't that he hadn't had women in the last fourteen years, because he certainly had. But not one of those women had moved him like Phoebe.

It must be some odd thing attached to a marriage license.

"Would you like me to go with you to visit your father? As a buffer, as it were?"

That was rather unexpected. "No need," he said. "I imagine you have things to do here, with the children." Clearly, she was nothing like his mother. He had been lucky to see the viscountess once a fortnight, if that. Not that he had missed her; how can one miss someone of whom one knows nothing?

"Nanny is more than capable of handling bedtime."

"I'll be home for supper," he repeated.

He shifted his stance, and for once it wasn't a response to pain. He was hard as rock, for no good reason other than that his wife was looking at him as if she were worried about him.

"Must we do that *tonight*?" she asked, swallowing again.

Griffin's mind was filled with images of himself tumbling her onto the bed and tearing off floaty layers of clothing. But even as his mind offered a dozen reasons why he should take her with dispatch, like any self-respecting pirate, her eyes stopped him.

They were dark with strain. Of course she didn't want to fall into bed with a burly stranger who strode into her house and declared himself her husband.

He could wait. They had a lifetime ahead of them.

He wanted to earn a place here, in this warm, happy house, full of illegitimate children, nursemaids, and one beautiful woman with a stubborn chin. Not to steal it, or force it.

He wanted that—*her*—more than he had ever wanted anything in his life.

Nine

$\mathcal{B}$iddulph Barry, Viscount Moncrieff, lived in Walford Court, an hour or so from Phoebe's house. It had been the country seat of the Barrys for generations, the place where Griffin grew up.

Sitting decorously in a carriage—because the very idea of slinging a leg over a horse made him feel faint—Griffin kept thinking about the fact that Phoebe didn't know his father well. It sounded as if the viscount had not embraced his son's wife.

He was unsurprised. His father was obsessed by the rituals and traditions of the nobility. It had undoubtedly nearly killed him to realize that he would either have to sell his son to a merchant's daughter or lose the ancestral estate.

Unfortunately Griffin had lusted after a life in which titles had no meaning, where a man earned honor from use of his own strength and wit.

He and his father had spent his childhood at loggerheads. Consequently, he wasn't all that bothered when he woke to find himself at sea, under the command of a disreputable scoundrel named Captain Dirk.

Piracy was a perfect revenge . . . an antidote to his father's vainglorious love of the aristocracy.

In fact, he hadn't even bothered to write to his father for years after he left England, not until James's father, the old duke, died. That death had been a shock for both of them, but especially for James, who knew damn well that his father had died wondering whether his only son was dead or alive.

It gave a man to think. Griffin's father knew he was alive because he had instructed his agent to reassure his family on a regular basis. And he had sent home gold as well. His father had been compelled to sell his son to a merchant; Griffin's money ensured that his younger sisters did not have to suffer the same fate.

But when James ascended to the duchy in absentia, Griffin realized that perhaps he should be in closer touch with his father. So he had written him a letter, telling him bluntly that he had become a pirate, even though by then Griffin and James were de facto privateers. He didn't see any reason to sugarcoat the truth.

His reception at Walford Court could not have been more different from his arrival at Arbor House.

His father had always aspired to a dukedom.

Apparently he'd used Phoebe's dowry to good effect; the estate now looked as if aping a dukedom was as good as owning one. No less than six footmen bowed as Griffin entered, not to mention the butler, who'd had another fourteen years to perfect his starched, sour look.

"Good afternoon, Mears," Griffin said, handing over his greatcoat. "You're holding up well."

Mears was far too dignified to respond to a personal comment. Instead, he bent his head a glacial inch, giving Griffin a good look at the powdered top of his wig.

He must have heard about the piracy. Or he didn't like the tattoo. Or he was just a wizened old bastard with a stick where none ought to be.

"Welcome to England, Sir Griffin," Mears intoned. "On behalf of the household, may I extend our best wishes on the occasion of your return."

He paused, but Griffin didn't see any reason to exchange flummeries.

"His lordship is in the study," Mears stated. "If you will wait in the drawing room, I will inquire whether Lord Moncrieff is available." His eyes skittered to the tattoo and away again. Too bad Griffin had left Shark at Arbor House; Mears would likely faint at the sight of him.

Griffin considered pushing his way into the library to greet his father. But he was too old to cross swords with Mears.

He had only waited in the sitting room a moment or two before the door opened. He looked up, expecting to see the butler, but his father was on the threshold.

The viscount had grown older. Deep grooves ran along the sides of his mouth. His hair had turned silver. He still stood tall, shoulders squared, and he didn't look frail.

But he was much older.

"Father," Griffin said, inclining his head, uncertain what to do.

The viscount walked toward him without a word, his face showing no expression. But then he reached out and pulled Griffin into his arms. "My boy," he said, his deep voice catching. "You came home. You finally came home."

His arms were strong, and for a moment Griffin had a fleeting memory of being embraced like this before. But how could that be? He hardly remembered seeing his father, who was always in London, sitting in the House of Lords.

Griffin cleared his throat, feeling distinctly awkward. His right hand was clutching his cane, but he patted his father on the back with his left. "I'm here," he said, trying for a cheerful tone. "Come home like a proverbial, piratical bad penny."

When his father pulled away, Griffin discovered to his horror that Lord Moncrieff's eyes shone with tears. "I thought I would never see you again," he said, ignoring Griffin's foray into weak humor. "I imagined you dead at sea, cut to pieces by strangers or drowning in a storm."

"There were some thorny moments," Griffin said, "but I'm back."

His father touched the poppy tattoo. "The mark of your profession?"

"Of my ship. The *Flying Poppy*." Griffin hesitated, then added, "I must sit down, Father."

Lord Moncrieff sprang back. "You're wounded. You lost a leg!"

Griffin's smile was reluctant, thrown over his shoulder as he limped to the sofa. "My wife came to the same conclusion. But no, I managed to escape the fate of a wooden leg. I'm merely recovering from an injury."

"If you lost a leg, I would expect you to replace it with solid gold," his father said, sitting down opposite. "Mr. Pettigrew has given me biannual reports regarding your estate, as you instructed. It seems there's a great deal of money to be made on the high seas."

"Did he tell you that we have received royal pardons?"

"Actually, the Prince Regent did me the favor of forwarding that news himself." His father's smile spoke volumes. Griffin had thought his pardon was the result of a very large ruby, but it seemed that Viscount Moncrieff may have played a hand as well.

"I received several letters this morning indicating that the Duke of Ashbrook made a rather dramatic entrance into the House of Lords," his father continued.

Griffin nodded. He was experiencing something close to vertigo. When he last stood on English soil, he was a youngster, forced to marry a merchant's daughter whom he'd never seen in the flesh. He had been furious, rebellious, alienated from his father. Now that same father was revealing a dry sense of humor Griffin had certainly never known about.

Oh, brave new world.

"I want to offer my deep apologies, Son," the viscount said now. "If I'd known how deeply you loathed the marriage, I wouldn't have forced you to it. I was devastated when you fled the country."

"I didn't run away due to my marriage," Griffin said.

His father wasn't listening. "I thought about the match very carefully before I agreed to it. Your wife is from the merchant classes, true. But she was beautiful, docile, trained in every possible domestic art. I truly thought she would be an excellent spouse for you."

Griffin nodded, opened his mouth again.

But his father barreled on. "Of course, now there are the children."

Griffin would have thought that his father's reaction to the idea of a cuckoo inheriting the title of Viscount Moncrieff would be near violence.

"I hadn't kept up more than a remote acquaintance," his father said, his eyes abjectly apologetic. "The children were presented as a *fait accompli*."

"I understand," Griffin said.

His father leaned forward. "I didn't think you were ever coming back. How could I tell Lady

Barry that her life would be childless? It would be cruel."

"I understand," Griffin repeated. But he didn't. His father didn't care that his own blood would not inherit the title?

The viscount had always trumpeted their ancient blood, the accomplishments of their long-dead ancestors. Griffin had come to loathe the very mention of the first Viscount Moncrieff, a repellant beast who had slavered at the feet of James the First. In Griffin's opinion, he received the title of viscount as a direct payment for personal favors of an intimate nature.

His father had never liked that suggestion, though there was a bawdy letter upstairs from the king that confirmed Griffin's impression.

"I must return home for supper," he said abruptly. He felt a bit like a man who was addicted to drink. He wanted to go home and see Phoebe.

He wanted to talk her into changing her mind and going to bed with him immediately. Even if that didn't happen tonight, he wanted to kiss her for the first time since their wedding.

His father's face fell, wrinkles sagging into place. "Of course."

"Come with me," Griffin added hastily. "There are plenty of rooms in the house, from what I saw. Are any of my siblings home?"

"No, they live with their own families now. Your youngest sister married two years ago. They will be very happy to hear that you are home safe."

Griffin rather doubted that, but he was willing to leave it an open question. The return of a pirate was unlikely to be seen as an unmixed blessing. Except, perhaps, by his perplexing father. "So you live here alone?"

At that, his father smiled. "I maintain a full household, as you surely saw. I've been working on a new bill that I'll present to the House in the next session, so I have a proper component of secretaries as well."

"Leave them," Griffin suggested. "Let's go to Arbor House and see what Phoebe has for dinner."

"See what Phoebe has for dinner?" the viscount repeated blankly. It was obviously a more informal notion than he had ever considered.

Griffin heaved himself to his feet. He didn't want to adhere to the foolish stiffness that governed the lives of the aristocracy, and he had a shrewd idea that Phoebe agreed with him. "I want to see her. She's the only wife I've got, and I've known her for approximately one day. This afternoon I barely managed to talk her out of annulling the marriage."

"That would be extremely difficult," his father said, looking startled. "And ill-advised."

"So come with me," Griffin said. "I could use the help. I have no idea how to make polite conversation. We didn't have any aboard the *Flying Poppy*, as you can imagine."

"Actually, I can't imagine," his father said. He got up and pulled the bell cord. Mears popped through the door. The butler didn't even bother to pretend that he hadn't been hovering within earshot the whole time.

"Tell Crafts to put together a bag, if you please," the viscount said. "I'll be joining my son and daughter-in-law for supper this evening. I may stay the night."

There was a strain of pleasure in his voice that made Griffin smile. When he considered a return to England, he had never imagined that he might find his father lonely, or happy to see him.

"Have my carriage brought around, if you please, Mears," Griffin bellowed after the butler. The man's back became visibly rigid, but he turned about and bowed silently.

"Just as if you never left," the viscount remarked. "Poor old Mears. He has such passion for propriety; must you tease him?"

"Teasing implies affection. We share a mutual loathing."

"Would you like to visit your old bedchamber? I kept everything just the same in case you returned."

"Unfortunately, even looking at those stairs makes me sweat. I'm going to save my strength to totter to bed this evening."

His father frowned. "What caused your injury?"

"A lucky bandit managed to slash James's throat and my leg just before expiring. He was damn close to taking off my crown jewels. If *that* had happened, I wouldn't have come home."

"Then I'm glad to hear it didn't."

Griffin felt a surge of restlessness. He wanted to be wooing his wife, making sure she hadn't changed her mind in his absence. "Let's go."

"Are you that eager to see Lady Barry?"

"Yes."

His father's eyes lightened. "I didn't pick so terribly, did I?"

"No." There was something raw and powerful in his admission. "No, you didn't."

Ten

Generally speaking, Phoebe ate her meals with the children. She saw no point in dining by herself, and it was much more congenial—if sometimes wearing, given Nanny McGillycuddy's conversational style—to listen to the children's chatter. She'd had enough of solitary dining in the first seven years of her marriage.

But Griffin had said he was returning home for supper. She would have a grown-up seated across from her at the dining room table, a rather fascinating idea.

She planned a menu with the cook—three courses instead of her usual two—and instructed the downstairs housemaid to set the table in the dining room. Then she ordered a bath and sat in it for a good forty minutes, trying to calm her mind.

And not succeeding.

Griffin was her husband, and he didn't want to

break off the marriage. She could already tell that what Sir Griffin Barry didn't want to do, he didn't do. She could see it in every lineament of his body, in the set of his jaw.

She raised her leg in the bath and watched water roll off her knee and down her leg. It had been one thing to face her wedding night when she was twenty, with the confidence of feeling both delectable and young. She had been utterly certain that her young husband would find her enticing.

There was something smoldering in Griffin's eyes that told her he still felt that way, but she was no longer so assured.

She soaped her knee for the fourth time. Two thoughts kept chasing themselves around her head: the first was a memory of her mother talking of tearing pain. That didn't sound any better now than it had fourteen years ago. And the second and more important was that she was old. Practically wizened. Dried up. Over *thirty*.

It made the blood roar in her ears to even think about that number. On her marriage night her breasts and her waist had been perfect. Now her hips were rounder, and her bosom was larger. Her breasts hadn't kept the teacup shape they'd had at seventeen.

Griffin, on the other hand, had only improved over the years. He was everything a woman ever dreamed of in the privacy of her own bed. His eyes, shoulders, even thighs, even . . . She had seen what he looked like from behind.

Now *he* was the delectable one.

She swallowed hard.

"Are you ready for me to wash your hair?" her maid asked, jolting her out of that train of thought.

"Yes," she murmured.

"An exciting day," May said, as she poured jasmine soap onto her hands and then began massaging it into Phoebe's hair.

"Yes."

"If you don't mind the presumption, my lady, Sir Griffin is as handsome . . . well, as handsome as ever a man was! Even Nanny said as how he was fine looking."

"Nanny? Really?"

May laughed. "She said a man with those thighs could father ten children and we'd have to teach you how to plead a sick headache."

"Hush," Phoebe said, and May quieted, which just meant that Phoebe went back to worrying.

By the time her maid was rinsing her hair, Phoebe had reconciled herself to the fact that her marriage was going to be consummated that very night.

For all Griffin had promised to wait, she wasn't stupid. Everything about him was strung tight. She was a challenge that he meant to conquer, his feelings all the more acute for the debacle of their wedding night. There was something hungry in his eyes that sent a thrill right down her legs. He *craved* her.

She felt as if her blood was overheating. She stood up, determined to put on clothes before May noticed that she was trembling slightly.

Then it struck her that she didn't have any seductive clothes, gowns designed for a man's appreciation. All of her clothes were retiring, costumes that informed the world that she was not a debauched woman, even though she had no husband.

May handed Phoebe a length of toweling and then turned to the wardrobe. "The blue gown will be just right. I'll remove the fichu that tucks into the bodice." Her smile was naughty, which made Phoebe wonder.

Her maid was not married. Phoebe had never seen her smile like that.

The blue gown was made of the lightest of lightweight cottons, so thin as to be transparent, although of course it had an underskirt.

It *had* an underskirt, because even as she watched, May began ripping the lining away. Too busy pulling out the small stitches, May didn't even look up at Phoebe's gasp.

"He's a pirate, my lady. A *pirate*. You have to make him stay in England. We need a man about the house. You can't keep a pirate at home by wearing a little cap on your head and pretending you're as bloodless as a Quaker."

Anxiety spilled into Phoebe's stomach again. Even her household didn't think much of her chances of keeping Griffin interested. Not given that she was an old woman of thirty-four, likely infertile, probably wrinkled in places she had never thought about.

With a silent groan, she straightened her shoulders. If only he'd come home five years ago. Or even four years ago, when she was thirty. Thirty seemed better. Vastly younger than thirty-four.

"No corset," May said, "and no chemise, either."

Phoebe had never dreamed of such a scandalous way of dressing. She opened her mouth to refuse—and paused. What did she know of these matters? Nothing. Maybe wives seduced their husbands nightly by leaving off their chemises.

What couldn't be avoided must be endured.

She allowed May to dress her in the remains of a perfectly good gown, without a scrap of underclothing, which made her feel the veriest trollop. And reminded her that she had to inform Griffin about the children's parentage immediately. The moment he came in the door.

May piled her hair on the top of her head in a disheveled bun, leaving strands to curl around her ears. Then she produced a little box.

"What's that?" Phoebe asked suspiciously.

"Kohl," May said. "We'll brush it on your eyelashes."

"No."

"But my lady . . . look, I have some lip color as well."

"No." There was no question in Phoebe's mind about this. She wouldn't disguise what she was, and who she was.

Obviously, Griffin intended to sleep with her. But if she didn't quicken with child after six months, he might well leave. Meanwhile, she wasn't going to pretend to a youth she no longer possessed.

But at least she would have him first. For a time. Under her anxiety was a kind of brewing excitement. After all, she'd been alone for years. When male eyes met hers on the street, she turned her head instantly. Part of the reason she avoided society was because men, even gentlemen, tended to assume things about a woman whose husband lived overseas. Or, in this case, on the sea.

They assumed she was lustful and lonely, and desperate for marital pleasures. She had never been such, and had received any such advances with disdain.

But now . . . slowly . . . she was realizing that no matter the reason that Griffin wanted to consummate the marriage, it meant that she could try those things. Perhaps she *would* have a child of her own. Perhaps it wasn't too late.

May adjusted Phoebe's necklace and stepped back. Without a fichu tucked into the bodice, her gown barely skimmed her nipples. If she pushed her knee forward, she could clearly see the shape of her thigh.

She began to shake her head, but May overrode her. "This is what you're wearing, my lady."

Phoebe frowned. Had she really lost control of her household to the extent that not only Nanny but also May felt free to order her about?

"You look beautiful," her maid said. "Just look at yourself, my lady. Really *look*."

Phoebe really looked.

She was beautiful. That is, still beautiful. She had grown up with her father's confident belief that he could barter her face and dowry against a title. But her mother had never fostered vanity. "The tilt of your nose is nothing to be proud of," she would say. Phoebe had grown accustomed to ignoring her appearance.

Looking critically at the glass, she could see that while her air of dewy youth had evaporated, there was a kind of sensuality to her lips and her breasts and even the curve of her hip that made up for it.

"Yes," May said. "There you are." She sounded as smug as a preacher on Sunday afternoon. "You'll do. That pirate's a lucky man, and he knows it."

Phoebe needed to go downstairs and check with Cook, see if the table had been set properly, make sure the children were tucked into bed. But she turned at the door and took a final look at the mirror.

Her father had bought Griffin the first time, but it was up to her this time. She wasn't bartering herself for a title.

She wanted the body behind the title.

She wanted Griffin at her side, for as long as she could keep him. She wanted a man—Griffin—to look at her with bold hunger, even if he tossed her on the bed, for all the world as if she were a possession rather than a woman.

The air she drew into her lungs felt overheated, bringing with it a swell of agonized longing.

To belong to him. To own him. To caress and explore him.

She had never looked at men's bodies closely, but somehow she had done so to Griffin. After only an hour or two in his company, she could trace the shape of his chest in her mind, the way it swelled from a narrow waist. The shape of his arse, muscled and powerful and altogether male.

Sensual images shot through her mind. It was as if a dam broke somewhere deep inside and a flood of erotic longings broke free. She could imagine herself caressing all that golden skin. Kissing it. Putting a hand between his legs, where no good woman ever even glanced.

Kneeling before him . . .

She hurried from the room so that May wouldn't see her face.

All this wild energy couldn't be normal. Men and women couldn't walk about feeling this madness racing up their legs.

Now her imagination had broken free, it was offering her image after image. She saw herself running to greet Griffin at the front door. He snatched her into a kiss so fierce that her head bent back against his arm. Their desire was so heady that they sank down in the entry, right there, on the floor, and she pulled him on top of her, shameless and joyful.

She was tempted to slap her own cheek. This was lunacy. As if something like that could happen. What about the children? The servants?

Had she lost her mind? She felt like one of those widows whom the ballads made fun of, the ones who walked about ogling young men.

Yet she didn't want to ogle young men.

She only wanted one man, one pirate with a tattoo and a limp.

Her husband.

Eleven

$\mathcal{G}$riffin was rather shocked to discover that he enjoyed talking to his father during the carriage ride to Arbor House. The viscount was fascinated to hear that Griffin and James had imported curry and lumber to England, birdcages and silks to Spain.

"So you really weren't pirates," he said finally.

"I started out that way," Griffin said frankly. "I was never the yo-ho-ho, walk the plank type of pirate. But I captured many a ship, took everything of value, and sailed away."

"You made your first fortune as a highwayman," his father said, the corner of his mouth twitching. Then: "Was there anything I could have done to steer you into a more ethical profession?"

"I doubt it. There's no way for an aristocrat to prove his manhood here in England, let alone to win that manhood. My future was handed to me on a silver platter, bound up with a royal patent. I wanted—no, I lusted—to pit myself against other men. To fight."

His father sighed. He was tall and lean and scholarly by bent. Clearly, he hadn't the faintest ambition to take on a man in a battle to the death.

"I must resemble Mother's side of the family," Griffin said cheerfully. "At any rate, piracy proved the life for me. I fought with every possible sort of weapon, and survived sea battles, not to mention storms. I can sail and steer a boat around the most dangerous shoals in the world."

"How on earth are you going to live in England?" his father asked, his tone bleak. "There's nothing to pit yourself against here. Is this a mere visit?"

"No," Griffin said. "I'm wounded. At thirty-one, I'm ready to rest on my laurels. I'm not fool enough to try to man a ship with a bad leg. Pirates fight like trapped badgers, and I'd be dead in six months."

"His Royal Highness told me that you and the Duke of Ashbrook were responsible for dismantling a number of ships involved in the slave trade. A disgraceful, disreputable business."

"Yes." Griffin hated to think of those particular ships. What they found there made them sick at heart, even after he and James sent the human cargo back to their own shores with a heap of gold coins and the slavers' ships to boot.

"You'll need something to do," the viscount said. "I've a judgeship open. Justice of the Peace for Somerset. You can do that."

"Something to do," Griffin echoed. "Why, aren't gentlemen supposed to do nothing, Father?"

His father raised an eyebrow. "I busy myself."

"In fact, we rarely saw you, if I remember correctly."

"My work is important. The nobility of this land stand at the monarch's shoulder to rule with him, and beside him. But I do wish I had seen more of my children."

"I can't see myself a judge," Griffin remarked. "From criminal to justice overnight? It doesn't seem possible. I know nothing of English law."

But his father grinned. "You were captain of a ship for over a decade, Son. There must have been many a sticky situation for which you acted as arbiter. The prosecutor for the Crown will inform you of the relevant laws."

"Ah."

"You can begin on Monday. There's a backlog of cases, since Pursett died last month. I've been dragging my heels about appointing another justice."

"Monday!" Griffin exclaimed. "Where does this court meet?"

"A mere half hour from Arbor House," his father said, a distinct note of satisfaction in his voice. "We'll have the formal investiture, such as it is, at eight in the morning, and you can begin listening to cases at nine."

"Nine in the morning? The same morning?"

His father looked at him. "There are men sitting in jails across the county because no one has been sworn in to listen to their pleas."

Griffin suddenly broke out in a howl of laughter. "What?"

"There's the father I remember. You always had a way of pointing out the *right* and *moral* way to do things, Father. In your eyes, there was never a different way."

"I hardly think—," the viscount began.

"It's all right," Griffin said. "I'm old enough. I ran off and became a criminal under all that pressure, but I believe I'm old enough to live up to your expectations now."

"Are you saying that you took up a life of piracy in reaction to my—to me?" His father looked horrified.

"Absolutely not."

The viscount lapsed back into the corner of his carriage, looking shaken. Griffin had always been a good liar, and clearly that hadn't changed. It was not easy to be raised by a nobleman who put his duty before his family. But it did explain why his son became a criminal famous through three seas, if not seven.

Not that it's an excuse, Griffin thought to himself. Just an explanation.

In fact, it was time for amends. Likely he would be in the courtroom at 8:00 a.m. on Monday.

But at the moment . . . there were different amends that he had in mind.

Twelve

$\mathcal{P}$hoebe had rarely been so horrified as the moment when she realized that one of the gardeners—stuffed into livery for the occasion—was ushering not just Griffin but also Viscount Moncrieff through her front door. She had been sitting in the drawing room, sipping a glass of sherry and trying to distract herself from the kind of heated images that, she was quite certain, no proper lady would ever entertain.

She had been failing miserably, immersed in an absurd fantasy in which she happened on Griffin while he was bathing, when she startled back to attention as the door opened—and she heard the aristocratic tones of the viscount.

Terror struck her heart. She was wearing a transparent dress, with little more than a ribbon keeping her nipples from the open air.

She started to her feet too late.

Griffin was at the drawing room door, tossing his greatcoat behind him to the footman. He surged into the room, brewing with energy.

Phoebe's heart sped up and her whole body tightened.

He froze for a moment and a look flashed through his eyes, too quickly for her to read. Was it shock? Surely it wasn't horror. Though perhaps one didn't expect one's wife—

When had she become such a worrier? She pasted a smile on her face and moved toward her husband and the viscount, who had nudged his son to the side and entered the room. "Lord Moncrieff, it is indeed a pleasure to see you. I wish the children weren't asleep so that they could greet you as well."

She didn't see Griffin's father very often, but they had achieved a kind of easy distance. They didn't understand each other, but they respected each other.

Though it would all be different now that Griffin was home. He was the glue that would either bind the viscount into their family, or allow them to fall apart again.

"An astonishing and happy day for both of us," the viscount was saying as his hand briefly tightened on hers and then let go. "You look lovely as always, my dear."

"Ravishing," Griffin said. The word calmed her worries. For today, for tomorrow, for a time at least, her husband wanted her.

By the time they reached the supper table, she

would have revised that statement. Her husband was consumed by lust. Griffin kept brushing her hand. His touch made her shiver, and then he would laugh, a full-throated pirate's laugh. They were seated opposite each other, as was only proper, but somehow his foot kept straying toward hers.

And his eyes . . . the way he looked at her! She never dreamed that it was possible to say so much with one glance. She could have sworn that he saw straight into her mind and stole those fantasies that her imagination kept throwing at her.

After the first course, his glances became like some sort of drug. Every one intoxicated her, made her heart beat even faster. All her woman's parts grew hot and tight, but when she shifted uneasily in her chair, he took note and her restlessness was answered by the flare of pure lust in his eyes.

All that time, the three of them talked decorously of the viscount's upcoming bill in Parliament and his plan to appoint Griffin as Justice of the Peace— which, frankly, Phoebe couldn't imagine.

The viscount renewed the gentle request he always made, that she begin attending the assemblies in Bath, and she refused. And then suddenly remembered that she had a husband who presumably had an opinion of his own, but he was laughing silently. He didn't care about assemblies.

He would never care about the assemblies.

She let her gaze thank him, let her smile take on a kind of Cleopatra knowing that wasn't drawn from anything but the erotic pictures she saw in her mind.

The viscount dropped his napkin and, in the absence of footmen, bent to retrieve it himself. Griffin caught her eyes and deliberately, slowly, licked the slice of pear he held in his fingers before slipping it into his mouth.

Phoebe blushed, feeling her body tighten until it almost hurt.

Finally it was time to retire to the drawing room. As Griffin came around the table to pull out her chair, leaning on his cane as he walked, she had the impulse to rise and walk toward him, but she thought better of it. Wounded lions didn't like to be reminded of their limitations.

He brought her to her feet, and then, turning his back to the viscount, said quietly, "I don't know about you, but I just spent that meal thanking God you aren't a virgin."

"Hush!" Phoebe yelped, her cheeks undoubtedly as red as an apple.

"I'll be lucky if I make it out of the drawing room without backing you against the wall and taking you right there."

"You mustn't say such things," she scolded, glancing at his father. The viscount was smiling obliviously from the door, and she could hardly acquaint her husband with the truth about her lack of experience before an audience.

Once in the drawing room, Griffin sprawled on the small sofa beside her, his broad thigh pressed against hers. She was breathless, giddy with excitement. But somehow she managed to keep her voice to its usual cadence, even though every time he shifted and pressed his leg against hers, she felt a melting wave of desire.

They talked of the estate attached to Arbor House, of the fields and men whom she employed. Griffin casually put a hand behind her back. Callused fingers played with her curls and then stroked her neck, caressing her, teasing her. Phoebe pressed her knees together tightly, feeling herself turning pink once again. She was amazed that the viscount peacefully talked of crop rotation without catching the tension that sang in the air like a high note of music.

Griffin talked of farm work too, but in his mouth it all took on a different intonation. The viscount talked of crops; Griffin turned to fertilization, a smile curving his bottom lip. He had no shame, flicking glances at her under golden eyelashes that told her without words that he was more interested in plowing *her* than the north, or south, or west fields.

What's more, his clever fingers were making the wanton imagination that she'd suddenly discovered spark with images of him touching her in places where she had never imagined a man would touch, or would want to touch. Finally she leapt from the sofa and announced she had to fetch her knitting.

"What are you making?" Griffin inquired, as seriously as if she'd betrayed a talent for architecture.

"A vest for Colin," she told him. "He is growing terribly fast."

"The children are a credit to you," the viscount said, smiling.

Griffin frowned, seeing that smile. He would have sworn that his father would never praise children got illegitimately, no matter how charming.

But then the viscount was standing, claiming to be tired, and Phoebe was issuing a charming refusal to even think of his leaving the house at this hour. It would have taken a stronger man than his father to reject her appeal.

Griffin had the sudden feeling that he would spend the rest of his life doing whatever she asked him to do. So much for the captain of the *Flying Poppy*, the man who answered only to the wind and the waves.

Oddly enough, he didn't mind the idea. There wasn't room for regret, not when hungry yearning filled every inch of him.

He didn't crave only her body, either. He wanted all of her, the sweet elusiveness of her, that drop of melancholy, the bright intelligence with which she countered his father's arguments.

All of it. All of her.

Thirteen

$\mathcal{P}$hoebe had no sooner turned from escorting the viscount to his bedchamber than her husband pounced on her from behind, spinning her so that his laughing face loomed above hers.

Griffin's voice was totally male, hungry and deep. "Your bedchamber or mine, Phoebe? Let me just add that there'll be no *yours* or *mine* after tonight. We'll share the bed and the chamber."

It was everything she'd been dreaming of for hours. She felt a flash of panic. "I have to check the children."

"They're asleep."

"I always look in on them, kiss them goodnight."

"I want to kiss *you*, not a child."

He bent his head and she pulled away. "You can't kiss me just outside your father's bedchamber!"

He pulled her through the next door before she

could take a breath, then he pushed the door shut and backed her against the wall without taking his eyes off her face. "Where are we?"

She was giggling helplessly. "A guest room. What if this was Nanny's bedchamber? Or the nursery?"

He had one forearm braced against the wall over her head, while the other gripped his cane. His eyes were dark and as hungry as his voice.

"Does your leg hurt?" she asked.

"Yes. And I don't give a damn."

"We should sit down." It came out in a little gasp.

"Lying down is better," he said with a wicked smile. "It doesn't hurt when I don't put weight on it. Does this room have a large bed?"

"No," Phoebe managed. That gleam in Griffin's eye was probably outlawed somewhere in the world. He was standing so close that she could smell leather, wind, and, faintly, a salty maleness that was more intoxicating than champagne.

"I haven't kissed you in fourteen years," he said conversationally.

"You haven't kissed me ever!" She remembered every moment of their shadowy wedding night, and it was far too businesslike to have included kisses.

"After the ceremony, in the church. Your lips were softer than I had imagined a woman's lips could be. It was utterly terrifying."

She giggled again and her heart lightened. There was something about his rueful, quirky smile that made anything seem possible. Even marriage.

"Truly." He brushed his lips against hers. "You're only more beautiful now, so it's a good thing that I grew a pair of balls in the interim. You were too much for me."

"Maybe I'm still too much for you," she said daringly.

He ran a finger down her forehead, over her nose, caught on her lip. "Quite possible," he said, whispering it. Then he finally bent his head and kissed her. Really kissed her. His tongue slid between her lips. It was strange . . . but it made her breath ragged. Rather timidly she began to kiss him back, realizing that kissing was a kind of intimacy, a conversation, a way of making love.

Her tongue tumbled over his. He nipped her lip; she pulled his head closer to hers and opened her mouth again, coaxing him back.

A while later she had forgotten that they were standing against a wall in a room she rarely entered. She couldn't hear anything beside her own breathing, a faint gasp whenever he left her lips to nuzzle her cheek, her jaw, her neck, before returning to her mouth.

"If I visit the children with you later," he said finally, his voice a hoarse thread, "could we retire to our bedchamber, Phoebe? I want you. Feel this. I have the opposite problem I had as a youngster." He took her hand and pressed it against the hard length in the front of his pantaloons.

"I've been hard as a poker for most of the day. Please let me make up for our wedding night."

For a moment Phoebe didn't answer. She couldn't. Her fingers had curled instinctively, measuring the pure size and strength of his organ. Union didn't seem physically possible. Yet heat pooled between her legs, and the only reason she wasn't begging was because she couldn't get her breath.

"Yes," she whispered back, moving her hand against him. Griffin could obviously feel her touch through his breeches, because he groaned and arched his body, thrusting against her fingers. In response, her own desire grew almost painful, a raging lust, to give it the proper word. A lust to see, to touch and feel and taste him.

"If we don't move, I'm going to take you right here," he growled.

Her heart leapt. That would be just as she had imagined. The image flew through her mind again of the two of them sinking to the ground and simply *rutting*, like animals in heat.

Beside herself, she moaned and leaned into a hot, wet kiss. There were sounds to this sort of kissing, the rasp of breath, the smack of lips shifting places, the groan that came from one throat and was swallowed by another.

He was crowding her now, his large body pushing hers against the wall, a muscled thigh shoving between her legs. His left hand, the one not holding his cane, slid from her hip to her bottom in a caress that lit her skin on fire.

All that fire swept the place where their bodies connected, even though they were wearing clothing.

"I've learned something about you," Griffin said into her ear, his hand moving slowly from her bottom to the small of her back.

"Mmmm." She had pulled up his shirt so that she could slide her hands underneath the cloth. His chest was ribbed with muscle, barely dusted with hair. She wanted to light every lamp and candle in the house so she could see what she was touching.

"You're wild," he said, clearly surprised and utterly delighted. "I married a wild woman. You merely pretend to be demure." He was crooning it, his mouth trailing fire across her jaw and down her neck.

"I don't think so," she gasped, torn between a wish to be truthful and a wish that she could be that woman he obviously wanted.

"No wonder you couldn't wait fourteen years for me to come home," he said, his voice deep and understanding.

"No," she gasped.

"Don't talk."

His voice was a velvet command, and she let him lick her into silence, loving the way his tongue sparked little trails of fire on her skin. He kissed her until she was writhing, hands biting into his shoulders, and then he suddenly nipped her earlobe. She cried out, her body consumed with flame, and she couldn't keep the words in, no matter how he commanded.

"I want you," she said, her voice a near sob. "I want to . . ."

He spun, jerked open the door. "My bedroom?"

"Four doors down on the left." She was pressing kisses on his jaw. He seemed to have forgotten his injury as he steadily walked her backward, moving through the shadowy corridor while kissing her.

Somehow they made it through the door. Phoebe found herself sitting on the bed, watching as Griffin undid the buttons on his coat and slid it off his shoulders.

It was fascinating to watch a man undress, sensual and somehow deeply intimate.

"Do you like what you see?" he said, pulling off his waistcoat.

She nodded.

"I plan to watch you undress for the next fifty years," he said conversationally.

Something that was wound tight in her heart eased.

He kept switching his cane from hand to hand as he pulled off his clothing. "Would your leg hurt less if you were lying down?" she asked, her voice quavering a little. "Would you like me to help you undress?"

He shook his head and his shirt flew to the side. Phoebe gasped. His chest was just as she had imagined, golden skin stretched over tight muscle.

"Swimming in clothes is tiresome," he told her. He bent over to pull off his boots, grunting as he pulled off the right one.

She started to her feet. "May I help?"

"Yes," he drawled. "Kneel before me, and I'll show you precisely where I need help." His laughing eyes spoke volumes about what he'd like her to do—and removing his remaining boot had nothing to do with it. Besides, the boot was already gone; now he was ripping free the buttons on his breeches.

Startled, she laughed, stumbled, and fell backward onto the bed.

He threw himself down beside her on his side. He was utterly gorgeous, naked and virile, his hair rumpled and that little flower under his eye somehow emphasizing his masculinity.

"The seventeen-year-old in me would like to point out that, contrary to expectation and your truly dazzling self, I am still up to the task."

Her eyes fell between his legs, laughter bubbling out, trailing off at the sight of him. He drew his hand down his length, preening.

"Show-off," she said, wrenching her eyes away.

"Wounded male vanity." He gave himself another slow caress and she found herself watching again. "I'd rather you did this for me."

Fourteen

$\mathcal{P}$hoebe's dress was driving Griffin mad. Well, that and her lips, dyed ruby dark from hard kisses. The gown was a bluish color, its material so frail that he could see the line of her thigh. It had no bodice to speak of, so every voluptuous inch of her was on display, waiting for his touch.

It was a dress that might well belong to a harlot in a high-class brothel. It made him wonder who she'd worn it for before him, before he shut the thought away in a dark corner of his mind.

That part of her life was over. Over.

But he wanted that dress off her. And he didn't want her to ever wear it again. That wasn't a gown that one's wife wore, even if she had taken a lover.

And yet . . . she had looked as startled as a virgin when he touched himself. She hadn't been frightened in the least all those years ago. As he remembered it, she had briskly pulled up her nightgown and lain back on the bed like the embodiment of every boy's wet dream.

"Do as you will," she had said, or something to that effect.

Now she was just as luscious, her curls spilling over her shoulders and her nipples standing out against the frail material of her bodice, begging for his touch.

"Come here, Phoebe," he said. He couldn't help it: his demand came out with the tone of a pirate captain who was never disobeyed.

The little smile that curled her lips looked remarkably like mutiny. She didn't move.

With one swift grab, he pulled her against him and then rolled on top of her. She was soft and yielding, with the kind of generous curves that haunted a man's mind, making him long to return home and grope his wife secretly behind a door.

Even his leg ceased to hurt in the face of a sensation so raw that a groan came from the back of his throat. "Damn, what you do to me," he whispered, pulling a few stray hairpins from her curls and tossing them to the floor.

She bit her lip, a flash of white teeth making her lip even darker. He thought about those ruby-colored lips closing around his most private part, and another groan broke from his throat. "I want you so much."

"I am your wife," she whispered back. "You can have me. I mean, you *do* have me."

The words burned into his heart and had him

shaking from head to foot. But he couldn't simply plunge into her.

There was still that trace of fear at the back of her eyes. Her lover had probably been a smooth and sleek Englishman. And here she was with a brute of a sailor.

He had to seduce her.

Gently.

"You are my wife," he said, loving the sound of it, rolling them both onto their sides. "My only wife." Her hair finally tumbled down over his fingers. He pulled her close and kissed her again. And again. They kissed and kissed, sweet and hot and unbearably sensual. He didn't let his hands leave her hair, twisting until every finger was knotted in silk strands.

She didn't touch him for the longest time but kept her arms locked around his neck as if she was pretending that they were both clothed. As if she hadn't noticed that he was stark naked, trembling with the wish that she would caress him.

Finally her fingers slid to his shoulders, and then down his back. He groaned, and gasped, "Touch me." He'd never heard that tone in his own voice before. But he shook off the thought.

"You're so powerful," she whispered, her feather-light touch sending streaks of heat straight to his groin. He imagined those slender fingers straying below his waist, and grew impossibly harder.

"I will be gentle," he stated, a vow and a promise.

"It's all right," she whispered back. He was drinking up the husky edge in her voice and hardly heard what she said. "I know it will hurt and I don't mind."

"Hurt?" He frowned at her. "I'm large but not monstrous." But her fingers were skimming the curve of his arse, and he was spending all his brainpower curbing himself so he didn't lunge on her like a wild beast.

"Would you mind very much if I ripped your gown?" he asked, trying for a polite air. He really hated that gown and all it implied.

"Not at all. I greatly dislike this gown."

He frowned. "You do?"

"It's not proper," she said, the corners of her lips turned down. "You may destroy it." She wasn't agreeing: she was commanding.

Without another word, he put both his hands on her bodice and ripped it straight down the middle.

She was exquisite . . .

And totally naked.

"No corset," he said, once he recovered enough so that he could breathe. "No chemise? Has English fashion changed so much while I was gone?"

"No," she admitted. "Not at all. I thought I'd die of embarrassment when your father walked into the drawing room. I was convinced he could see how shamefully I was attired."

Another pulse of that unwelcome wish that his wife wasn't quite so experienced, that she didn't know to leave off her undergarments when greeting a man. He pushed it down, away.

"I had no idea," he promised her, "and neither did the viscount. Believe me, I was looking."

Phoebe's breasts were voluptuous and plump, overflowing his hands like a gift from the gods. He ran a hand down the curve of her hips, the length of her legs. She lay before him, naked, flawless, a sweet expanse of perfect skin and sultry curves waiting to be caressed.

"You're perfect, Poppy," he breathed. And then heard what he had just said.

She scowled. "My name is not Poppy. I know you've been with other women, but you have to remember my name."

"I'll never be with another woman again," he said, cupping her face in his hands and bringing his nose close enough to touch hers. "I'm going to spend the rest of my life in this bed."

"No Poppies?"

"Never. Could I call *you* Poppy sometimes?"

"No!"

"Not even when I want to make those beautiful eyes stormy?"

"No." She was an uncompromising woman. He made a mental note to call her Poppy on regular occasions. Obviously, it was his role in life to make certain that his wife laughed.

"No going to sea?"

"Never again without you. I'd like to show you Paris sometime." Tired of talking, he took her mouth, one hand curving under her bottom, pulling her hard against his crotch.

They kissed until he realized that he was in danger of losing control, pinning his wife down and having his way with her.

"You're bad for me," he murmured, leaving her mouth and kissing his way down her throat.

She had to clear her throat to answer. "Why?"

"First you made me impotent. Now you're threatening to turn me into a six-second miracle."

"A what?"

"A misfiring pistol," he said, a laugh rumbling in his throat. For all he was ravaged by lust at the mere sight of her, he actually had an iron grip over himself. He would not lose control until he had wiped out the memory of Colin's father, so that his wife never thought of the man—whoever he was—again.

He'd reached her breast, so he licked and nuzzled and suckled until she was begging him wordlessly, her arms trying to pull him closer, her legs clenching together. "Please," she kept begging. And then commanding, "Now, Griffin!"

There was no reason to obey her, not this time, so he kept on going, down past the curve of her stomach. He glanced up to see a horrified expression on his wife's face.

That just made him grin. Apparently, there was something *he* could teach her in the bedroom. He was skilled . . . she was a woman . . . the outcome was inevitable. And she was wildly responsive, after she got over her initial qualms.

In fact, it was a mere moment before she screamed, her body twisting up before she fell into a surprised, limp heap. He didn't stop. He was reveling in the pure carnality of her lusciousness, in her sleek, wet beauty. So he bent his head and started over with a wantonly sensual kiss, one that broke every rule and demanded utter surrender.

Phoebe surrendered, oh so sweetly. He let the pirate side of him enjoy holding her down, pleasuring her even as she tried to pull him up.

He kept going until her breath was coming in little sobs, her body bucking against his, her eyes glazed.

Then he brought his hand into play, and with just a rough caress and a twist of his fingers, her whole sweet little body tightened around his fingers and she screamed again, falling apart.

It was time.

He came up and over her, pausing for a moment to enjoy the sweet triumph of knowing every luscious inch of her was suffused in pleasure. Her skin stretched like the finest silk over her bones, sweet and creamy, without even a freckle.

Or, more to the point, the faintest stretch mark.

He frowned.

His wife's skin was unmarked, except a trail caused by kisses that must have been rougher than he thought. "Phoebe!" he growled.

She opened those beautiful blue eyes.

Perhaps they would always be able to read each other's thoughts. A little smile instantly curled his wife's lips. "There's something I keep meaning to tell you," she whispered, her voice a husky, sensual invitation. No virgin could . . .

"Damnation!"

Fifteen

$\mathcal{P}$hoebe could have laughed at the astonishment on Griffin's face, but her heart was too full. "It's good news, isn't it?" she asked. "From your point of view, that is?"

"Good," he repeated. He looked as if she'd struck him over the head with a big rock.

She nodded.

He spread his hands across her stomach. She instinctively tensed her muscles to try to draw it flat. She had a curve there. The truth was that she had curves everywhere.

"You didn't sleep with another man." His voice was raw with an emotion she couldn't quite recognize. Relief? "You aren't accustomed to eating dinner without underclothes."

"What? No!"

"You never wore that blue gown for a lover?"

"Absolutely not!" She felt a little indignant at the very idea. "You think I have a *wardrobe* just to satisfy my illicit desires? My maid took off its underskirt because she wanted to make sure you found me desirous."

"Absurd."

She scowled at him.

"As if any red-blooded man in the world could resist you. Now I wish I hadn't ripped the gown." There was laughter in his voice again, but relief, too. Relief and joy and a bedrock strain of desire. "Or rather, I wish I'd jumped off that boat and swum back to shore and tried again. Or that I'd remembered I was married and been faithful to you."

She snorted. "Under English law we aren't yet married, you know. Not until the marriage is consummated. My father told me, the moment I confessed that you were gone."

"You lied?"

"I lied."

He cupped her face in his hands and dropped a kiss on her lips. "Thank you." And: "I don't deserve you."

"No, you don't," she whispered back. "Remember that."

"The children?"

"My cousin died when Alastair was born. Her husband asked me to care for them. He left for the Bermudas and died of a fever only two months later."

"Worthless sod," Griffin growled, picturing Colin's father under his foot. "He should have stayed with his children."

But Phoebe was smiling at him, and the thought slipped out of his head. "They call me Mama. Still, I tell them about their mother, and we visit her grave now and then."

Despite all the emotion, his body was urgently making its demands known. He'd had a cockstand for hours, and he couldn't wait much longer.

"You'll be a wonderful father for them," she said.

The three little ones had already stepped into his heart, that scrappy bravery they showed ten times as dear now he knew they were orphans. "We'll adopt them."

"We already did." Phoebe had the lazy smile of a well-satisfied woman playing around her lips, but he was still in the grip of a ravening hunger.

Strands of hair fell over her voluptuous curves, playing hide-and-seek with a pink nipple. He clasped her breasts with a possessive joy that he had never felt before. "Phoebe," he murmured, bending to lap that nipple. "Could we discuss the children later?"

A tiny gasp, and then: "Yes."

It was a long night. Griffin worked his way down his wife's body again, making certain that she understood that every splendid inch of her was *his,* had been kissed and claimed. In turn, he threw himself on his back and let her touch him everywhere.

"Virgin curiosity," he grumbled, his muscles shaking as he fought to keep control as her fingers glazed his most sensitive parts.

"Exactly," she said. But the gleam in her eye seemed more suited to a pirate queen than a virgin, even as she decided that touch needed to be supplemented by taste. His self-control was on the frailest of threads . . .

Still, she was a *virgin*.

Finally he rolled over, plundered her mouth as he braced himself above her. Her eyes weren't glazed any longer: they were clear, desirous, and passionate. "Yes," she sobbed, "please."

Griffin knew at that moment that he would never experience anything so wonderful again in his life. "This might hurt."

"I know," she said, "just do it. Please!" Her fingers were clenched on his forearms.

He thrust into the sweetest, tightest, heaven-sent . . .

There were no words.

By some miracle, he managed to hang on to his control enough to pause. "Phoebe," he growled, "are you all right?"

"No," she whispered.

"Pain?" He dropped a tender kiss on her mouth. She wiggled and he sucked in a breath. "No."

"No pain?"

She wiggled again. "It's just that I want . . ."

He withdrew in one smooth movement.

"*More*," she said, her voice husky, craving. "More. I want more of that."

He gave her more. At some point he realized that he had been wrong: he hadn't had the best experience of his life already, because surely that came later that night, when Phoebe woke from a nap.

She crawled on top of him and he woke to find a delectable, fragrant woman sinking onto his very willing self.

At which point his very own pirate queen leaned over and whispered, "Sir Griffin Barry. My husband."

Surely that was the best moment . . . but then there was the next morning in the courtyard, when Phoebe described herself as insatiable, beckoned to him like a "crazed widow" (her term), and pushed him up against the wall. They barely made it into the dairy, and all the time he was pounding into her, smothering her cries with his kisses, he could hear Nanny McGillycuddy calling.

Sixteen

The story thus far has taken but a single day . . . but this final chapter happens later, after days had blurred together like shining beads on a string: luminous, joyful, slipping from pleasure to pleasure, into a memory of the best summer of their lives.

Even in all that joy, one night stood out. It was in the dog days of summer, when September was still breathing sluggish, summer dreams, and snow seemed like an old wives' tale. The lake water was warm even in the morning, and the lawn of Arbor House was burned by the sun and disheartened by the pounding of little slippers up and down its slope all day long.

Far from keeping the children out of the lake, Griffin encouraged amphibian habits. This particular day, court had been in session only in the morning, and he had the children in and out of the lake all afternoon. By now they had all learned to swim, though none as well as Colin, who was a veritable fish. Shark had tied a wooden seat to a willow tree; it swung out over the lake and they took turns dropping, screaming, into the water. They raced little wooden boats back and forth and quarreled over a dead fish that Alastair discovered floating belly up.

By six o'clock, when Phoebe and Griffin came around to give goodnight kisses, all three children were already dreaming, brown as berries, exhausted and happy. Colin, Margaret, and Alastair had changed since June. When Griffin first met them, they had been scrappy but vulnerable, with the wariness of children who aren't entirely sure that the world is a safe place.

Now they swam and ran and played with a blithe sense of invulnerability. They were the pirate kings and queen of their world. They had Papa to protect them against everyone, including and most especially pirates, and Mama to cuddle them (when Papa wasn't), and Nanny to scold them, and Lyddie to ignore them, so they could get into mischief now and then.

To their minds, their parents had no greater ambitions than to wrestle and play and soothe them.

But, of course, their parents sometimes waited impatiently for bedtime, played chess with an eye on the clock, stole kisses that no one saw, and counted the minutes until twilight fell.

This evening Griffin kept Phoebe and Viscount

Moncrieff in stitches with tales of the idiot prosecutor for the Crown, one Barnardine Hubble.

"So Hubble looks down at Margery Bindle and he says, with all the pompous clearing of his throat and twitching of his wig that you can imagine, 'Miss Bindle, can you confirm that you believe your baby was conceived on the evening of August eighteen, when the defendant came through Bath in company with his theater troupe?' "

"Poor woman," Phoebe said. "Caught by a player. Some of them are wickedly handsome."

The sideways glance her husband gave her, which said without words that she was not to ogle good-looking actors, was quite satisfying.

"So," Griffin continued, "Margery agrees that the baby was conceived on the evening of August eighteen, and Hubble demands, 'What were you doing at that time?' "

Phoebe broke into giggles, and even the viscount smiled. "The chamber went into an uproar," Griffin admitted. "I couldn't stop laughing myself, and afterward Hubble huffed around the back rooms complaining about a lack of dignity in the courtroom."

"He's right. There is no dignity in your court," Phoebe said, putting down her fork. If she didn't stop eating, she'd be as round as a church steeple in a few months. "Tell your father what happened last week with the doctor."

Griffin and his father were becoming fast

friends, though naturally they never said such a thing aloud. They were too used to considering each other enemies, when to Phoebe's mind they were more alike than different.

"Dr. Inkwell is fascinated by dissection," Griffin said, waving a paring knife as if to illustrate the doctor's technique. "Alas, a Mrs. Crosby claimed that he dissected her husband while still alive, even though the man's death was attested to by two doctors."

"Poor woman," his father observed. He was peeling an apple in one neat spiral.

"Only Hubble would be fool enough to prosecute the case. He began by cross-examining the good doctor. 'Before you began the dissection, did you check for a pulse?' The doctor said no. 'Did you check for breathing?' The doctor said no."

"Shouldn't he have checked something of that nature?" the viscount asked.

"Hubble asked if it's possible that the patient was still alive," Griffin continued, "and Dr. Inkwell said no, because his brain was sitting in a jar on his desk."

A slow smile curled the viscount's lips, the same smile that Phoebe saw countless times a day on her own husband's face.

"And then Hubble asked, without skipping a beat, 'But could the patient have still been alive?' "

"This is the part I love," Phoebe put in.

" 'Absolutely,' snaps Dr. Inkwell. 'Mr. Crosby is undoubtedly alive and practicing the law.' "

They frightened a sleeping sparrow with their

laughter. She started from her nest and flew in a circle around the courtyard before settling in the old oak.

They had been dining early so the viscount could take himself back to his own house and spend the next day working on the most important bill that the House of Lords would see that quarter.

"Tomorrow," Phoebe called, blowing her father-in-law a kiss as he took his leave.

There were no lonely corners of Griffin's heart anymore, but had there been, his father's grin as he left would have soothed them.

Griffin had a family now. Hand in hand, he and Phoebe wandered down the lawn to the water, and from there climbed into the flat-bottom rowboat, and from there ended up in mid-lake. They began with a twilight swim and ended up naked in the boat.

It was that sort of evening.

He was lying flat on his back, enjoying the slosh of warmish water that was playing around his back. Phoebe was on her knees, perched over him, and he knew that any moment now the queen of the pirates would make him happy.

But probably not until he begged.

Which he was going to do, as soon as he'd had enough of stroking those luscious breasts, and then down the slope of her stomach, and . . .

The slope of her stomach.

"Phoebe?" he asked. "Is there something you forgot to tell me?"

She looked down at him, tossed her hair over her shoulder in a way that made her breasts plump in his hands. "Sir Griffin, have you noticed that I like to choose the right moment to make important announcements?"

"I have."

"I have no time for that now."

His hands slid down, into the hottest, wettest place on the whole boat. His wife gasped and dipped to kiss him.

He kissed her hard, saying without words what was in his heart.

Then she straightened and let him guide her with strong hands, let him drop her at just the right angle, let her cry echo across the rippling water and into the quiet night.

"You are my heart," he said, thrusting into her, fierce, out of control as always, beside himself.

She smiled down at him, hair wet and finger-combed, looking like Venus perched on a clam-shell rather than atop a battered pirate. She looked like a boy's wet dream. She looked like his wife.

"I love you," she gasped as he thrust up, at just the angle that he knew she liked the best. "And, Griffin?"

"Yes?" He wasn't really listening, concentrating on making her come before he completely lost his claim to manhood.

"We're having a baby," she cooed.

"You choose now to make your announcement? *Now*?"

Her hands were clutching his shoulders, and

he saw her eyes go luminous, pleasure-filled. He lost control then, but it was all right, because they reached that moment together and tumbled down into a river-soft silence together.

And then when he had carried her off the boat— with a leg that was stronger than ever—he laid her gently on the grass and whispered, "So we're having a baby?"

Her eyes were tender and unbearably loving. "Yes."

"Our fourth," he said, stretching out beside her. "Do you think we have a boy or a girl in here?" He cupped her stomach.

"I don't know. A little viscount, perhaps?"

"I would like Colin to be the viscount," he said, feeling a prickle of guilt. Colin was his right-hand man.

"Colin would hate to be a viscount," Phoebe said with a laugh. "He is going to sea, Griffin. You know he is. You simply need to concentrate on making sure that he never becomes a pirate."

"Of course not," her husband murmured.

And distracted her again.

Epilogue

$\mathcal{I}$t was fair to say that the courtroom of the Justice of the Peace for Somerset was infamous. Certainly among smugglers, solicitors, and ne'er-do-wells. Sir Griffin Barry, Justice of the Peace, had a way of talking to a man who'd been hauled in for beating his wife that could make a hardened criminal turn ash-white.

"He's a maverick," Mr. Calvin Florand said to his young associate, Mr. Edwin Howell. Howell had just entered the Inns of Court, and Calvin always made a point of taking a new associate down to Somerset for a few days. They spent their days observing the court, and their nights pulling apart flagrant violations of law resulting from the doling out of justice. Calvin reckoned that Howell would learn more about justice—and the limits of the law—in three days of watching Justice Barry's court than in a whole year of sitting in a classroom.

Just now Howell was watching Sir Griffin with round eyes. His Honor never looked precisely justice-like—how could he, given that tattoo?— but he looked particularly dangerous today. He wasn't clean-shaven, and his wig, rather than giving him the air of an English gentleman, made him look like a lion at a costume ball.

"Does he always look like this?" Howell asked in a low voice.

They watched for a moment as Sir Griffin leaned over the bench and gave the defendant a hard stare. The clerk had just read aloud a criminal complaint against one Charlie Follykin, who was charged with buying three and a half "tubs of spirits" for thirteen shillings a tub in France and transporting them across the Channel, with intent to resell them in England for four pounds each.

"How do you plead?" demanded the clerk.

"A pox o' your throats!" Charlie spat.

The prisoner looked like a man who expressed his appetites with abandon. He had a large stomach, a large mustache, and a glossy sheen to his eye that suggested unswerving overindulgence in spirits.

As the silence wore on, Sir Griffin leaned over and said, "Did you drink half a tub before or after selling it?"

"Never drink what I could sell," Charlie assured him. Apparently, even Charlie understood that insulting this justice would not be a good idea.

"Then you meant to sell it. He enters a plea of guilty," Sir Griffin directed. The clerk scribbled on the court docket.

"I'm curious, Charlie," the justice said, fixing the prisoner with a gimlet eye. "Exactly how did you get to France?"

"Get to France?" Charlie said, letting fly with a tremendous belch. "I never do. I won't. I've been drinking all night, and I'm not fitted for it."

"You must answer His Honor's questions," admonished the clerk.

Charlie looked blearily up at the bench. "I'll not go to France, even if you beat my head out with billets."

The clerk was clearly distressed at this lack of reverence, but the judge merely looked amused. Finally, when it seemed that Charlie was getting the better of the court, Sir Griffin stood up. He walked down from his seat, carefully turning back the wide velvet sleeves of his robes.

The clerk faded backward, leaving Charlie mumbling to himself and looking at the floor.

"You!" said the justice, when he was standing before the prisoner.

Charlie jumped. There was something about that voice which clearly woke him out of his trance. "Huh?"

"Do you want me to knock you into next Monday?"

"No," Charlie said hastily.

"Tell me why in the blazes you are in this court on a trumped-up charge."

Charlie peeked at the justice, then looked back at the floor. "I was supposed to guard the tubs," he muttered. "Eight shillings a night."

Sir Griffin walked around and climbed up onto his chair. "Right," he said briskly. "The prisoner changes his plea. Not guilty, here by reason of collusion. Who turned you in, Charlie?"

Silence. The clerk darted forward and poked the prisoner in the back.

Charlie just looked confused.

Sir Griffin leaned over, and a flash of real annoyance crossed his face. "Follykin, this is the eleventh time I've had you before the bench in the last four years."

"Not that many," Charlie said, looking rather appalled.

"My wife gave birth to a baby yesterday. Do you think that I want to be here, breathing the foul air coming from your mouth?"

Charlie shook his head.

"Babies cry all night," the justice said reflectively. "I know what happened here, Follykin. Your friends talked you into taking the fall for the smuggling because you fell down on the job of guarding the tubs, drank the brandy, and then let the assizes find you."

"Only had a sip or two," Charlie protested.

"You didn't mind because you like the jail, don't you? I've heard the jailer's wife has a rare hand with a pasty."

"She does," Charlie agreed.

"Right." The justice slammed his hammer onto his table. "The prisoner is condemned to four days hard labor, not for importing spirits, which he didn't do, but for the crass stupidity of wasting my time so he can get his hands on some Cornish pasties. The four days hard labor will be carried out in the children's foundling home, where I would expressly note that after being given a thorough cleaning, the prisoner should be put to rocking babies. All day. And most of the night. He can bed down in a storage closet."

Charlie looked up at the judge, a tragic look crossing his face. "Don't do that to me, Your Honor," he begged.

The clerk prodded him with a stick. "Move along, Follykin. You know His Honor doesn't ever change his mind."

"Why should you have a better night than I will?" the justice demanded. He took off his robes, tossed them into the hands of a waiting clerk, and left the courtroom without further ado.

"That's bollocks," the young lawyer whispered. "There wasn't any procedure. He threatened the prisoner. He sentenced him to hard labor even though he was innocent, or at least partly innocent. And that kind of hard labor . . . I've never heard of it. A storage closet isn't jail!"

"Right," Calvin said. "Now I happen to know that the jailer's wife provides the very inn we're staying at with pasties, so let's retire, shall we, and discuss the finer points of the actual *use* of English law in our courtrooms."

Outside, Griffin climbed rather stiffly into his carriage. These days his leg gave him a twinge only when he was dead tired.

He was dead tired.

Fred had come into the world screaming as loudly as he could, and he hadn't stopped yet.

When Griffin reached his house, Fred's wailing had upset his sister Sophie, who was crying as well, and what with one thing and another, Alastair and Colin were up, too. The only child peacefully sleeping, in fact, was Margaret. Griffin appeared at the nursery door only to find that his poor wife had the desperate look of a woman in need of rescue.

Griffin took Fred and popped him into the cradle; wonder of wonders, he fell asleep. Nanny took charge of Sophie, Lyddie took Alastair to the kitchens for a glass of milk, and Griffin picked up his poor wife, tired as she was, and carried her all the way down the hill to the river.

They sat there for at least an hour, just staring at the water and ignoring the faint sounds of mayhem that continued to issue from the house. The moon turned the water into a shimmering silver plate.

Griffin thought there was probably nothing more lovely than to have his wife's round bottom in his lap and to rest his chin on her hair and feel her breathing against his chest.

After a time Colin came trotting down the hill with a bundle in his arms, trailing a bit of pink blanket.

Phoebe rose and took Fred—crying again—then settled down in a different chair to feed the child, who appeared to have the appetite of a future giant.

Colin leaned against his father's shoulder in a companionable sort of way.

"I like the way you brought Fred down here," Griffin said, winding his arm around his eldest son's shoulder. "Good man."

"Had to be done," said the pirate.

"A man's got to do what a man's got to do."

Fred burped, and Colin wrinkled his nose. "Do you think he'll sleep any better tomorrow night? He doesn't seem to sleep at all."

"Probably not," Griffin said. He looked over at his wife's bright hair. He could just see the curve of her cheeks as she murmured to their new son.

"Do you suppose you could stop having babies now?" Colin asked with a sigh. "There are five of us, you know. It seems like an awful many."

Griffin's heart swelled with the pure joy of the moment. All those years on board ship, he'd grappled with adventure and death and mayhem. He thought he was proving himself, but he didn't really understand what it was to be a man until he returned home.

"Five seems like a good number to me," he said, hauling Colin's lanky body over the side of his chair and into his lap.

"I'm too old to sit in your lap," Colin protested, his skinny legs flailing a moment. But then he settled against Griffin's shoulder, and two seconds later he was asleep.

Griffin reached out and took his wife's hand. "I love you," he said quietly.

Phoebe smiled at him. She was more beautiful

than she'd been when they married, more beautiful than she'd been when he returned from the sea. She would only get more lovely every year . . . and he would only love her more.

"Damn," he said quietly. "I don't even know what to do with the way I feel for you, Phoebe."

She smiled again, her eyes luminous in the moonlight. "Just love me, Griffin."

He raised her hand to his lips. "There's no question of that, my darling."

She narrowed her eyes. "Don't you dare . . ."

"My darling Poppy," he said smugly.

A Note from Eloisa

There's nothing more irritating than a story that ends with a loose thread! So, you may be wondering, who won the bet? Which pirate proved the more seductive, Griffin or James?

The answer can be found by comparing Griffin's success here to James's success in *The Ugly Duchess*, my most recent fairy tale. That novel is spun, obviously, from Hans Christian Andersen's "The Ugly Duckling." My version puts together a duckling and a pirate, with a touch of "Cinderella"— and a dash of Coco Chanel. Theo, the duchess in question, is a witty, lovable heroine. And of course, James (and Griffin) sail the seven seas, tattooed and muscled and altogether delectable.

If you like rewritten fairy tales, I'd love to introduce you to my series. So far I've written *A Kiss at Midnight* (a version of "Cinderella"), *When Beauty Tamed the Beast*, and *The Duke Is Mine* (a version of "The Princess and the Pea"). The last fairy tale is probably the least well known. Remember the story of a princess who arrives at the castle gates in the middle of the night and is put to the test to see if she is a "real" princess—by sleeping on one hundred mattresses and a pea, among other things? I had a great time figuring out how to get those mattresses into the plot. (And the pea! The pea was another challenge.)

That's probably the most fun aspect of rewriting fairy tales: how does one take the structural underpinnings of one story and weave an entirely new, fresh story around them? I'm very happy to announce my next fairy tale will be a version of *Rapunzel*, the story of a golden-haired girl locked in a tower. Mine is called, quite fittingly, *Once Upon a Tower*, and it publishes in June 2013.

If you enjoyed the length of "Seduced by a Pirate," I have quite a number of novellas that make perfect reading in a waiting room (I've taken to reading on my phone, and I love it). Two are loosely connected to my version of fairy tales, "Winning the Wallflower" to *The Duke Is Mine*, and "Storming the Castle" to *A Kiss at Midnight*. "A Fool Again" is another e-novella, connected to one of my earlier novels called *Fool for Love*. Of course, all my novels are available in electronic form. Want to read more about them? I have excerpts, inside information, and even some photos that inspired my characters on my website, www. eloisajames.com.

And, as always, you can find me either through

email (Eloisa@eloisajames.com) or on Facebook: www.facebook.com/eloisajamesfans. Please check in and tell me what you thought of "Seduced by a Pirate" and "With This Kiss."

Yours,

With This Kiss
Part One

One

August 1827
Arbor House
Home of Sir Griffin Barry

$\mathcal{B}$y the age of ten, Lady Grace Ryburn had a clear understanding of her place in the world. Her mama, the Duchess of Ashbrook, made certain that her four children knew precisely how to behave in any conceivable instance, and Grace was a dutiful eldest daughter.

She had impeccable manners. She never sat on the grass, or climbed trees, or behaved in any fashion other than that which behooved a member of the peerage. She spoke three languages, played the pianoforte, and painted landscapes (poorly) and portraits (surprisingly well). She was kind to servants, old people, and dogs.

She was boring.

Grace's little sister Lily, two years younger, was not boring. Lily never walked if she could run. She ripped her frocks, spilled her milk, and gave people sparkling looks and disobedient smiles. She didn't obey anyone's rules, including the duchess's.

Their father said that Lily was a force of nature. After years of observing her sister, Grace came to understand what her father meant. Because she was so pretty, Lily didn't have to behave. She had been adorable as a baby, and now, at eight, she was dazzling.

There was one good thing about not being the center of attention, like Lily. Grace could sit inconspicuously at the edges of rooms and watch people's faces—the way their jaws moved, the way they blinked, the way their foreheads wrinkled when they talked. She watched the way grown-ups responded to a girl like Lily versus a girl like herself.

Since Grace was plain, quiet, and not sparkly—but very smart—she came to the obvious conclusion that it was risky to misbehave. Without being pretty, she couldn't command love and forgiveness the way her sister could.

So Grace minded her Ps and Qs . . . until one August night, when her family was staying at Arbor House, the country house of Sir Griffin Barry and his family. The Barrys spent every December at Ryburn House, and the Ryburns spent every August at Arbor House, and that was the way it had been for Grace's entire life.

Most of the year, the Ryburn estate ran smoothly, with over one hundred servants weaving and interacting, all devoted to the comfort of the duke, the duchess, and their four children. But in August, many of the duke's servants were sent back to their own homes and most of the furniture was put under Holland covers. The great estate of Ryburn House fell to a sleepy summer silence as Grace and her family made their way to Arbor House, which had only twenty servants to take care of all of them: Sir Griffin and Lady Barry and their five children, and the duke and duchess and their four children.

It was chaos. It was glorious. The ducal progeny dreamed of it all year long. They talked longingly of days when they were in and out of the lake all day, when the air was lazy and sweet with the smell of new-mown hay, and when the children often didn't bathe at all.

At Arbor House, the Barrys' nanny ruled the nursery, and the Ryburns' nannies found themselves curtsying to her. Nanny McGillycuddy believed that children, even little lords and ladies, shouldn't have too much supervision. There weren't nearly enough maids, and no footmen at all, and their parents picnicked with them on the grass. Ordinarily, the duchess wouldn't dream of sitting on a blanket and eating outdoors. She just wasn't the type, any more than Grace was.

But when the two families were together, everything was different. Sir Griffin and Grace's papa had been pirates together, sailing the high seas, and so they told stories of sea battles, and once in a while they would actually drag out their rapiers and stage a mock fight for all nine children to watch.

Grace generally found herself watching Colin, instead. In her heart of hearts, she thought Sir Griffin's eldest son was the most handsome boy in all England. He was tall and lean, and his shoulders already showed definition. He had a strong jaw and tumbled chestnut hair, but it was his eyes that she thought about most. They were periwinkle blue, a color she couldn't capture with her paints, no matter how many times she mixed and remixed.

She wasn't alone. Even her mother—whom everyone called the most elegant woman in England—laughed, and said that if *she* had been introduced to Colin at an impressionable age, she never would have given her husband a second look. That would make the duke growl and scoop his wife into his arms, pretending that he was going to carry her off to his pirate's lair.

Colin was the kindest boy she knew, too. Once, when she was a little girl and skinned her knee, he had wrapped it up in his own handkerchief, and had told her how brave she was. Ever since, she had felt brave.

Now that he was a big boy, all of sixteen, she was too shy to hop into his lap the way Lily did. But earlier in the evening, she had leaned against his shoulder while he told a story about a sea dragon and a pirate treasure.

In the middle of that night Grace was woken by a moan that had come straight through the wall next to her bed. Her room was next to Colin's, so the noise had to have come from his bedchamber. She sat up, wondering if something was wrong.

A lady could never enter a gentleman's chamber. That was a big rule, one of the biggest rules her mother had impressed upon her.

But Colin was almost like a brother.

When she heard a second moan, she jumped straight out of bed, and without even thinking about it, made her way into his room.

"Colin," she whispered, putting a hand on his shoulder. "What's the matter?"

"I'm hot," he said with a ragged moan. "Terribly hot."

Grace headed for the washbasin, wrung out a cloth, and brought it back to the bed. She wiped his face, trying not to get the bedclothes wet. "I'll ring for a maid," she told him, settling the neatly folded cloth on his brow.

"No maids will come," Colin said, with another moan. "Nanny McGillycuddy is old. She's too old to get out of bed."

Grace frowned at that, because she realized that his fever must be terribly high if he thought he was in the nursery. On the other hand, he might be right about the maids. In her mother's household, maids always came within two minutes of a bell, but the same could not be said for Arbor House. "I could fetch our nanny," she offered.

Colin flung himself on his side, and the cloth

slid off from his head to the floor. "I'm so hot. I shall die in this desert."

"Don't be silly. Of course you won't die." Grace reached over so she could feel his head. That's what her nanny always did when she was ill.

He grasped her wrist and squinted up at her. "It's Lily, isn't it? You're my favorite. I'll love you forever, if you'll please give me some water, sweet Lily."

Grace froze. He thought that *Lily* was coming to his aid?

There were times when Grace was so jealous of Lily that she wanted to scream, and this was a perfect example. Colin liked Lily so much that he didn't even realize that Grace was standing right next to him. The truth of it pinched her heart and made her angry.

The glass on his bedstand was empty, so she went back for the pitcher. She brought it to the bed, but before she could fill the glass Colin sat up and reached toward the pitcher.

"Let me pour you a glass," she said, pulling back as he grabbed at it.

"You're a brick, Lily," he said. "You're the b—"

His voice broke off as the pitcher upended on his head. Water struck his face and ran in a flood down his chest and even splashed onto Grace's nightgown.

For a moment, she felt only satisfaction. She wasn't such a good girl right now, was she?

Then a terrible feeling gripped her stomach. She had poured water on Colin, who was ill. Dying, maybe. Never mind the fact that he was laughing, albeit weakly.

She ran for the door, crying, "Mama!"

Her mother bundled her back to bed, and Grace lay there, sleepless, until the noise stopped next door and she knew that they had moved Colin to another room because his bed was wet.

The next morning her mother said, "Sweet pea, you should have rung for a maid when you realized Colin was in need of help. And how *did* he end up soaking wet?"

"He moaned, Mama. I heard it right through the wall." She couldn't stop herself from telling the rest. "He thought I was Lily, and he said that he'd love me forever. I mean, he'd love *Lily* forever."

Her mother raised a slender eyebrow. "Why would he love Lily forever?"

"If she would give him some water." Grace swallowed. She'd never had to admit to naughtiness before. "So I gave him the water."

Her mother pressed her lips together tightly, as if she were trying not to laugh. Then she said, "Grace, you do know that one never throws water at a gentleman, no matter how irritated one might be?"

Grace nodded.

"And a lady never visits a gentleman's bedchamber in the middle of the night, *particularly* if she hears moaning?"

Grace didn't quite follow that last part, but she nodded again.

The duchess stooped and gave her a hug. She

smelled so good, like wildflowers and silk. "It sounds as if Colin deserved it," she whispered.

Her mother was like that. She understood things.

Grace leaned against her shoulder for a moment. "He thought I was Lily," she repeated, unsure why that hurt so much.

"It was because you are a young lady who doesn't even sleep in the nursery any longer," her mother said, giving her a kiss. "Colin wouldn't dream that you would be wandering the halls . . . but Lily, of course, is another matter."

"But he said that *she* was his favorite."

"He's changed his tune this morning. He can't believe that she overturned a pitcher of water on his head!"

Her mother's eyes were dancing, and that made a little giggle bubble up inside Grace.

"He won't die of a chill?"

"Absolutely not. He's already feeling better."

No one else ever learned the truth. Lily was furious when Colin told the whole drawing room that she had been the one to break his fever, and perhaps save his life.

"I wouldn't save his life if he paid me a half a crown!" she told Grace later. "He's a horrid boy and I think it's mean of him to tell everyone that I poured water on his head. Not that I wouldn't, because I *would*!"

Lily's eyes gleamed in a way that Grace recognized, but she didn't really care. She'd caught Colin's fever, and it was making her head ache.

The rest of the feud became family lore among the Ryburns and the Barrys. Lily marched down to the lake and carefully skimmed off all the frogspawn she could find. Then she sent the youngest maid in the household to Colin's bedchamber with a plate of hot toast spread with "beef jelly," the better to strengthen him.

Colin ate every piece.

Two

Two years later
December 1829
On the way to Ryburn House

Colin Barry, the eldest son of Sir Griffin Barry—but not heir to his father's title, as he'd joined the family by way of adoption—was absurdly pleased to be home for Christmas. Although in point of fact he wasn't headed home; after leaving his ship, he had picked up his brother Fred at Eton and they were on their way to the country house of the Duke of Ashbrook.

He hadn't been in England in more than a year; he'd been at sea, fighting the wind and the waves, wearing the uniform of the Royal Navy. His father had taught him everything he knew about sailing, and inasmuch as Sir Griffin had been a notorious pirate—before he became an equally notorious justice of the peace—Colin had an unfair advantage over other young men his age. Those lessons explained why he was carrying with him a commission from His Majesty's navy stating that Mr. Colin Barry, midshipman, had received a commendation from Rear Admiral Sir George Cockburn.

Colin saw that commendation as an expected step on the way to being the youngest captain ever to be given his own ship in the Royal Navy. He had a burning wish to make his father proud, and since he knew perfectly well that his mother would never allow him to become a pirate, a naval captain was next best.

"How are all the Ryburns?" he asked Fred.

Fred shrugged. "Grace and Lily are fine. The twins are still in the nursery."

"How is the terror herself, Lily?" Last time he'd seen her, she'd been an eight-year-old with the temper of a young devil. Her own mother nicknamed her The Horror. Of course, that had been two years ago.

"Annoying," Fred said shortly. "She thinks she's grown up and she acts like a romp. Grace is much better."

It was hard to imagine Lily becoming a young lady. Whenever he thought of her he got a little lurch in his stomach, remembering the frogspawn she'd tricked him into eating. Not to mention the toad she put in his bed a few days later.

"Oh!" Fred said, looking up. "One thing did happen. Grace almost died; did Mother write you about it?"

Colin frowned. "She mentioned an illness, but I didn't realize Grace was truly in danger."

"Something is wrong with her lungs." Fred looked away, out the window. "I hate that."

"I'm sorry," Colin said gently. "Will she get better?"

"Of course she will!" Fred scowled at him and bent his head back over his book. "I have to learn this Greek."

Colin nodded, not that his brother noticed. There were five siblings in his family: himself, Margaret, Alastair, Sophie, and Fred. Given the four in the Ryburn family—Grace, Lily, Cressida, and Brandon—nine children had tumbled about together for large stretches of his childhood. To lose one would be inconceivable.

Lily was the loudest and the naughtiest Ryburn, which made it all the more unexpected when they were greeted by a charming young lady, who curtsied with a sprightliness that made her perfectly groomed curls bob around her shoulders, and generally behaved like the daughter of a duke. Even so, Fred regarded her with a healthy skepticism, and Colin felt a bit wary himself. There was something about Lily's smile—no matter how charming—that suggested she was enjoying her own performance.

"My poor darling Grace is closed up in the nursery, which is *such* an insult for a young lady of twelve," the duchess said, after a few minutes. "You did hear that she's been ill?"

"I was very sorry to learn that," Colin said. "I hope she's feeling better."

"She's much improved. We may take her to Spain after Christmas to see if sunshine might help her turn the corner. Do go and see her. Grace always loves news of you."

"In the nursery, you said?" Colin felt rather sick at the thought. Grace was the quietest of the ducal progeny, but he hated to think of her confined to bed.

He climbed the stairs as Lily's giggles drifted from the sitting room behind him, punctuated by the duchess's laughter. A moment later he poked his head around the nursery door. Grace was sitting up in bed, her vivid red hair in a braid. Her fingers looked very delicate, holding a book.

Colin froze. It was the one thing he hated about being in the navy: the fact that people died. Not just men on his ship, but the enemy as well. He was haunted at night by images of a man he'd shot falling into the waves, and of a man on fire after the mainsail had broken out in flames.

He shook himself. Grace was not dying. She had improved. The duchess said so.

She looked up. "Colin!" Her face lit up. "I'm so happy you're back safely!"

He walked over to her, and sat down at her bedside. "Poor Grace! You've grown as thin as a pennywhistle." He took her hand, which was as white as her face. His heart was thudding in his ribs. He had hated learning lessons about death at sea; it was even worse to encounter that threat at home.

"I'll be better in no time. Mother and I are going to travel to Spain after Christmas. What about you? Have cannonballs been whizzing past your ears?" Her hand tightened on his. "We worry about you so."

"A cannonball did hit my ship last month," he admitted.

"That must have been awful."

He looked down at her fingers against his sun-darkened skin. "It was, rather. I don't like to think of you almost dying, Grace. No more of that."

"I don't intend to die," she replied, with the kind of quiet dignity that characterized her.

Colin studied her face for a moment and then smiled. She had a little pointed chin and huge gray eyes; she looked a bit like an elf. "How old are you, if you don't mind my asking?"

Grace turned up her nose. "I'm a young lady, so you mustn't ask that sort of thing."

"You're twelve," Colin said, remembering. "My goodness, by the time I next have leave, you'll probably be dancing your way through your first season."

She shook her head. "It's years away, and you must come home sooner than that. Besides, I hate dancing."

"It's impossible to imagine a young lady who hates dancing," he said teasingly, adding, "though in truth, so do I."

"I prefer to paint. I've had to spend a great deal of time in bed, so Mother bought me some proper watercolors." She reached to the side and handed him a sketchbook.

Colin opened it and found himself quite startled. Grace's paintings weren't the sort of ham-handed jumbles that he and Margaret had created at the same age. The first page held a vivid painting of a lop-eared dog. The paws weren't quite right, but he would have recognized that dog anywhere, simply by the look on her face. "Old Bessie," he said. "Mother wrote me that she'd passed away."

"We buried her under the flagstones by the buttery," Grace said. "That's where she liked to sleep, in the sun."

Colin turned the page and discovered a portrait of a young maid, and then a window with clouds visible in the sky beyond, and finally an apple just on the verge of turning soft. "I think you're brilliant," he said, meaning every word. "I could never do anything approaching this."

She beamed at him, and her smile was so beautiful that Colin blinked. Grace generally stayed in Lily's shadow, and to be honest, he hardly thought about her. But now he realized that Fred could be right: Grace might well be the more interesting of the two sisters.

The thought made him uncomfortable. She was a twelve-year-old girl, for heaven's sake. And he was eighteen, a grown man. He rose to his feet and bowed, picking up her hand and kissing the back of it.

"Lady Grace, I hope you are entirely recovered very soon."

Her eyes grew round. She had extraordinary eyelashes, as thick a fringe as he'd ever seen.

"Oh!" she said, pulling her hand away quickly. "I expect I shall."

Colin got out of the room feeling rather queer. He was the eldest child in the Griffin family, and he had watched as his own siblings and the duke's babies arrived. They were all *family*, nothing more than that.

It was just odd to think of Grace and Lily growing up, that was all.

Three

Two more years have passed
December 1831
Ryburn House
The Duke of Ashbrook's country estate

The year Grace turned fourteen, Colin walked through the door in a uniform, and her heart gave one big thump and never beat exactly the same way again. He had grown even taller. His shoulders were very wide, and his cheekbones much more pronounced.

Her family flew from their chairs and everyone clustered around, exclaiming at the fact he'd been made a lieutenant. Grace didn't quite dare join them, but all day she secretly watched him whenever they were in a room together. When her mother declared that she was old enough to join the adults at supper, Grace walked down the stairs white with excitement.

Sir Griffin happened to be in the entry, and he looked up at Grace and then smiled. He was a justice of the peace, and Papa had been trying all morning to talk him into running for Parliament, before his father died and Sir Griffin had to take up his seat in the House of Lords.

But she didn't think he would run for Parliament; he liked going to court half the day and then playing with his children or sweeping his wife off for a private talk. She loved her own mama and papa dearly, but they were busy all day long.

Now Sir Griffin waited until she reached the bottom step and said, "Lady Grace, you are exquisite. How did you manage to grow up while my back was turned?"

Grace dropped into a deep curtsy and smiled at him. "I am not quite grown up yet."

He offered his arm. "Your mother showed me the painting of Fred in which you caught his snub nose perfectly. I think you show a positive genius with a brush."

Sir Griffin sat her beside Colin, stopping to ruffle his oldest son's hair, just as if he were eleven instead of twenty. "Why don't you do a portrait of this ruffian, Grace? It would give us something to swear at when he decides to visit the fleshpots of Europe rather than return home where he belongs."

Grace had no idea what "fleshpots" were, but they didn't sound very nice.

"I'd love to have you paint my picture," Colin said cheerfully as she sat down beside him. "As long as you don't bring along that naughty little sister of yours."

"I tried to paint her portrait last week, but she wouldn't sit still long enough."

Colin laughed. "Lily is like a sprite, isn't she? Flying on to whatever mischief she can make next."

Grace could have sorted him out regarding Lily. She wasn't nearly as interested in mischief as his own brother Fred was, for example. She was just high-spirited. Papa said he was planning to move to Scotland when she came of age. Mama said that Lily was just like her father.

Deep in her soul, Grace resented the fact that everyone talked about Lily all the time. "I rode my first steeplechase," she told Colin, ignoring his foolish comment about sprites: Lily couldn't fly. And she was even worse at riding than Grace was.

"That's brilliant! Any luck?"

She shook her head. She'd fallen off after about ten minutes, and had been taken home by a groom. "So is it fun being at sea?"

"Fun?"

"Yes, fun," she prompted. "You always said that the best thing in the world would be to go to sea and never step foot on the shore again. So I was wondering whether it is as much fun as you thought it would be."

"There are moments that are great fun," Colin said slowly, then stopped because his mother asked him something from his left.

"Which moments?" Grace asked, when that conversation was over, and she had his attention once more.

"There's nothing better than being chased by a storm. It howls up behind you, and it takes everything you've got to outwit it."

Grace could almost imagine it because of paintings she'd seen in the National Gallery. "Isn't it wet and cold? Aren't you afraid?"

"Storms are not always cold. If you're in the Tropics, the water can be warm as your bath, but even so a storm can whip it up so that it froths like cream."

"I shouldn't like that."

"You might surprise yourself. There's a wonderful burst of excitement that comes from skimming before a wind that's going faster than even the swiftest bird can fly."

Grace shook her head. "I don't care for excitement."

"You don't, do you? It's Lily who inherited the pirate sensibility."

Lily again. Grace was tired of hearing about Lily.

"What parts are not as much fun?" she asked.

His eyes darkened a little, the periwinkle blue going navy. Like seawater in a storm, she thought, or her father's favorite waistcoat. Her father liked somber colors, though her mother always tried to put him in magnificent purples.

"Oh, you don't want to hear about that."

Grace sat up a little straighter and gave him a polite smile. She was her mother's daughter and had excellent manners. She knew that one never argued at the table. "I do wish to hear about that," she pointed out. "Otherwise I would not have asked."

Colin grinned at her. "Do you always mean precisely what you say?"

"Yes." Grace didn't have a gift for fibbing. She was fascinated by the way people tried to hide their thoughts. More than anything, she liked watching the secrets people had in their faces. But she knew perfectly well that she didn't have any secrets herself, and no ability to hide them if she did. "Do tell me what you don't like about being at sea."

"Sometimes it feels as if the ship has fallen out from under your feet, and you suddenly realize the water beneath you is fathoms deep: I don't like those moments."

Grace shivered. "I wouldn't, either. Especially because that water is full of fish who would like to eat you."

"Not all of them," Colin said. Then he told her about fish that had lights on their noses, and eels whose tails whipped the water so it looked as if a current went through it.

But Grace was nothing if not tenacious. "What else don't you like about being at sea?" she asked, some time later.

Colin's smile went crooked. "You never give up, do you?"

"Why should I?" Grace asked. "If I want to know something, I mean?"

"Right you are," he muttered. "Well, I have to say that I don't like fighting. And that's a problem because I'm in the navy, and the navy is all about fighting."

"Do you fight with swords?"

"Mostly with guns." His face closed shut and his eyes went the color of the ocean at night, not blue but black.

"When you are fighting, do you wish that you were home instead?"

"There's no time for it, not in the middle of a sea battle." He stopped but then he added, "After, when we're cleaning up from the fight, I want nothing more than to watch Fred and Lily misbehaving, or see my father and yours behaving like idiots at the dinner table."

"Idiots?" Grace frowned at him. "Papa is never an idiot. Don't you have maids to clean up for you on board ship?"

"No," Colin said. "There are no maids in the navy, Grace."

"I could write you a letter now and then," she offered. "If I knew where to send it, that is. I can describe to you what's happening at home so that you can picture it, even if you are washing the deck."

A faint smile touched his lips. "I would love any letter that you would write me. If your father forwarded it to the Admiralty, they would send it on to me in a dispatch."

And that was how Lady Grace Ryburn began writing to Colin Barry, Lieutenant. Her first letter was quite short, and included a frank truth: "I hate Lily. Last night she cut off the fingers of my favorite pair of gloves because she thought it was funny."

Colin wrote a note back, saying that he'd had a rotten week, and her letter about the gloves made him laugh.

So Grace started trying to find stories that might make him laugh in the midst of the worst days. She described her brother taking all of their father's neck cloths and turning them into sails for toy boats. She wrote when the chickens escaped and perched on the housekeeper's clean linens. She even put in a little watercolor of a hen roosting on a sheet.

She told him the plots of plays they saw in London, and what their governess said about them. Once she even wrote down an entire song that Lily learned in German, sending it along with an ink drawing of Lily singing with an agonized expression.

In fact, she found herself writing about Lily quite a lot. Lily *was* funny. Besides, no matter how much Grace resented her sister, she loved her even more. Grace tried to make her own life sound as interesting, but it wasn't.

At some point, she began painting very, very small portraits (because she had to make them fit between the folds of a sheet of pressed paper), and many of them were of Lily, too.

Mostly, Colin didn't write back, but when he did, he always thanked her, and he always asked what Lily had got up to lately.

By two years later, Colin hadn't managed to return to England, but Grace was still writing to him twice a month.

Both families got used to asking Grace how Colin was doing, and after a while she began forwarding his letters to Sir Griffin and Lady Barry. Colin was not communicative, it seemed. The occasional letters he sent to Grace were the only ones he wrote at all.

"He has a best friend," she told them all one December. "His name is Philip Drummond and he's a lieutenant as well. Colin says that Philip is a better sailor than he is."

And the following August: "He and Philip are assigned to the West Africa Squadron. Their ship is trying to protect people from being stolen from Africa. He says slavers fight like demons when they're caught."

"He's a chip off the old block," her father said, smiling at Sir Griffin and raising his glass. "You raised a good man, Coz."

But Grace remembered how much Colin hated fighting, and didn't care whether Colin was good or not; she just wished he could come home.

Four

$\mathcal{F}$red snorted. "If you don't fall for Lily, you'll be the only man for miles around who hasn't."

"She can't be sixteen," Colin said, raising an eyebrow.

"She's fifteen, the same as I am. She was swanning about Bath in July, flirting with anyone in breeches."

"Are you hoping she'll wait for you?"

Fred scowled. "She's still a horror, if you ask me. I like Grace better, but she's older than me."

The sun slanting low through the carriage windows caught Fred's cheekbones and his wildly curling hair, and Colin thought that his brother—especially after he grew into his ears—would be as likely to cause swooning as Lily.

Not that Fred cared. He wanted to be an astronomer, and because their parents were quite unconventional in insisting their children learn more than how to dance a reel, Fred spent his time studying planetary motions and the like.

"So what else has changed at home?" Colin asked, settling back into his corner of the carriage. He felt a bone-deep sense of happiness at the idea of spending a few days at Arbor House.

"Nothing," Fred said, turning a page. "Alastair made a fool of himself over Lily in December, not that she paid him any mind. He's had a hopeless infatuation for years now. It was embarrassing to watch."

"I find the idea of Lily as a heartbreaker extremely hard to imagine," Colin said.

"She's the biggest flirt in five counties, that's what Father says. Though he likes her."

"He does?"

"Everyone does." Fred thought about it for a moment and then offered, "I think because she's so pretty, but at the same time, she makes you feel comfortable to be talking to her."

"A very wise assessment. Is that enough to make every young man in her vicinity fall in love?"

Fred rolled his eyes. "She's the daughter of a duke; everyone knows she has pots of pirate gold for her dowry; and she's bigger in the front than most girls her age."

"That would do it."

"She'll love you. She's up for a challenge."

"What do you mean?"

"Just that. At an assembly, she likes to line up all the eligible men and knock them down like nine-pins. You weren't around this year, so she hasn't knocked you over yet. I'd say that you'll be desperately in love with her by the end of the first day."

"Why should I be at risk, since you aren't?"

"It depends on whether you remember what she's really like. I shall never forget."

"And that is?"

"Horrid. Frogspawn horrid."

Colin nodded. "She might well have changed, though."

"You never know who you're really talking to," Fred said darkly. "You wait. Lily looks as sweet as pie. But underneath? *Frogspawn*."

"*A*re you truly only fifteen years old?" Colin asked, a few minutes after being charmed by an utterly engaging young lady, who had her mother's elegance and her father's looks. "And are you sure that you are *Lily*?"

She threw him a sparkling glance. But as a dashing young lieutenant encounters many a sparkling young lady, Colin just grinned back at every minxlike look she gave him from under her lashes, until she burst into laughter.

"Yes, do give up," he said, answering her unspoken comment. "I know that you have ambitions to be the most hotly sought-after young lady on the marriage mart, but I'm not available."

Lily's face lit with honest laughter was so much more seductive than her flirtatious glances that Colin actually felt a flash of attraction. "I shall be," she confided. "Mother only allowed me to go to select events this year, but next spring I shall make a proper debut."

"In London?"

"Of course. Grace will be coming as well as she hasn't debuted yet. Mother is throwing the town house open and there will be a ball held in our honor . . ." She chattered on and on, but Colin didn't listen. He just relaxed into the tinkling prettiness of English conversation. It felt so far from the powdery, acrid smell of cannon smoke. The way bright red blood falls to the deck and seeps between the boards.

With a start, he pulled himself back together. This year, for some reason, he was having trouble leaving the fighting behind on board ship, where it belonged. He needed to buck up and be a man.

"All right," Lily said, tucking her hand through his arm. "I can tell that you're not listening."

"Forgive me," he said, wondering what he had missed. Her smile was so impish and yet delightful that he smiled back, despite himself.

"You are finding me utterly tedious, and why shouldn't you?"

"I find you delightful."

"Pshaw!" she said, laughing. "You would have been my first beau in uniform, but I suppose I shall meet some others in the spring. A lieutenant! We're all so impressed, Colin. Father said that he thinks you'll be an admiral before you reach thirty, at this rate."

Colin made himself smile. "I don't see Grace anywhere. Will she be joining us?"

"Oh, she'll be down by the lake," Lily said. "Probably writing *you* a letter. Do go see her."

Grace was indeed down at the lake, sitting under a willow and working on a portrait of her brother, Brandon. She had heard a "halloo" and a lot of shouting behind her, up the hill toward the house, but she didn't move. With so many children milling about, there was always some sort of excitement brewing.

She had discovered that putting tiny flecks of red where someone didn't expect to see them gave depth to a piece of clothing, no matter how tiny. She realized it after putting her face as close as possible to a portrait by Hans Holbein in the ducal gallery.

Holbein's portrait was of one of her ancestors, a stuffy, bejeweled duke. Hers was of a naughty boy, but the effect was the same.

She was so intent on painting that she was unaware someone was approaching until a hand came down on her shoulder, and a big body came between her and the water glinting on the lake.

It was Colin.

She looked up at him without a word, cataloguing—the way she always did—the curl of his eyelashes, the deep blue of his eyes, his high cheekbones. The way his thigh muscles bulged as he squatted before her. The way his shoulders seemed much wider than they had been the last time she saw him. Just like that, her heart began beating so quickly that she felt a bit dizzy.

"Hello there," he said, smiling at her. "How's the best correspondent in the world?"

Grace felt her cheeks flood with color. "I'm fine. I'm so happy to see you home safe, Colin." She looked him over. "Without an injury. It's just marvelous!"

"Yes, well," he said, with an odd flatness in his voice. "I'm lucky enough to have all fingers and toes accounted for. What are you painting?"

"I'm making a portrait of Brandon." She frowned down at her paints as she tried to figure out what was wrong with Colin's voice. Surely it was a good thing not to be injured?

"Brandon is not my favorite ducal progeny," Colin said. "You are, darling girl, with all those wonderful letters. There were times when I would have gone stark mad but for thinking about the stories you told me."

"Are you still blockading the slaver ships?" she asked, wishing that she could think of something clever and funny to say.

Colin sat down next to her. "That I am, Grace. That I am."

They sat for a while and looked out at the lake.

"And do you still hate the fighting part?"

"Your letters help."

"Do you ever read poetry?" she offered. "Maybe that would help as well."

He threw her a glance that warmed her down to her toes. "You're overestimating me, Grace. I'm no good with words. I try to write you back, you know. I sit there and I can't think of anything to say because it's all—" He stopped.

"If you hate it that much," she said, after a moment, "you must leave the navy."

His jaw tightened. "I can't give it up. It's the only thing I know how to do."

"You could learn something else. There's no point in doing something you loathe so much."

There was silence.

"You *do* loathe it, don't you?"

He said nothing. Colin answered her letters so rarely that she found herself reading the few lines he wrote over and over. Yet it felt to her as if his anguish stretched all the way from the coast of Africa to England.

"Does your friend Philip Drummond hate it as much as you do?"

"No."

"What's Philip like?"

"Much more cheerful than I am," Colin said, shooting her a glance from under his lashes. "He likes excitement." A little shudder went through him.

Grace saw that with a sinking heart. "You must resign your commission, Colin. Sir Griffin could get you out."

"There's no way out, Grace. Not without dishonor."

"Dishonor is better than death," she insisted.

Rather than look at him, she stared at the drying paint on her brush.

There was more silence, the only sound the lapping of lake water. "They've all died around me," he said, finally. "Everyone but myself and Philip. They call us the golden twins, because no matter what happens on board, we walk off without a scratch." He reached out his hand before them. "Not even a scratch, Grace. Do you see that?"

She thought it was the most beautiful hand she'd ever seen: large and indubitably male, a strong hand. It bore no resemblance to the pampered hands of the aristocratic boys she'd met. "I am *glad* to see you haven't injuries," she said, giving it emphasis.

"It's a curse."

A big black swan drifted up to shore. "Don't look him in the eyes," Grace warned. "He's cross most of the time. Your father says he's a devil in disguise. If you meet his eye, he'll get out of the water in order to snap at our toes."

"As you told me in a letter," Colin said, smiling his lopsided smile. "I take it this is Bub, short for Beelzebub, the Prince of Darkness himself?"

"Why is it like a curse to walk out of a battle unwounded?" Grace asked. It had to be asked, even though her stomach clenched into knots at the idea of Colin's being wounded.

"There's all this smoke, and when it clears, the men are dead. All around you. Or crying." His voice was hollow and utterly calm. "Dying men cry for their mothers, Grace. They do. There's nothing you can do for them, but make promises you can't keep."

"That's awful," she whispered.

"You must wonder why I don't write you more often. I'm not good with words. I use up all I have, writing those mothers."

"I'm sorry," she said. And then she came up on her knees, put her palette to the side, and pulled at him until her arms could go around his shoulders. "I'm so sorry."

He resisted for one moment, and then gave in, arms going around her waist, holding her tightly against his big body.

It was a moment Grace never forgot. The sun was hot on her back, and because she was on her knees, and he was seated, her head was slightly above his. She tried not to think about the fact that his shoulders and his back were muscled, because he was hurting. Even if there weren't any wounds on the outside, he was injured.

After a while he pulled away and looked at her. His eyes were the dark blue of the ocean just at twilight. "You are quite special," he said, his voice deep and low. He put a finger on her lips.

Grace felt that touch to the bottom of her toes.

Then he stood. "Would you like to return to the house now, Lady Grace?" He held out a hand to her.

She accepted his help and stood, trying to figure out what it all meant. She loved him. She felt it in every part of her being. It would break her heart if he died; she might never recover.

But she couldn't say that to him, and he didn't seem to share her feelings.

"I understand that you and your sister are to debut next season?" Colin's voice had turned coolly pleasant, the voice of a family friend.

Did he like her? Did he care at all?

When he left a few days later, she still had no idea.

So she took up her pen and began a letter to him, about the escapades of the two youngest Barrys, who had decided to run away from home.

She wrote nothing about herself, or the golden twins, or the curse.

He didn't reply to her next two letters, and sent only a note after the third. From the cursory letters he sent, she had the feeling that he skimmed hers and tossed them aside. And yet, stupidly, she couldn't stop writing and rewriting her descriptions, sometimes staying up all night working on a miniature watercolor to slip into a packet.

She had always signed her letters, *From Ryburn*, or *From Arbor House . . . Lady Grace*. But one night in a fit of rebellion, she changed her signature. *Your friend, Lady Grace.*

He sent one of his infrequent replies to that one. It was only three lines long, but she took it as a sign he approved.

Five

May 1835

$\mathcal{G}$race's debut went about as well as she had imagined it would.

Lily shone in the ballroom. She danced like the sprite Colin imagined her; she laughed at all the young men, and they adored her for it.

By the end of May, four men had asked for her hand, and one of them was heir to a marquess.

Grace had one proposal, from a thirty-eight-year-old widower with three daughters.

The only bearable part about it was that she made the miserable experience sound rather funny and bright in her letters. She painted pictures of abject suitors collapsed at Lily's feet. She painted her desperate swain with a child in each arm and one on his shoulders. She told Colin about his brother Fred knocking over the punch bowl at Lady Bustfinkle's musicale because—as it turned out—he had drunk far too much punch himself.

She never wrote a word about what it was like to sit at the side of a ballroom even as the music made her feet long to dance. She made it sound as if London gentlemen adored shy girls who had no clever conversation.

She had realized by now that she wasn't ugly, except perhaps in comparison to Lily. She was quite acceptable, with a heart-shaped face and nice eyes. Thanks to her mother, her gowns flattered her slender figure and red hair.

But she simply could not sparkle. And at times she felt so desperately shy that she could hardly speak.

Then Colin wrote one of his rare letters, congratulating her on having a brilliant season.

She couldn't bear the fact that she had, in essence, misled him. So she sent a little self-portrait as a well-dressed mouse sitting in the corner of the ballroom, watching everyone dance.

She didn't put the truth of it down in words.

Words were hard; painting was easier.

He didn't write back.

She told herself that he was silently sympathetic, that he was wishing he were home to dance with her.

Then she tried to believe it.

Six

May 1836
The Duke of Ashbrook's townhouse

Colin didn't return to London again until the following year, when Grace was nineteen. The night before his ship was due in Portsmouth, she was sick with nerves.

By two days later, she was just sick. He was definitely in London; her own parents had seen him and he had told them warmly—according to the duchess—how much he appreciated her letters.

But he hadn't called on her. She didn't want appreciation. She was old enough to know exactly what she *did* want.

"Perhaps he'll come to the ball tonight," Lily suggested. Then: "Do you suppose that the fact Lord Swift sent me violets means that he is serious?"

Grace didn't feel precisely jealous of her sister. She would hate to be the center of attention the way Lily was; she was much more comfortable dancing with second sons and future vicars. She actually liked sitting at the side of the room, where she could watch the dancers. It wasn't easy to memorize a face well enough to be able to paint it the next morning or, sometimes, that very night. If a face was so interesting that she was afraid she would forget details, she might stay up half the night painting, much to her mother's dismay.

In fact, she didn't pay young gentlemen much attention unless they had interesting features. According to her mother, that explained why they paid her even less.

She didn't care.

She was in love, and although it was difficult to imagine a future with Colin—given the fact that he hardly ever wrote her, and never a word about anything personal—she couldn't help herself. Loving him was as natural as breathing. And as essential to her as her ability to paint.

That night, the family went to a ball thrown by the Duchess of Sconce. Grace danced a few times, and sat down to supper with her sister, a flock of Lily's admirers, and Lord McIngle, a Scotsman who was showing signs of becoming an admirer of her own. Even though he wasn't old, or widowed, or half blind.

Supper was just over; she had curtsied to Lord McIngle and was following her sister into the crowded ballroom, when there was a rustle through the room.

Grace turned. Colin was standing in the door. All around her she heard whispers; after all, he had recently been made captain of his own vessel: the youngest Englishman ever to receive that honor.

His uniform was magnificent, dark blue with gold trim and gold buttons all over his chest. The gleaming, bronze-colored epaulets on his shoulders made him look outrageously manly. His cravat was lace, and (she thought) the white emphasized the darkness in his eyes.

She loved the fact that he carried a secret in his eyes, one that he had never let out, except once, on the shore of the lake.

She instinctively started toward him, but made herself stay still and allow him to come to her. Lily always said it was important for gentlemen to pursue ladies, rather than the other way around.

That frozen moment gave her an excellent view of the most romantic thing to happen in London in ages, or so everyone said the next morning. As Colin walked down the steps, there was one of those accidental, miraculous partings of the crowd that happens even in crowded ballrooms. Colin was at one end, bowing before Lady Sconce, straightening, looking up . . . and Lily was at the other.

In the bright light of the ballroom, Lily looked—to Grace's objective eye—as beautiful as a true fairy sprite. She wore a pale gown suitable for a young lady, but because the Duchess of Ashbrook had a hand in the fabric, Lily sparkled with a subdued gleam that made her skin look flawless, and her hair blazed like rubies on white velvet. She had a perfect figure, round in all the right places, and slim everywhere else.

Grace's heart sank to her toes with a thud. She was wearing her most beautiful dress, the one that made her look like a Renaissance queen, or so her mother said. But she—and her mother—knew that an ordinary girl, no matter how sweet her expression, couldn't hold a candle to Lily. No one could. And it just made it worse that Lily wasn't vain about it. Even though she still had moody spells, she was a genuinely nice person.

The joy on Lily's face when she saw Colin walk into the ballroom was entirely unfeigned. And the look of utter shock, and then dazed awareness that came over his face . . . entirely unfeigned.

Having spent a few years in London ballrooms, Grace could diagnose love at first sight as well as anyone. Colin had just fallen in love. And Lily? Perhaps Lily had as well. She had a weakness for men in uniform. She was smiling at Colin, holding his hands and smiling up at him with such unmitigated pleasure that Grace wanted to weep. Or vomit.

She felt that, too. She felt just as joyful that Colin was home safe, that he had survived all those sea battles and whirlpools, and made his way home with prizes and accolades, though she didn't care about those. She just cared that he was home, rather than five fathoms deep with his bones turned to coral, and all the rest that Shakespeare wrote about drowned men.

And then, as everyone sighed with delight, the young lion returning with the vice admiral's special commendation asked Lily to waltz with him.

Grace watched from the side of the room as Colin twirled Lily, one hand lightly clasping hers, the other around her waist. When they were opposite Grace, Lily's head fell back and her curls fell over Colin's arm. She was laughing, looking up at him. When Lily laughed, as their father always said, the world laughed with her.

Grace watched until they neared the doors to the portico, saw Colin's face light with pleasure, saw the way he bent toward Lily as if he were a frozen man and she were a fire.

Then she turned and walked, very precisely, to the entryway. She shook her head when the butler offered to fetch her mother, telling him instead that she wanted the Duke of Ashbrook's carriage drawn up immediately. Then she asked him to inform her mother that she had a headache.

She fled.

Seven

*C*olin took one look at the exquisite, laughing Lily and lost his heart. He had entered the ballroom feeling rather cold and sick. She had looked at him, then laughed, and held out her hands.

Lily was everything battle wasn't: she was exquisite and fragile and utterly precious. The very sight of her told him that there were things in the world worth fighting for.

He danced with her, and that was even better. He could hardly believe that they used to refer to her as The Horror.

"How can *you* be naughty Lily?" he said, looking into her dazzlingly beautiful eyes. She was dainty, and yet perfectly shaped, like a statue of Venus. And she smelled so good . . . the sort of perfume that reminded him that there were rooms where no one crumpled to the floor with a cry of pain, where there had never been a smell of death and decay, where there was always another glass of champagne to drink.

He forced his jaw to relax. He had made up his mind not to think about that sort of thing. To leave it behind. Only a weakling would let memories follow him like a trail of wailing ghosts all the way from Portsmouth and into a ballroom.

The good thing was that Lily knew nothing of war. He almost didn't want to see Grace because she knew too much. She knew that he hated the navy. He was afraid merely seeing her might unman him.

He took no pleasure from the ocean anymore. All that was subsumed with his loathing of battle.

But here, with Lily, he felt different. He could feel his heart lifting. *This* was the way out of the maze of fear and memory: dancing and laughing with an enchanting woman who knew nothing of war, who had a dimple in her cheek, who smelled like roses. He twirled her faster and faster, letting the tempo guide his steps.

In the ballroom, there was no death and blood. No tears. No letters to be sent to mothers.

He smiled down at the lovely lass in his arms. Her lips were the color of spring roses and her eyes were soft and affectionate. Lily was like a whirlwind made of laughter. The faster they twirled, the more she loved it, leaning back against his arm and giggling.

After their dance, he asked for Grace. But he was secretly glad when it turned out that she had gone home with a headache.

"She never would have left if she knew *you* were coming," Lily told him. "She absolutely adores you, though I don't know why. You obviously don't deserve it!"

Over her fan, her eyes shone with a merry, wicked light. Around them pretty girls swirled, their dresses light and airy against their perfectly shaped bodies, arms gleaming in the candlelight, lips rosy. He traded Lily to a sleek young lord who told him, languidly, that he had deep admiration for the navy. "The bravery," the man said, waving his hand. "All the courage you chaps display. Quite remarkable."

He danced with a friend of Lily's, who had bouncing curls and shining white teeth. In fact, her teeth were rather mesmerizing, and he found himself imagining her head as a skull, but then he forced the image away—*away*—and managed to put himself back in the gaily turning ballroom.

"More champagne?" The evening was drawing to a close, but Lily and her friends were as fresh as daisies, as beautiful as they had been hours ago.

He took the glass, perhaps his fourth, perhaps his eighth, and met Lily's eyes with a smile. He was sure it was a smile because he turned his lips the right way.

"I want to meet your friend, Mr. Philip Drummond!" she said.

"You know of Philip?" For a moment the two worlds collided; with an effort of will he pushed the other one away.

She laughed, gaily. "Of course I know of him—

from the letters you've sent Grace, silly. We all know Philip or, rather, Lieutenant Drummond now, isn't it?"

He managed only half a smile this time and tipped up the glass of champagne. "Drummond is a capital fellow. A great friend."

"Where is he now?"

The champagne rushed down Colin's throat in an angry rush of bubbles. "With his family in Devon."

"Oh, of course!" Lily put a hand on his sleeve. "Colin, it's time to go home."

He frowned down at her.

Her eyes were sympathetic. Everything you'd want a wife's eyes to be. "You've had too much champagne," she told him. And then she came up on her toes and, to his utter horror, wiped a tear from his cheek. "Come on, old thing," she said, tucking her arm under his and towing him off toward the door. "I expect the navy doesn't give you much champagne, do they? We must have Father send you a case in the diplomatic bag . . ."

He stumbled along with her, letting a stream of words carry him to the door, whereupon his father appeared from somewhere, and then he fell into the darkness of the carriage.

"I don't sleep much," he told his father, blinking because Sir Griffin was a little hazy in the dark carriage. "But I think it will be all right tonight."

"I'm so glad," his father said, but he sounded sad.

So Colin added, "Because of the dancing. Because of Lily."

"Lily?"

His father sounded a little dubious, so Colin made the statement even more positive. "When she's there, and I'm dancing with her, and she's smelling of roses in late summer, I don't think so much. She's my tonic." He swept his hand in the air and accidentally hit the wall of the carriage.

His father's hand landed on his knee, warm and steady. "I love you, Colin. We all love you."

What was the point of saying that? He would have asked, but all the champagne swept up into his head and he collapsed into the corner of the carriage.

In the end, the memories invaded his sleep, anyway.

But when he woke up, he remembered that it was Lily who had chased them away.

$\mathcal{T}$he next morning, her eyes shining, Lily told Grace that Colin had come to the ball. Apparently he had asked for Grace, but no one could find her, and finally their mother had told him that she had a headache, and he had said he was sorry to hear that.

And to tell her how much he appreciated her letters.

Grace decided at that moment that there would be no more letters.

Colin paid a call that morning, but Grace refused to leave her chamber. Lily popped her head in, and said that Colin was taking her for a drive in the park, and did Grace wish to come?

Grace was so consumed with love and anger and anguish that she shook her head. "I'm painting," she said. "You know I paint every morning."

"After all those letters, don't you wish to see Colin?" Lily asked, looking surprised. "I'd think you'd be dying to say hello to him. He's even more handsome now, Grace, I promise you that. And it was so sweet when he became a little tipsy on champagne last night. I shall tease him about it."

Much later that evening, after supper had come and gone (Grace ate in her room), her mother looked in, gave her a hug, and said, "Darling, are you certain that you don't wish to say hello to Colin? I expect he finds it confusing, given that you have written all those letters. He's coming tomorrow morning as well."

She swallowed and said, "He's fallen for Lily, hasn't he?"

The duchess opened her mouth . . . and shut it again.

"Hasn't he?" Grace asked in a hard little voice. She had seen it happen. She knew.

"I believe Colin has discovered Lily's charm," her mother said, finally. "But that doesn't mean that he won't discover yours as well."

Grace rolled her eyes. "I might as well be invisible when Lily is near, Mother. You know that."

"I disagree." But mothers are mothers, and Grace knew better than to trust her mother's opinion.

The duchess caught her up in another hug. "You are my dear, darling Grace, and any man who doesn't see what a wonderful woman you are doesn't deserve to kiss the hem of your gown."

Mothers say things like that.

Grace managed to avoid Colin for the three short days of his leave, and when the following Wednesday came, and her father bellowed for her letter so that he could forward it to the Admiralty, she said, very simply, that she would write no more letters.

Her father always maintained that he was nothing more than a battered old pirate, with a great scar across his throat and a tattoo under his eye. But Grace never saw him that way, and when he opened his arms, she flew into them and nestled against his heart.

"Perhaps that's best, sweet pea," he said, encircling her in a hug so tight that she could hardly breathe. "You can't write to the man forever, after all."

She shook her head, feeling her hair rumple against his chest. "It's getting embarrassing."

"Someone else should take up the torch," he said.

Tears prickled Grace's eyes. "Lily hates writing. She'll never do it."

"He's an old man of twenty-five. We should have stopped it when you became a young lady."

"He's not old," Grace said, sniffing a little.

"But he's not a lonely boy any longer. No more letters, Lady Grace, and that's an order from your father."

She nodded and let a tear or two darken his silk neck cloth before she pulled away and stood up straight.

"I saw you talking to McIngle a few nights ago." Her father very kindly ignored her tears as Grace dug a handkerchief from her pocket.

"I like him," she said, managing a wobbly smile. "He has such an interesting face."

"It's not all about faces. He's a good one. I would have taken him on my crew in a moment." That was her father's highest praise.

"But Colin . . . I . . ."

Her father drew her back into his arms. "He asked for her hand before he left, dearest."

For a moment Grace didn't even hear what he said over the ringing in her ears. Then her heart started beating again, a sort of death march. She'd known it. She'd known it the moment she saw Colin's eyes meet Lily's. She saw the joy in his face.

"What did you say to him?"

"The same thing I say to anyone who asks. No daughter of mine will marry before she is twenty, no matter how dear a family friend her suitor may be. And frankly, that goes double for Lily. I want her to be a bit steadier before she contemplates a match. Your mother and I are firmly against youthful marriages; you know that."

"It worked for the two of you," Grace managed. But her voice wobbled.

"Not at first," her father said. "Not at first."

At that moment, Lily herself drifted into the room, looking as fresh as if she hadn't danced away the night. "The world seems so *dark*," she said, pausing. "Colin has left to rejoin his ship."

Grace took a deep breath. "You'll see him on his next leave."

"But it won't be the same, will it?" Lily said. "Colin dances so beautifully. I feel as if I'm flying when we waltz."

"I thought the two of you looked lovely together."

Lily narrowed her eyes. "I thought you left the ball before he arrived. He should have asked you to dance before me!"

"I didn't give him the chance," Grace said hastily. Hell had no fury like Lily if she thought her older sister had been spurned.

"He should have found you," Lily said indignantly. "You've been writing him for half your life. That was remarkably impolite of him. Perhaps I'll write him and say so!"

The duke wrapped an arm around each of them. "I'll write the lad and let him know that you won't be writing any longer, Grace."

She nodded.

"I shall write him instead," Lily said. "I promised. And he *is* a family friend, Papa."

Grace's heart warped at the idea of not taking up her pen to write Colin. What would she do with her life? Sometimes she felt as if she lived merely to find the funniest moments and put them onto paper, to capture a face so amusing that it would make Colin laugh in the midst of battle.

But she didn't touch her pen. She cried a great

deal that week, but she didn't write a word. By Sunday, she had pulled herself together. She couldn't live merely to write letters to a person who rarely bothered to answer her.

She had obviously created a romance in her head and heart that didn't exist. She was always imagining what he was thinking in response to her letters, but she must have been wrong. Perhaps he didn't even keep her letters.

That saddened her, but it also made her angry. If someone had written *her*, written her every month for years, she would have searched him out immediately on her return to England. She would have danced with him all night, if she could. She would have thanked him herself, not just sent a message through her sister.

She wouldn't have proposed to someone else. Not ever.

The crate came the next morning. Inside was a simple wooden box, marked with her name. She opened it cautiously, finding rumpled pink silk with a slip of paper on top. Her name was written on the paper, with a simple *Thank You.*

For a moment she felt sick, physically ill, as if the ground was pitching under her feet.

"Oh, look!" Lily crowed, looking over her shoulder. "I knew Colin couldn't be so impolite as to not thank you for all those letters. He should have asked you to dance, but this is even better." She plucked up the silk cloth that lay on top before Grace could stop her. Below was a neat line of small round bladders. "What on earth are those?"

"Please let me do that," Grace said. But she was too late; Lily had already grabbed one of the bottles. "It's a pig's bladder filled with paint."

"A *bladder*? Ugh!" Lily cried, dropping it. "It's all wired shut, Grace. How on earth will you get the paint out?'

Grace took it back. "You pierce the bladder with a tack and then replace the tack to keep the paint from drying out."

In all, there were eleven different colors. One was cadmium red, but there were others that she hadn't seen before: a beautiful deep green, the color of a cedar tree. A blue that was so clear that it looked like a summer sky. Another blue that shaded into violet, the color of twilight over the sea.

She scooped up the box and trotted up the stairs, heading for her bedchamber.

The duke stepped out of the library, and she heard Lily explaining the gift. She froze at the top of the stairs when her father called her name, looked down, and saw him standing with his arm around Lily. They looked uncannily similar.

"No letters," he stated.

"I do have to thank him."

"A brief note that will advise Colin it is your last letter."

She nodded.

"I'll write him for you," Lily said cheerfully. "But only once, unless he replies. I would never write the way you did, Grace, without getting responses. You were far too kind to him."

Grace made it into her bedchamber and closed the door before she started crying, which was quite an achievement.

In all her years of correspondence, she had received at most one letter every few months. Of course, some of Colin's letters might have gone astray. But she had stopped pretending that he was writing her as often as she would wish.

Yet, if he was in love with her sister, he might well write Lily. The pain hit her so hard that she actually sank to her knees on the carpet, clutching the wooden box, wondering how one lived with a broken heart, especially when one's beloved is married to a sister.

It was humiliating to think about how she wrote him long, boring letters, as if she were his maiden aunt. Worse, each one had been a love letter, though he hadn't known that.

At last she got to her feet, walked over to her writing desk, and wrote a short note, thanking Colin for the paintbox and explaining that her father felt it was no longer appropriate for them to correspond. Then she sat down and made the best painting of her life.

It was a miniature, no bigger than her palm. But she painted it on a small square of canvas, so that, if wrapped in silk and carried in his breast pocket, it wouldn't fade or chip, like the watercolors she'd sent him before.

It was a portrait of Lily, laughing.

Grace worked all night, surrounded by candles that kept burning out, so she had to replace them, rubbing her eyes. She had to finish. She had to put Colin out of her mind, give him this last gift.

Then it was finished. Lily gazed out of the picture, with all her laughing exuberance, her innocent seductiveness, the sweetness that stopped her from becoming vain.

It was very tiresome to love one's rival, she thought before falling, exhausted, in bed.

When she woke up, late in the afternoon, the painting was dry enough to be sent off. She wrapped it in silk and then a soft piece of vellum, and went downstairs to give the packet to her father to be dispatched to the Admiralty.

When she unwrapped the vellum to show him, he held the miniature very delicately in his huge hand and stared at it in silence for a moment.

"You have a great talent, Grace."

She knew he was right. She had captured Lily. It was the only thing she had to give Colin, since he didn't want her.

The duke reached out with his other hand and caught her against his side. "All this love you have inside you, sweet pea . . . it will make some fellow very happy."

She nodded. She was exhausted, but she also felt clean and emptied out. Her love wasn't gone, but she was ready to let it go.

She had built an imaginary *thing* between herself and her childhood friend. But adult relationships didn't spring from letters. They came from the sort of happiness that Colin had felt when he saw Lily across the ballroom, and when he kissed Lily's hand.

That was an adult relationship. Someday, someone would feel that for her. But it wouldn't be Colin.

"Thank you, Papa," she said, resting her head against his shoulder.

"I won't allow him to marry Lily," he said, touching the painting with a finger. "He couldn't see what lay before him. I won't give him another of my girls to overlook."

Grace shrugged. "It's all right, Papa. I've put him behind me."

The duke wrapped up the painting again. "Colin has to be the stupidest man I know." He paused. "Actually, I have a lot in common with him."

Grace sat down on the sofa and drew up her feet under her. "Do you mean because you went away to sea and left Mama behind?"

"Exactly," her father said, going back to making a neat package of the painting. "I was worse than Colin, actually, because I was already married to your mother, and I knew I loved her."

"But she told you to leave," Grace said, repeating the story that they all loved. "She told you to leave and never come back, and you didn't return for seven years."

"That's right," the duke said. "Given my profound stupidity in obeying her, I can hardly say anything about Captain Barry's idiocy." He looked up, and suddenly he looked like a pirate again.

"Of course, if he comes around here and tries to woo either of my daughters, I'll disembowel him."

Grace laughed. "Sir Griffin wouldn't like that."

"He wouldn't, would he?" The duke's laugh welcomed a fight with his closest friend.

"I think I'll go take a bath," she said, tired to the bone.

"I'll send this out," he said. "And I'll put in a note from myself as well."

Grace continued up the stairs. She didn't really care what her father wrote in that note.

Eight

*L*ily's letter arrived six weeks after Colin left London. At first he thought, happily, that it was a letter from Grace, and then felt ashamed on opening it. He had fallen in love with Lily; of course, he should welcome her letter above anyone else's.

Even now the memory of that ball—the pretty girls, the delicious food, the intoxicating champagne—made him grin. *That* was the England he longed for, and by marrying Lily he would be a part of it. She had always been such a sweet, laughing presence, even as a child.

Lily's letter was written in round, rather childlike script.

Dear Captain Barry,

I went to three balls last week and danced until well past midnight at each of them, but they weren't as

*much fun without a bosky captain at my side. Papa
says that it is improper for me to write you, but I
thought I would anyway. I like breaking his rules.
I tell him that it keeps him young. This week we are
looking forward to two balls, a masquerade, and a
musical breakfast. London is quite a whirl of gaiety.
When I think how tedious you must find your life,
it quite breaks my heart. If you found your way to
Paris, I'm sure you would be happy. I think that the
French court must be like heaven on earth. How I
wish Papa would take us there! I do hope this letter
finds you well. I'll probably stop here, as I'm not
much of a writer—I prefer dancing.*

Colin read the letter four times. It was manifestly
the letter of a charming young lady. Of course her
life was a whirl of gaiety. Of course it was.

That night he lay in his berth staring up at the
wood planks above his head. A small spider had
found its way on board, and it was building a
web, hoping to catch flies. There were no flies on
board ship that Colin had seen.

He watched as the spider carefully, carefully
dropped a slender, elegant line of silk from the
ceiling to the wooden wall against which his
berth was fixed. It was very busy, quickly running
back to its origin point, adding more radial lines,
then, beginning at the center, a spiral of connect-
ing threads.

After a while, he read the letter once again,
squinting in the candlelight. Lily's gaiety shone
from every word. She would make some man,

a man with dancing feet and a dancing soul to match, a beautiful wife.

He would not be that man.

There was peacefulness in that realization. He let it sink in, watching the spider weave its spiral lines. Lily's light gaiety would never work for him, and all the darkness he carried would drag her down to earth if he married her.

He had been changed by the war, by the deaths he'd seen and the deaths he'd caused. There was no going back, not when rivers of blood ran through a man's dreams.

He folded the letter and put it on the floor at his side. It wasn't Lily's fault that her prose suffered so greatly in comparison to her sister's. When one of Grace's letters arrived, he could and did spend hours thinking about what she'd described.

The spider retreated, curling into a ball so small that he hardly saw it. Candlelight gleamed along the gossamer threads, as the spider waited . . . waited. Colin snuffed the candle and lay there, unwilling to sleep, to risk the dreams that tormented him every night.

If only the letter had come from Grace . . .

It wasn't Lily's fault that she wasn't as intelligent as her sister. Nor as witty and kind. That wasn't fair: Lily *was* kind. But she was shallow compared to Grace.

She was a waltz, and Grace was a hymn. He turned over in bed and went to sleep, thinking about it.

*C*olin didn't realize for another month that there would be no more letters from Grace. After all, sometimes weeks passed between dispatches from the Admiralty.

He thought nothing of it at first, and not much the second week. But by a fortnight later, he was pacing the deck at night. The fourth week, the West Africa Squadron was still waiting for orders. And there was no escaping the fact that Grace's letter should have reached him, perhaps two letters arriving at the same time, as they sometimes did.

It was his own damned fault. He had gone to the house two mornings in a row, but they had told him she was ill. Perhaps there was something wrong with her. She would never have avoided him . . . not the warm, loving Grace of her letters. She was as dear to him as his own sister; surely she knew that?

She must be dying, he thought, with a cold thump of his heart. Dying, and no one had told him. Scarlet fever, perhaps. Or her lungs—perhaps they were still weak.

But then he remembered the way Lily's eyes had shone during the ball, and the way she'd laughed when he took her for a ride in the park, and the way he grew infatuated with her, so much so that he lost his mind and actually told the duke that he would like to marry her. Lily would never have laughed like that if her sister were dying.

He had felt a tremendous pulse of relief when

the duke said no. He had been a fool, a damned fool.

Lily, beautiful, laughing Lily, wasn't the answer to his problems. He shouldn't have thrown away his resolution to avoid marriage at the first sight of a pretty English lass.

Of course, she was *Lily*. He was predisposed to love Lily, given the way she teased him and amused him since she was a young girl. He'd never forgotten that Lily had saved his life when she'd entered his bedroom, realized he was in a fever, and dumped a pitcher of water over his head.

Now that he was older, he knew that a pitcher of water over the head wouldn't save anyone's life. But it was a funny story.

The frogspawn was another.

A package for him finally arrived well into the third month after he sailed from England. By then he had reread all the letters Grace had written him, starting with the ones where her handwriting was large and uncertain. He worked his way slowly through the years when she was learning Latin and tried to write him funny sentences in the language, and through her watercolors, which grew more and more intricate and assured. He reread her stories about their two households, looked for a long time at the portrait of his parents kissing under the mistletoe and at the picture of Fred covered with mud after falling off his horse, carefully replacing each one in the waterproof box in which he kept them.

His whole life was caught up in those pages. Or rather, it was the life he missed because he was in the navy.

That would have been the only life worth living, though he usually didn't admit it to himself.

The packet—for a packet did finally arrive—was larger than the usual letter. He didn't let himself open it for two days. It had to be the final one.

Of course, he had always known that the end would come. Grace would marry someone, and what would her husband think about her sending letters to another man?

It was enough to make Colin consider marrying her himself, but it was stupid to marry a woman merely so that she would continue to write him letters.

Even if those letters were the only thing standing between him and madness.

When he finally opened the package and saw that the enclosed note held only three sentences, he clenched his jaw so hard that it hurt for a day.

Then he read it, the cool, precise letters that shaped her words, such unwelcome words, over and over. She always signed her letters, *Your friend, Lady Grace*. But this one just said, *From London . . . Lady Grace*. Finally, he unwrapped the portrait and looked at it, numbly.

It was a portrait of Lily, which was nice. She was a pretty girl, Lily. She glowed like a naughty angel, and Grace had caught that quality perfectly.

He put it to the side and read the letter again, along with the accompanying note from the duke.

Her father thought it was inappropriate for them to correspond? Her father? The duke? The duke thought . . .

He remembered, suddenly, the rash way that he had said to the duke that he would like to marry Lily someday, if she thought it was a good idea.

Of course the duke didn't want Grace to correspond with a man in love with her sister.

He had been an ass, worse than an ass.

A young midshipman skidded to a halt and snapped to attention before him. "Orders are in, Captain," he said, managing not to pant.

Colin nodded. He folded up the portrait and put it in his breast pocket. He would take it out later. He always looked at Grace's work over and over, to see if he could distinguish all those tiny brushstrokes that came together into such clever portraits, and this was the best portrait she'd ever sent him.

It wasn't until they were well out to sea, the wind pushing them over the waves on the way to intercept another slaver ship, that he understood what that portrait meant.

Grace had given him what she thought he most wanted.

Lily.

The thought made him almost lose his breakfast over the rail. It had all gone wrong, that visit. He didn't want Lily. He didn't even want to look at her portrait, no matter how fresh and pretty she was.

Grace's letters had kept him alive for these last

few years: kept him from madness, even from suicide. He had friends like Philip who weathered battles with equanimity, who saluted without blinking an eye as their friends' bodies were consigned to the ocean. He wasn't like them. He didn't sleep well for days after an engagement. The splash of a body being buried at sea echoed in his ears for hours after it happened.

But he had had Grace's letters, those lovely songs about life in a different place, in a different key, where blood and death weren't the only reality.

He should have told her that. Written more often. But so often when he took up his pen to write, all that came to him were images of men dying, and how could he tell her about something so horrible? So he wouldn't write, and he told himself that, obviously, she didn't care, because she kept writing.

One problem was that he was an unmitigated idiot.

The other was that he was sailing toward Freetown, in Sierra Leone, and they wouldn't be back on English shores for nine months.

A few days later he pulled out the portrait again, but when he looked at it he suddenly felt as if it were painted in tears. Lily smiled, but the brush of the artist had wept. He clung to the railing, a pain gripping his heart that made his vision black for a moment.

There was love in that portrait.

Real love, not the sort of love-of-a-brother affection he had for Grace.

She would get over him, of course. All that love and warmth and humor she offered . . . there were probably a hundred men at her feet every night.

She could have accepted any number of proposals over the last years. She'd always written wryly of the London season, making it sound as if she hovered on the margins of *ton*.

But she was irresistible on paper, and would be more so in person.

Even so, in the grip of vanity, he decided that she had waited for him since she debuted. That she would still wait for him. He just had to make it home alive and whole.

And then he would marry her. It was the least he could do to thank her for all the wonderful letters. He pushed away a small voice that spoke of selfishness. He wouldn't propose in order to get more letters, but to thank her for those he had already received. And because he loved her; he really did.

Months passed, the way they do at sea, the days carelessly thrown away in a billow of cannon smoke and men's lives. One day he received papers indicating that he had been awarded yet another prize from the Royal Navy. The HMS *Daedalus* was to be commended for meritorious service in the line of duty. And they gave him, as its captain, a large amount of money.

Philip, his first lieutenant, saluted him with a shot of their carefully rationed brandy. His parents wrote. The duchess sent an exquisitely written note, with a scrawl on the bottom from the duke. Grace did not write.

He got a note from Lily, a dashed-off letter sending him love from all. She made a list and then said something about each member of their two families. Fred was "sent down from Cambridge, for nakedness. Papa won't say where but it must have been in public." Cressida was "sick after eating too many gooseberries." And Grace . . . "Grace is being wooed by a very nice man named Lord McIngle who says he's met you several times. Grace laughs, and says she likes him because he has never flirted with *me*, which is true enough. He has eyes for no one but Grace."

For a moment he wondered if Lily meant to phrase her last sentences like that. If there was censure implied between her lines.

But Lily wasn't complex or thoughtful, the way Grace was. She was dazzling and rather shallow, while Grace was full of mystery. A man could spend a lifetime learning all there was to learn about Grace.

He had kept every one of Grace's letters, but he sent this one of Lily's overboard with a curse at a man he'd never met, a Scottish lord who was winning—had apparently won—the only thing in the world that he wanted.

But later that day, he found himself writing a reply to Lily, anyway. He had never written Grace more than a paragraph or two. But he didn't feel that he could simply launch into the only questions that interested him: *How is Grace? Is she happy? Does she miss writing to me? Who the hell is McIngle?*

His letter stretched to five pages, reaching the important part—the only thing he cared about—on page four. He watched the thick packet disappear into the diplomatic pouch, destined for the Duke of Ashbrook's daughter. Not the right daughter, but *a* daughter.

That night he lay awake, pulsing with rage at the idea of Grace marrying a man he dimly remembered as a pleasant fellow, but not one who could protect her if highwaymen stopped her coach . . .

It occurred to him that brothers don't feel this sort of wild panic and rage at the idea of their sister marrying a pleasant fellow.

They didn't lie awake, picturing a sister in peril . . .

The crucial fact: *she wasn't his sister.*

And he didn't feel brotherly toward her. Not at all.

A couple of weeks later, the HMS *Daedalus* encountered the *Loki*, a Baltimore clipper slave ship.

This time, when the smoke cleared, Captain Barry didn't walk out unscathed. His second-in-command, Lieutenant Philip Drummond, assumed command of the vessel, and carried out plans that Sir Griffin Barry, with approval of the Royal Navy, had put in place long ago: If Captain Barry was injured, he wasn't to be dropped off on shore to recover. Nor was he to wait about for a British naval ship to fetch him home.

Captain Drummond put ashore at Casablanca, where he bought the fastest clipper he could find, hired a crew, and had the wounded captain carried aboard, accompanied by his personal batman, Ackerley. And then he and all his men lined up along the gunwale in a salute, and he was the only one who didn't have tears in his eyes as they watched one of the golden twins being taken away on a stretcher.

But when Drummond turned back to the deck, he was captain of the *Daedalus*.

Nine

January 1837

$\mathcal{T}$he day that Colin's letter arrived was not a happy one for Grace, especially when Lily asked her if she'd like to read it. Grace saw pages and pages covered with Colin's spiky writing and shook her head.

She went upstairs and sat down, refusing to cry. She was the daughter of a duke. She was not a dying swan who would spend the rest of her life mourning a man who didn't love her.

That afternoon she dressed with special care for a drive with Lord McIngle. She selected a new and especially flattering pelisse, made from violet cashmere, with black braided silk trim and a wide black velvet belt with a silver buckle.

Just before His Lordship was due to arrive, she

popped into her mother's sitting room to show herself off.

"You look exquisite, Grace," the duchess exclaimed, getting up from her desk. "And even more important, you look happy."

"I am better," Grace said stoutly. "I'm not the first to have suffered through a childhood infatuation. Colin never even kissed me, so I haven't the excuse of saying I was misled."

Her mother gathered her into her arms. "I knew that Lily's letter would feel hurtful." And then: "But I am glad to hear that Colin didn't give you reason to believe that his affections matched yours."

"Quite the opposite. All those years, he never wrote me back more than a line or two. He didn't seek me out when he was on leave . . . not to mention the fact that he fell in love with Lily. I feel like such a fool, Mother!" It burst out of her.

The duchess leaned back, her hands on Grace's shoulders. "You are *not* a fool, darling. It is never foolish to love a good man. I'm just sorry that he didn't reciprocate your feelings—and even sorrier that your father and I didn't cut off the correspondence years ago."

"I do believe my letters were healing. So I'm not sorry I wrote them."

The duchess looked at her searchingly. "You are such a good person, Grace. I don't know how your father and I managed to produce such a generous, wonderful young woman."

"Don't forget fanciful. I made up a whole romance in my mind. When Colin didn't answer a letter, I would make up the answer he *should* have sent me. Before I knew it, I was in love."

"I do wish I could have spared you that lesson," her mother said. "Especially your pain in seeing that letter he wrote to Lily."

Grace shrugged. "It forced me to realize that I can't hide from the truth. There's a glaring contrast between the four-line letters Colin wrote me, and the five-page letter he sent Lily. He must truly love her."

"I'm not so sure that I agree about Colin's feelings for your sister. Your father and I *are* agreed that he is not the person with whom Lily should spend her life. But the more important thing, darling, is that you find someone who will realize precisely how precious you are. It's obvious to everyone, for example, that Lord McIngle is wildly in love with you."

"He is, isn't he?" It was quite nice to see John's eyes light up when she entered a room. "I know this is petty, Mother, but I so appreciate the fact that John has never even looked in Lily's direction."

"John, is it?" her mother said teasingly. "Your father and I like your John very much. We would be very happy to have him join our family."

Lord McIngle arrived so promptly to take Grace for a drive that one might think his carriage had been lurking around the corner.

But no, Grace thought, John McIngle would always be on time. She could count on him. He was steady, and warm, and unfailingly respectful.

John had been wooing Grace for quite a while now, so she knew the pattern of their afternoon excursions: John would tool his curricle to Hyde Park, where they would make a circuit, stopping to greet friends.

Grace's shyness had prevented her from forming many intimate friendships, but John was so convivial that all of London adored him, or so it seemed. She found herself chatting and laughing with his friends as if they were her own—and, indeed, some of them were becoming so. It felt wonderful.

After driving once around the park, they would retire to Gunter's Tea Shop for an ice. But this time, John handed Grace into the curricle and asked, "Do you mind if I take you on a short excursion to one of my favorite places in London, Lady Grace? It is entirely respectable, I assure you."

Grace smiled at him with genuine pleasure. He was such a *nice* man. No woman in the world could be offended by a question asked by a man with such adoring eyes. "I would be most happy, Lord McIngle."

"*John*," he reminded her.

"John," she repeated.

He didn't drive terribly far, and then stopped the curricle in front of a small church called Grosvenor Chapel. His tiger took the reins, and John helped Grace from the carriage. They walked silently through the nave and out a side door, into a pretty little walled graveyard. There was no sense of grief here, just the buzzing of honeybees, happy to have found so many rosebushes in the heart of London. A narrow brick path wound its way between the gravestones.

"How beautiful!" Grace exclaimed, her fingers twitching because she was so sorry not to have her sketchpad and a pencil. She looked up at John. "How on earth did you find this exquisite secret?"

"My mother is buried here." His expression was not at all tragic, but boyishly wistful. "I always visit her when I am in London; I have the feeling she is happy here."

"What a lovely thought," Grace exclaimed, thinking how adorable his matched set of dimples were.

Then he took both her hands in his. She looked up with a start. The sun was shining on his hair, playing on his thick curls. His voice was as earnest as his eyes were yearning.

"I knew from the moment that I saw you that you were the woman I wanted to spent my life with, and that my parents would have loved you as much as I do. Lady Grace, would you do me the inestimable honor of becoming my wife?"

With This Kiss
Part Two

Ten

Grace told herself frequently how happy she was to be engaged to Lord McIngle—John, as he insisted she call him. He was a good man, with a lovely voice and brown eyes. She liked his dignity, she liked his kindness, and she thought they would be very happy together. She especially liked the fact that he had an estate in Scotland.

Scotland was a long way from London. Far enough that a woman could nurse a broken heart until she forgot all about it, until the laughter of children and the kisses of a loving husband wiped away the stupid infatuations of her youth.

John often arranged small treats for Grace, things that he knew she would enjoy. Most importantly, he didn't pretend that painting was only a lady's pursuit, as watercolors were for most young ladies. One day he gave her a miniature of

Sir Walter Raleigh, a delicate painting of the slender, lovelorn aristocrat.

"He understands you," her mother said, deep approval in her voice. "This is a precious antique, Grace. He truly loves you."

"I know he does," Grace replied, keeping her voice light and happy.

"He's a good choice," her father told her. "A good man."

Both her parents had a little knot in their brows every time they looked at her, but by the time a month had passed, Lord McIngle—John—had become a welcome addition to their family.

Lily teased him mercilessly, calling him Old Sobersides. She was the only one who argued with Grace. "He's not a good choice for you," she insisted. "He respects you too much."

"Respect is good," Grace said, thinking of how Colin slighted her letters. "I want respect."

"It's not enough."

"He loves me!"

"Not the right way."

Finally Grace turned on her sister in a rage. "Don't you see, Lily? Must you make me say this aloud? No one will ever love me in the *right way*, not in that feverish way that men fall in love with you. I'm not that sort of woman!"

Lily cried, and Grace ended up crying, too.

Sobersided John thought she was pretty. He kissed her frequently (if respectfully), and she enjoyed it. He gave her a new set of paints. The morning after that gift, she handed Colin's paints to her siblings, and used John's instead.

Later that night she stole back the most beautiful blue, the lapis lazuli. She put it in a drawer with her lingerie and pretended it wasn't there.

The day John gave her a sable paintbrush, she told her parents that they should set the wedding date.

Eleven

$\mathcal{O}$nly a few days out of Casablanca, a storm blew them off course. Colin lay in the dark, counting the days as they passed. He was out of the navy, honorably discharged. He should be glad about that.

He was safe, if not entirely sound. He should be glad about that too.

He was going home, to England, to Grace.

And that's where any happiness died. By now Grace might have married McIngle.

He had had a plan to steal her away from McIngle before he was injured.

But now . . .

He was a selfish ass, but he wasn't a complete bastard. He couldn't steal her from her fiancé when he wasn't a whole man.

The thought made his headache worsen. The doctor had instructed the mate to give him a dose of laudanum every morning and night to control the headaches and (he suspected) to keep him tamely in bed. He didn't care. His idiot batman, Ackerley, periodically appeared by his bed and told him to open his mouth, and he did.

But there was an unexpected side effect to laudanum. As he slipped in and out of sleep, he discovered that he was able to relive Grace's letters as if he were part of the events she had described in them. They were so vivid that he found himself in the drawing room, standing beside the duke and laughing when they realized that young Brandon had turned every one of His Grace's neck cloths to sails for his toy boats.

He sat by Grace's side as she painted naughty chickens, and watched with her as Lily flew about the ballroom, laughing her gilt laughter, the laughter of a woman who has never known pain or fear.

Grace knew both pain and fear. She knew them because of him. In his dream, he danced with her, holding her tenderly and dancing slowly. Not like the whirling waltz he shared with Lily, but a waltz in which every touch fired his blood. Because it was a dream, a laudanum dream, suddenly they were at Almack's surrounded by pretty ladies. Yet all the women faded into a kind of blurred prettiness, because the only woman in the room who mattered was Grace.

Her hair was wound high on her head with ringlets falling down her back. Her gray eyes smiled at him with a look that said she found him as delicious as he found her. They turned in the dance again, slowly, and his thigh brushed her slender leg, sending a flare of pure erotic heat up his groin.

He bent his head and brushed her lips with his. They were soft, rosy pink, and she was blushing because he was creating a scandal by kissing her in public. But he didn't care about society. The only person he cared about was in his arms, and he found himself tilting her head, hungry for her, near to growling . . .

The ballroom disappeared and they were on the lawn before the lake, under the spreading willow tree where he had watched her paint. But this time, rather than hugging him, she was lying on her back, laughing up at him. He had thrown all her hairpins into the lake, and bright strands of her hair were wound in his fingers.

He felt mad, crazed with passion and love and hunger. Grace looked into his eyes, and she saw the raw feeling that he couldn't control. She did something with the bodice of her dress and suddenly the whole garment disappeared.

And there she was. Pink and sensual and loving, pulling him down to her. He didn't have clothes, either, and their bodies met with lovers' joy, with a delirious pleasure. He couldn't pause to enjoy it, not with this pounding, driving *need* to be inside her, to own her, to know that she was his, rather than McIngle's.

He reared over her, savage and fierce, knowing his eyes were blazing down at her. All he wanted in life was to possess the woman who lay beneath him, who held his heart and soul in her hands.

Her legs fell open, welcoming him. She was wet and sweet, and at his touch she arched her neck, a broken cry coming from her lips.

She understood, she loved him anyway . . .

Just like that, the moment slipped away and he was back in Almack's, standing against the wall.

Grace was dancing a slow waltz, but it was with McIngle. She was smiling at the Scotsman, and there was all the warmth and love in her eyes that Colin had always assumed was his. Assumed like a fool, because he didn't understand what he had, and what he wanted.

He should have crawled to her feet every time he returned to England. He should have written back to every one of her letters, three or four pages to each of hers.

He should . . .

The laudanum dream was fading, and he grasped at it, trying to keep the bright image from evaporating, because even though Grace was dancing with McIngle, he could still see her, watch her smile, that quiet smile . . .

She was gone.

He woke, feeling the pitching motion of the ship taking him back to England. In his dream, he had been whole and untouched.

Now he was back to himself.

He could never go to sea again. Over the years he had won three purses while in the Royal Navy. He was far wealthier than he had ever imagined. Still, he couldn't take Grace from McIngle. When she saw him like this, she would leave McIngle, if they weren't already married, and come to him out of pity.

He would rather die.

He got out of bed, tripped on something, and fell to the floor. It knocked the wind out of him; when he recovered enough to push himself up to a sitting position, he discovered that he'd knocked over his chamber pot, and that he was wet.

He was . . . what he was.

It was over. He had pissed away the best thing that had ever happened to him—the love of an intelligent, funny, and utterly sweet woman—because he couldn't see outside his own stupid head.

It took painful, slow thinking, but he came to some conclusions.

One was that he couldn't take laudanum, not unless he wanted to dream about making love to Grace, only to wake with tears on his cheeks. A second was that he would rather die than have Grace come to him out of pity. He had to rebuff her, for her own good. Even if he spent his life knowing what an ass he'd been, mourning her, it was better than tying her to a husk of a man.

He discovered that making his way to the floor and pushing himself straight-armed up from the floor, over and over and over, allowed him to doze.

He pushed up a hundred times. A fortnight later, two hundred times.

He could nap, but he couldn't sleep through the night. Finally, when he hadn't slept for two nights, he took laudanum in desperation. And again, he found himself in the ballroom.

This time, Grace was sitting at the side of the room. She was the most beautiful woman there, her skin like sweet cream, her hair glowing like banked coals. And none of the fools around her saw it.

He did. Their host introduced them, and then he finally touched her hand. She looked up at him with surprised innocence, and he realized that in *this* dream, she didn't know him at all.

He could woo her the way a normal man would woo a woman he desired. A profound joy filled him, and he smiled at her . . . the dream progressed through balls and a musicale and a ride in Hyde Park. All the way through, he watched her with a kind of mad hunger, nourishing the little flame of her feelings toward him.

Time was different in the dream . . . after weeks, or perhaps months, passed, he knew that she was just as desirous as he was. She kissed him with an erotic longing that matched his own.

The kiss started to fade, and he realized, while still in the dream, that it was the laudanum, and not Grace.

Still, he held on to the moment with all his will. He didn't want to go back to the darkness, to the cabin that always smelled of piss, to the bed where he lay not so patiently, waiting for the English coast.

In the last moments of the dream, she gave him a private smile, a little wicked and a little tender, and whispered, "Come to me tonight, Colin. I miss you. I miss you so much. I love you . . ."

And he woke. Or rather, he thought he woke, but in reality he was just caught up in a different dream. He opened his eyes to find himself on board ship. There was a crack, like lightning, and the mast was falling into the ocean. All around him were screams. He looked down and saw with horror that there was a river of blood running over his boots.

After that, he threw the laudanum out the port-hole.

By the time the ship finally reached Portsmouth, he had come to a decision: Grace was not for him. He would go to the Ryburns' townhouse the first night, simply because his parents didn't maintain a house in town, and the duke and duchess would be mortally offended if he stayed in a hotel.

But the following morning he would leave for Arbor House. In time, he would buy an estate with his prize money, somewhere far from Grace. Though, of course, she might be living in Scotland with McIngle.

Good.

It would be dangerous to be near her. He was her childhood love, and now he knew he loved her too. All he had to do was revert to the sort of cold bastard who wouldn't answer the letters written by a twelve-year-old girl.

He could do that.

The miracle was that he had a heart that could break, considering what a cold bastard he was.

Twelve

June 12, 1837

$\mathcal{G}$race was in the entryway when the carriage bearing Colin Barry drew up, though she had no idea of that quite yet. She had just taken a cloak from their butler, Featherstone, as she and John McIngle, her new fiancé, were on their way to visit a private showing of Constable's watercolors and preliminary sketches, which John had arranged as a special treat.

Then Featherstone opened the door. Grace turned as John was helping her into her cloak, and saw a tall man on the step, a servant holding his arm. Time slowed and almost stopped. She recognized his hair first: longer than she'd ever seen it, curls and loops falling below his ears. His shoulders, his legs, his face . . .

Her eyes wouldn't accept what she saw on his face.

The black bandage. The way the attendant stood at his side.

It couldn't be—it *was*.

"Featherstone, I apologize for intruding," Colin was saying in response to the butler's greeting, his voice utterly calm. "I will make arrangements to move to the country tomorrow. But at the moment, if you would be good enough to tell the duchess that I have come for a brief visit, I would be grateful. My man, Ackerley, will arrange to have my trunk brought up."

With a silent jerk of his head, Featherstone sent a footman running in pursuit of Grace's mother. He was bowing, and never mind the fact that Colin couldn't see . . .

Because Colin couldn't see. He was blind. *Blind*.

Grace gasped aloud, reality finally burning into her mind. Colin turned his head toward her and she could have sworn that he could see through the linen cloth covering his eyes. But he said nothing.

He stood relaxed, seemingly at ease, in the midst of the butler, four footmen, John. Even blind, it was as if the other six men were kittens to his tiger. He was all muscle compared to John, his shoulders twice the size. A controlled strength always entered the room with him, and it hadn't lessened an iota with the loss of his sight.

She was still frozen in place when John stepped forward. "Captain Barry," he said, "you likely won't remember me, but I'm Lady Grace's betrothed, Lord McIngle. We met briefly at a musicale a few years ago."

Did Colin stiffen when John said the word *betrothed*? If so, it was an infinitesimal reaction.

"Of course," he said, bowing his head. John took his hand so naturally that Grace felt a pulse of deep affection for her fiancé. The feeling cracked the walls of ice that surrounded her.

John was still speaking in his friendly, easy way. "Would you like to enter the morning room while we wait for Her Grace?"

"The rose chamber is waiting for you, if you would prefer to rest," Featherstone put in. "And may I add how very glad we are to see you in England once again?"

Grace took his free hand in both of hers. "Colin," she said. "I'm here." To her chagrin, her voice shook.

He turned toward her voice. "Lady Grace." He simply stated it, without a smile. The bandage emphasized his hewn cheekbones and stern mouth. "It's a pleasure."

"I'm so—I'm so sorry to see you ill." He'd lost weight, she thought numbly. He looked pared down, like a storm god in a drought. That thought was so irrelevant that she actually shook her head.

"I am blind," he said. "I wouldn't precisely describe it as an illness."

She took a step closer, clutching his hand even more tightly. "Are you in pain?"

"No." His voice was even, without a hint of

anger. And yet a wave of silent rage struck her like a blow. "It happened almost six weeks ago, Lady Grace. I've become used to it." His body was rigid, belying the easy sound of his words.

She swallowed. Colin was a warrior, and she had the sense that he was fifty times more dangerous wounded than he had been whole. For an instant she stood, clinging to his large, callused hand. Was there a vulnerable slant to his lips?

The truth hit her like a stroke of lightning. Once again she was endowing him with the emotions that *she* wanted to see.

She dropped his hand. "Lily is not home at the moment." She forced the words out. "She'll be so happy to see you when she returns."

Colin nodded, and then unerringly turned toward John. "Lord McIngle, I would be most grateful if you would escort me to my bedchamber. Stairs remain a challenge."

It was amazing how he could calmly admit a need for help and still make it so clear that he was burning with rage at the very idea.

"Of course," John said, nodding to Featherstone, who preceded them up the stairs.

Colin didn't turn his head in her direction again. He simply walked next to John, managing to make it seem as if he were leading the Scottish lord, rather than the other way around.

Grace stood at the bottom of the stairs, tears pouring down her face.

Her mother ran out of the door at the back of the entry, and stood beside her, hand covering her mouth, watching as the three men reached the top of the stairs.

"He—he—" Grace couldn't make the words come.

"He's blind," her mother said softly. "Thank God, that seems to be all of it. Did you see other injuries?" The three men turned down the corridor and out of sight.

"All of it!" The words came out more harshly than she intended.

"Now Colin will have to leave the service," the duchess said. "Don't you see, Grace? The navy was killing him inch by inch, and now he can be done with it. It's a cruel thing to have lost his sight, but I'm so glad that he's alive." She picked up her skirts and began running up the stairs.

Grace hadn't thought her parents understood how Colin felt. But they had watched him grow from a child. No one who loved him could have missed the fact that his eyes had turned to dark pools.

A few minutes later her mother returned downstairs, accompanied by John.

"He's tremendously brave," the duchess was saying, her voice catching.

"He may well regain his eyesight," John said encouragingly, patting her hand. "I have heard of similar cases in which sight was lost from a cannon flare rather than a physical injury."

"I just can't bear it," her mother said with a little sob. "His parents will be devastated. And they're not even due back in the country until August!

James will have to send someone after them immediately."

She collected herself. "Featherstone, please send a message to Lords, asking His Grace to return. And send a carriage to Dr. Pinnacle in Harrogate Street, with a request that he attend us immediately. Queen Adelaide herself told me that Pinnacle is a genius when it comes to ocular matters. He lives in Mayfair; with luck we'll catch him at home."

As Featherstone began sending footmen hither and yon, the door opened again; it was Lily, returned from a ride in the park. A moment later, having heard the news, she was rocketing around the drawing room, touching things lightly. That was what Lily did when she was nervous.

John, laughing, followed her around the room, teasing her as she rearranged her mother's china ornaments.

The doctor arrived and was escorted upstairs. Grace just sat on the sofa, her knees clamped together, her hands shaking. She couldn't bring herself to speak. She didn't belong here, in this too-bright room full of people speaking too loudly. She should be with Colin.

It seemed hours before the doctor clattered his way back down the stairs, accompanied by her mother. Grace jumped to her feet.

The doctor was shaking his head. "I really cannot say what will happen, as I didn't dare to remove the bandage. But unless you can make your patient lie still in a dark room, Your Grace, he may well be permanently blind. In this sort of case, the patient must be protected from all disturbances, and repose in full darkness for six weeks. From what I understand, Captain Barry has had no proper care to this point. He should have had the bad blood let out after enduring that cannon flare, though luckily he seems lucid enough."

"We'll keep him in bed," her mother promised. "And in the dark."

When the Duchess of Ashbrook took that tone, she was *never* disobeyed. Colin would be flat on his back if she had to tie him to the bedposts.

"You won't have a problem for the next twenty-four hours," the doctor said, pulling his cape over his shoulders. "I gave him some laudanum. Given his size"—he said it distastefully, as if his patient was a giant of some sort—"I gave him a double dose. You will find him docile for some time, Your Grace, and I would be happy to visit tomorrow and administer the same again."

The duchess's brows drew together. "Did he agree to this medicine, Doctor?"

Dr. Pinnacle apparently caught the dangerous note in her voice.

"It was best for the patient," he said, putting on his gloves. "There are times when a doctor must overrule a patient for his own good, and this was one of them."

The duchess said nothing, but the moment the doctor left, she raised a finger in Featherstone's direction. "Be so good as to find another ocular expert, if you please." The butler nodded, bowed, and backed through the door.

"I suppose we might leave now," John said with a kind of relentless cheer that grated on Grace's nerves. "Everything is well in hand. Captain Barry will likely sleep well into tomorrow."

"My mother always has things in hand," Lily said, rearranging the ornaments on the mantelpiece again. "Where are the two of you off to?"

"Lord Burden-Sisle has kindly agreed to allow us to view his collection of Constable watercolors," John replied. "Would you like to join us?"

Lily wrinkled her nose. "Absolutely not. It sounds horrendously boring. I can't imagine how you'll survive, John."

"There are only six watercolors and some preliminary sketches," he said.

"But Grace takes forever to look at even one picture," Lily complained. "Haven't you seen how she peers at paintings, and then stands back, and then peers at them again? I was near to weeping with tedium the last time we went to the National Gallery."

Grace stood up. "John, if you'll forgive me, I wouldn't be able to enjoy the collection at the moment."

"But Lord Burden-Sisle made a special appointment," John protested. "He is expecting us."

"Lily will go with you in my stead."

Something in Grace's face caused Lily to leap to John's side, taking his arm and smiling up at him with her most dazzling smile. "You *will* take me, won't you, John?"

He scowled at her. "Not if you ply your wiles on me. I'm to be your brother-in-law, not one of those foolish puppies whom you dazzle in the ballroom."

"Shame!" she cried, drawing him toward the door. "I'll have you know that my swains are *very* intelligent men. I can't imagine why you would slander them in such a fashion."

He looked back, but Grace shook her head, so he bowed and left.

Thirteen

This time, Grace didn't wait for a moan through the wall. She ran up the stairs and straight into Colin's bedchamber. The room was in darkness, thick velvet curtains pulled across the windows; the only light came from a single lamp, turned down low. She took a deep breath, closed the door, and leaned back against it.

This was madness. Yet she couldn't stop herself.

Colin was not lying in bed the way the doctor said he must.

He was seated at a chair before the fireplace, almost as if he were staring at the empty hearth.

"Colin," she whispered.

He turned his head, slowly, far more slowly than he had earlier. She realized that his hands were gripping the arms of his chair as if he were in a ship on a tossing sea.

"Who's there?" he said, growling it.

"It's me, Grace." She walked over to him. "How are you?"

"What did they give me to drink?" He spoke through clenched teeth.

"Laudanum."

A flash of betrayal crossed his face.

"The doctor gave it to you," she cried. "We wouldn't have done it. He feels you should stay in bed."

He reached toward her, found her wrist, and gripped it. "I don't know whether I'm dreaming this or not," he muttered.

"You are not," Grace said, looking down at the way her small wrist disappeared in his hand.

He gave a sharp tug and she sat down on his thighs.

"Colin!"

"Are you a dream or not?"

"I most certainly am not! I'm Grace. Don't you remember me?" She was starting to babble.

"You're betrothed to McIngle, and God knows what he would think of the fact you're in a man's bedchamber."

"I'm breaking off my betrothal," she blurted out.

He said nothing to that. She shouldn't stay here, perched on his legs. Under her bottom she could feel his thighs as he shifted. He was all muscle, contained power.

Yet he was home safe. The bolt of joy that hit her was so intense that it swept away her panic about the state of his eyes.

"You should leave," he said, ignoring her announcement.

"What happened to your eyesight?" she asked, desperate to stay on this side of the door rather than on the other.

"A cannonball exploded directly in front of me," he said, his voice flat and uninterested. "The flash blinded me. I should lie down now."

She stood up, feeling a pinch of anger, but it was nothing new. He'd been rejecting her for years. The fact that he was pushing her away now was unsurprising.

She stepped away, and he stood up as well, but then he swayed slightly, his big body quivering for a moment.

"I'll help you," she said, taking his arm the way John had.

"I know where the bed is," he said, sounding even groggier than he had a moment earlier. He turned in the wrong direction. "I found my way to this chair from the bed after the doctor . . . What did the doctor do? I don't feel well."

"That's not the right direction." She tugged on his arm.

If the truth be told, she was still in love. She was greedy to be with him, to be next to him. She didn't care that he was blind. She didn't care if he never regained his sight, if he growled at her. Maybe she could take a position as his housekeeper, and he wouldn't realize who she was.

"You smell good, like a girl I once knew, but that

was a dream," he said, sounding tipsy, like Fred after he drank too much punch.

Grace gave him a little tug. "Your bed is this way."

His hip was pressed against hers, causing little ripples of fire to spread over her skin.

"Colin," she said, realizing that her voice had become husky and low.

"The bed," he stated. His arm went around her waist and he hauled her closer to him. "You have beautiful curves."

He really sounded inebriated. The drug must have taken hold.

"This way," she whispered, gently tugging him again. She managed to get him to walk a few steps, and then he toppled forward onto the bed and rolled on his back.

The door opened. "Grace!" She'd never seen her mother look so irate. "Out of this room, at once. Colin's incapacity is no grounds for discarding every rule of polite society."

"I'm coming," Grace said, shaking out a blanket and spreading it over Colin. He was so large that his feet stuck out the bottom.

"Grace!"

She turned her head and smiled giddily. "He's home, Mother. He's home, safe and well. I'm sure his eyes will heal. And if they don't, it doesn't matter because he won't be dead. He's *home*."

The duchess came to stand at her shoulder. Even with the bandage, Colin looked outrageously handsome, his lips cherry dark and full. "He always was a gorgeous young man."

"He still is," Grace snapped.

"I didn't mean that he wasn't. I'm worried for him. His life will be difficult indeed if he doesn't regain his sight."

"He will heal." Grace reached out and soothed the blanket over his shoulder. "Everything will be different now he's home."

Her mother looked at her, and then turned on her heel. "I think we'd better go to my sitting room and have a talk."

Grace pulled the blanket a little higher and made sure that Colin's arm was comfortably tucked against his body.

"*Grace.*"

She followed her mother.

Fourteen

By the time Grace reached the duchess's sitting room, she was feeling quite peaceful. She knew what she had to do, although, unfortunately, her mother would not approve.

"If it has even crossed your mind that you will throw yourself at that young man's feet," the duchess said the moment Grace entered the doorway, "I will personally bundle you into a carriage and send you to the country!"

No, her mother would surely not approve. Grace sat on a sofa, never mind the etiquette that insisted she should not sit before her mother did, and stated flatly, "I cannot marry John."

Her mother sat down beside her. "Darling, Colin wasn't a good prospect even before he was injured, much though I love him."

"He *will* regain his eyesight."

"That doesn't mean he will fall in love with you."

Grace swallowed hard. Her mother was not the sort of person who lied to make a person feel better. You could trust her to tell the truth, even if you might not wish to hear it.

Now the duchess leaned close and gathered Grace in her arms. "We never told you children the reason I threw your father out of the house after just two days of marriage, but it had to do with believing that he didn't love me. I would *never* wish that horrible experience on one of my children."

Tears threatened. Grace couldn't pretend, even to herself, that Colin loved her. Three hours earlier, he had turned his head in her direction and then away, without even asking how she was. He hadn't congratulated her on her betrothal. She was nothing to him. Less than nothing.

And yet she felt such a wave of love for him, the ungrateful beast, that she could hardly bear it. "He's hurting," she said, the words tumbling out. "I know him, Mama. He hated being in the navy, and the fact that he never got injured made it worse."

"How so?"

"He felt guilty just for surviving. They died all around him, you know. His men did. And they cried out for their mothers. He couldn't bear it."

The duchess's arm tightened. "That's terrible. I could see he was unhappy, but I had no idea he was so tormented."

"I don't want to love him." Grace stared down at her fingers, twisting together. "I *hate* the fact I love him, and you're right to say that he doesn't love me."

Her mother sighed. "I wish you were a little girl again so that I could give you a kiss and make it better."

"He's not in love with me," Grace repeated, "but I'm in love with him. That's the way it's been for my whole life, and it won't change. I almost feel as if I'm cursed."

"No!"

"Colin walked into the house today and my heart leapt, even though I saw he was blind in the same moment. I don't care about anything other than the fact he's home. I wouldn't care if he had lost a leg or both arms. It wouldn't be right to marry John, feeling the way I do."

"I've occasionally thought that John would be perfect for Lily," the duchess said thoughtfully, stroking Grace's hair. "He's steady and kind, and she needs both. And he's very intelligent." She left the corollary unspoken.

Grace shrugged. "As long as Lily doesn't marry Colin. I think of *that*, and I feel like a madwoman, Mama, I really do. Absolutely cracked." Her voice wavered, and she swallowed before adding, "I'll never love anyone as I do him. I'm not a baby, and I've loved him for years. He's all there is for me."

Tears rolled down her cheeks, and her mother handed her a perfectly pressed handkerchief embroidered with the Ashbrook crest. "Did I ever tell you about the time when your father and I were both young, and he had to lie in a darkened room or risk blindness?"

"No."

"Your father does not like to stand still for five minutes, let alone weeks. I fell in love with him sitting by his bed, and I never recovered from it."

"How old were you?"

"Ten or eleven, I think."

Grace was quite unsurprised to find that she and her mother fell in love around the same age. "Mother," she said, straightening her back, "I intend to bring Colin to Arbor House."

Her mother's face fell. "Oh, darling, I can't accompany you just now."

"I shall take him by myself."

"I know Colin is a family friend, but you are a young lady. Your maid would be an adequate chaperone for the journey, but you could not reside in Arbor House with him, given that his parents are not in residence."

"I can, and I will." Grace folded her hands.

"You will be compromised!"

"Yes."

A fascinated expression replaced her mother's frown. "Dearest, you do understand the implications of what you are saying?"

"I will not allow Colin to blunder about the country unable to see." She took a deep breath. "I mean to seduce him if I am able."

"Oh my goodness," the duchess said faintly.

"Gentlemen aren't like servants, you know. You can't simply order them to do your bidding."

"What is the worst that could happen? He will reject me. Again. But at least," Grace said fiercely, "I will have fought for him. I have to do that, at least."

"But—"

"I shan't marry anyone else," Grace said, cutting her off. "I expect it won't be so terrible being an old maid, unless Colin marries Lily. But I *know* him, Mama. If he doesn't regain his sight, he won't willingly marry either of us. He wouldn't want to be a burden."

Her mother was silent. Then: "I wouldn't be surprised if Colin isn't secretly in love with you. You wrote him all those charming letters for years. He may well need a little push, though *seduction*, Grace, is going too far, as I hope you realize."

"Yes, Mama."

She was never any good at lying. Her mother shook her head. "You are very like me, do you know that?"

Grace smiled. "Yes."

"I think there's a good chance that Colin will not agree to being accompanied by you."

"He certainly will not. I think it would be best if he were put in the carriage now. If he doesn't wake for hours, it will be too late to cavil."

"Colin is nothing if not honorable," the duchess pointed out. "The mere journey will compromise you, so there's no need for drastic measures. You can have a proper wedding night." She stood up and rang the bell. "In fact, I'll have our solicitor quietly obtain a special license and send it after you."

"I won't marry Colin unless I have managed to seduce him," Grace stated. "The last thing I want is a husband who was forced to marry me."

Her mother opened her mouth, but their butler opened the door. "Featherstone," the duchess said, "I believe that this regrettable dose of laudanum can be put to best use by bundling Captain Barry into the carriage and dispatching him to Arbor House. The doctor ordered complete rest and darkness, and this house is far too active. He will be more comfortable there."

Featherstone nodded. "I'll order the traveling carriage, Your Grace."

"Oh, and do tell Lady Grace's maid to pack her things. She will accompany him to the country." The butler showed not a flicker of surprise. He was, above all, a servant of the Duchess of Ashbrook.

"Darling," the duchess continued, turning back to Grace, "I have just realized that it might be best if Colin had left by the time your father returns."

Grace jumped to her feet. Her father would never allow her to travel with a man who didn't love her, especially if the duke had the faintest idea that his daughter was planning to seduce the man in question. "Featherstone, please tell Mary to pack a small travel bag so we can leave immediately."

"I'll send your clothes after you in the morning," her mother said, as the door closed behind Featherstone. "You must write a letter to John before you leave."

Grace bit her lip, thinking of John's adoring eyes. "Do you suppose that Lily could make him feel better?"

"That's a question for Lily and John, not for you. Tell him the truth, Grace. He will be bitterly disappointed, but it does a man good to have a broken relationship or two in his past. John is a bit too satisfied with himself."

"What if Papa sends after me the moment he hears what happened?"

"I think," the duchess said, with a wicked twinkle, "that you can count on me to distract your father."

And so it was that a slumbering Captain Barry was bundled onto one seat of the ducal carriage, and Grace sat down on the other. Another carriage followed with Colin's trunk, and his batman, and with Mary, Grace's maid.

Grace's heart beat quickly for the first hour of their journey. But at length, she relaxed. No one wants to think *too* closely about her parents' intimate life, but it would take an idiot not to recognize that the Duchess of Ashbrook could wind a pirate around her little finger.

It would be hours—perhaps an entire day— before His Grace knew that his daughter had disappeared.

Fifteen

Colin had fallen back into a laudanum dream, even as he struggled against it, telling himself that he had sworn never again to enter the dangerous world that left him with an aching heart and tears on his cheeks.

Colin was a man. Men don't cry. *Ergo*, Colin didn't cry.

Except when taking laudanum.

In this dream, he was in a carriage with Grace, which was interesting, because he couldn't remember being in a carriage with her before. He was blindfolded, unlike his other dreams, but he knew she was there. Somehow, he knew.

Since it was only a dream, he followed his heart and asked, "Are you there?"

He whispered it, but he heard a soft rustle of her gown, and then she was next to him, bending over him. She didn't wear perfume, the way her sister Lily did. He could smell Grace, a scent of lemon soap and woman.

A cool hand came on his cheek, and she murmured something.

He didn't care what she was saying. This was *his* dream, and so far it was going the way he wanted.

So he reached out and grasped her gown. She seemed to be wearing a traveling gown of some sort of sturdy fabric. He spared just a moment to commend his dream-making abilities. That was quite a realistic detail.

Dream Grace was still saying something, but rather than answer, he pulled her toward him. She fell onto his chest with a little squeak. The voice in the back of his head was laughing: *Graceful!* Not that she would appreciate the pun.

But it didn't matter. He began to shift their positions, which was hard to do when he couldn't see, and he spared a wish that his damned dream would give him his vision as he usually had while dreaming—but no complaining. He was too afraid that at any moment Grace would dissolve under his fingers.

Finally, he had her underneath him. His body felt massive in relation to hers, and he realized that all those exercises on board ship had probably made him even more muscled than he usually was. Good thing this was just a dream. An English lass would likely be put off by his size.

He cupped her face with his hand and tilted it toward his lips.

This time he heard her. "Colin, do you know who I am?"

"Of course I do," he told Dream Grace. "This is my dream, after all." Then he kissed her. Gently. The way a man kisses a woman whom he adores and hasn't seen since he left for the sea.

Her mouth was sweet as honey and sent an instant flame down his body. She seemed startled, frozen almost, but then she murmured something and her hand slipped into his hair. When they were both gasping for breath—nice touch of realism there—he let his lips slide from hers, and started kissing the line of her jaw, the arch of her cheekbone, the curl of eyelashes that had stunned him when she was only twelve and had made him feel like some sort of filthy old man.

But now she was twenty . . .

"How old are you?" he murmured.

"Twenty," he heard, which was like a benediction.

"Not twelve?"

He had to make sure of that. He'd have to throw himself out of the carriage if he had started dreaming about young girls.

"Of course not!" Dream Grace sounded indignant and a little cross. Everyone thought that the Real Grace was docile, but he knew the truth. She put a wicked sense of humor into her paintings.

He kissed her until she was whimpering, and he was rubbing against her, and then he came to himself enough to realize that he'd better move quickly. He hadn't dreamed about Grace in weeks, and this time, he wanted to actually take her instead of merely thinking about it.

Without a second thought, he braced himself on one arm, reached for her bodice, and ripped it free. There was a bit more verisimilitude to the whole affair than he had expected—in his earlier dreams, Grace's clothing had simply evaporated from her body. But this time, he actually pulled her body up from the seat. There was a sharp sound of cloth tearing, and she gave a little shriek of surprise . . .

The dream was going to dissolve; he could feel it in his bones. So he went back to kissing her, because if he couldn't have it all, he wanted every moment of her soft lips that he could have. She tasted of tea and faintly of sugar and mostly of Grace. When he was kissing her, he didn't mind that he didn't have his eyesight; he didn't need it. Everything he wanted to know he could tell with his other senses: the tremor that shook her body, the little moan when he nipped her generous lower lip, and the way she kissed him back, eager as any courtesan.

Some part of his mind reminded him that a dream wasn't real. But damn, he had conjured a wonderful Dream Grace.

His hand slid to her breast and even though he had to tear away yet another layer of cloth— this dream was irritatingly precise—he finally had a breast in his hand. It was the most delightfully rounded breast he could have imagined. It was perfect. He nuzzled her, and then kissed her nipple, and the only thing that made him sad was that he couldn't see it.

Suddenly he remembered that this was *his* dream. So he demanded, "What color is your nipple?"

Dream Grace was gasping in a way that made his whole body vibrate with desire. When she didn't answer, he commanded, "Tell me." He'd never heard that tone in his voice before. He sounded like a satyr.

Since he was a satyr, he might as well keep going. He moved back just enough so that he could run a hand up her legs, under her skirts. She still hadn't answered his question, but her breath was coming in little gasps, so he let it go.

Dream Grace had a mind of her own, it seemed. Or maybe she didn't know any more about her breasts than he did, because if he didn't know, she couldn't . . .

But the complications of dreaming up a naked person slipped away from him, because now he had a hand running up the luscious curve of her inner thigh. Under his fingertips, her skin was like the softest satin he'd ever felt.

He wanted to taste her, so he pushed off the seat onto the carriage floor. The floor was hard under his knees—again, congratulations to his imagination for realistic detail—but he wasn't going to complain.

He might have finessed it a bit if he was with a real woman, but this was his dream. He pushed the gown straight up to her waist and pulled off her drawers.

Dream Grace babbled with surprise, but he refused to listen. His imagination was correct in that detail: Real Grace, with her lovely air of dignity, would never allow herself to be debauched in a coach. She wouldn't be surprised, but outraged.

"This is *my* dream," he informed Dream Grace, putting a stern note in his voice.

Then he began licking her inner thighs, making his way toward heaven. He was almost there when the coach lurched and his lips fell directly on a silken tuft of hair. His mind told him the hair was likely a delicate red. His mind also complimented him on the clever way the coach motion had worked in his favor.

Dream Grace sounded urgent now. "Trust me," he said, silently telling his dream girl how much he adored and respected her.

Telling her that he would make love to her in a queen's bed or a stable, if she would give him a chance.

That she was the center of his universe.

It worked. Dream Grace caught his hand in hers, and then she kissed the tips of his fingers. The touch of her lips drove him mad.

He lowered his head and ran his tongue over that little twist of hair again, pushing her legs apart to make room for his shoulders. He had never tasted anything sweeter. What's more, he could hear Dream Grace's breath changing, coming even faster. Her hand tightened on his, but he still had one free hand. He trailed his fingers up the smooth skin of her thigh, up and down, finally came closer.

She twisted against him, murmuring words that Real Grace would never say . . . begging him, pleading with him.

He loved it. Dream Grace had no dignity and no restraint. She was all sensuality, with desire that sprang from her heart and body.

He ran a finger over her delicately. His hands had never felt so large and clumsy as they were at this moment. She screamed at his touch. The sound was pure pleasure, but he spared a moment to remind his imagination that it was *his* dream and virginity should have no part in it. He didn't want that scream to have a hint of pain.

Sure enough, Dream Grace was no virgin. She wasn't in the least uncertain. She had one leg draped over his shoulder now, and she was arching wantonly toward his mouth. She was soft and wet . . . He slid a finger inside her, gasping at how tight and hot she was. She screamed again, so loudly the dream coachman could probably hear her, and then convulsed around his finger.

He kept kissing her, luxuriously, slowly, with a kind of pleasure that he'd never indulged in before. She was gasping—panting, really—so he thrust another finger beside the first.

Her cry was so sweet and passionate that he almost spent himself there, on his knees. One thrust of his fingers and she was shaking again, convulsing, driving him into a fever of desire.

Damn, but he had a potent imagination. It was a good thing that he had thrown that laudanum out the porthole, because he saw now how easily a man could become addicted to dreams like this one.

The only thing that annoyed him was that he couldn't see her. But no complaining . . . He wouldn't wait any longer. He stood, braced himself against the swaying coach, pulled his placket open and her thighs apart, and said, "I want you." His own voice was so guttural, low and fierce, that he surprised himself.

Dream Grace wasn't the sort of illusion who argued with a man. As he put a knee on the seat, her arms came around his neck, and she pulled his mouth to hers.

Colin positioned himself at the entrance to her sleek warmth and then slowly began pushing forward. This dream was amazing. He was ecstatic.

No woman could possibly feel this tight and hot. No woman's lips were that lush. No woman could turn his loins to fire with nothing more than a squeak, like a mix of surprise and desire.

He pulled out, slow, and then worked his way back into her, shuddering with the pleasure of it. Then he caught her lips again, stilled because it felt so good, kissed her for a long moment, caught there between pleasure and movement.

Suddenly he had a pulse of anxiety—what if the dream ended?—and remembered, at the same moment, that the woman who had put a leg over his shoulder didn't need the sort of careful attention one might give a real woman. She was *his*, straight from his imagination.

So he pulled out again and then thrust, roaring aloud at the pleasure he'd never imagined . . . hadn't ever thought . . . His thoughts fell apart.

He loved her; she was his center; he was nothing without her.

For long minutes he had no other thoughts than the desperate heat in his loins and the blazing need in his body. He pumped fast, and then faster, one hand caressing her breast, the other balancing himself against the movement of the coach. He just wished he could see her face, see her head thrown back in exquisite pleasure, her lips open, her eyes glazed with desire . . . love.

Was she with him? Did it matter? She was Dream Grace, after all . . . She would be with him. She was pure sensuality, pure desire.

For a moment, he felt sad, missing Real Grace's complex, thoughtful mind. But his beloved would never be this sensual. She was adorable, and grave, and dignified.

The thought of Real Grace made it all roar out of him, all his love and despair and pure lust, moving from him to her in a storm.

Then . . . his knees were weak. He slipped free, consumed with deep thankfulness that the dream had finally—*finally*—allowed him to make love to Grace, rather than dissolving her into thin air just before they joined.

He was so damned tired that he could feel darkness swallowing him up. He stood, bumped his head on something, fell onto a seat. Grace was gone, of course. Just himself on a leather seat, alone again.

He missed her with a piercing agony, but the darkness was coming to swallow him up.

"Mine," he said, shaping the word clearly, just in case he never saw Dream Grace again. "You're mine, now."

He spoke to the silent air, of course. There was no one in his dream but him.

She didn't reply.

Sixteen

*L*ady Grace Ryburn wasn't a virgin anymore.

Not that the man who did the deed seemed aware of that fact. Colin was lying flat on his back on the opposite seat, one arm over his bandaged eyes, the other hanging free so that his fingers curled against the coach floor. He was dressed, but the front of his breeches gaped open.

And his member . . .

That was not a very attractive look, to Grace's mind. She had quite liked how he looked, before. In fact, she had almost reached out to touch him.

She had absolutely no wish to touch him now, but obviously, someone was going to have to button his placket before the coach stopped.

Then she looked down at herself, slowly recovering from the shock of it. Her gown was torn. Her chemise was hanging off her shoulder. Thank goodness, she never wore a corset while traveling, because presumably he would have bitten off the whalebone stays with his teeth.

Worse, there was a smear of blood on her leg. And she hurt. In fact, she hurt quite a bit.

Tears pressed the back of her throat, but she made herself think it through. She'd enjoyed it, until the actual possession, so to speak—which she found most unenjoyable. It was rather surprising to find out how much she disliked that part of the marital act, since her mother had always led her to believe that it was great fun from beginning to end.

Colin had had fun all the way through. But then she felt a flash of guilt. Lord knew whom he thought he was making love to. He hadn't chosen her. The thought of Lily skittered across her mind and she shoved it away. No, he was surely thinking of a mistress, some woman he'd made love to before. Not Lily. That woman, whoever she was . . . she was *his.* He had said so, in a hoarse, possessive way that thrilled her to her toes.

The jealousy she felt was blinding, and entirely unwelcome.

Frankly, Colin had been like an animal, mad with desire. She shivered at the thought of how he had lost himself inside her, and then found herself shivering again with a delicious pulse of heat.

The wonder of it was that she had somehow managed to seduce him, even though she could hardly congratulate herself on her effort. He had simply taken matters into his own skillful hands.

Slowly, she sat up, wincing, and pulled off the

remnants of her gown. Her mother had trained her long ago to be prepared for an emergency such as the luggage carriage going astray, so her traveling bag was in her carriage, and contained another gown.

It took a few minutes to wiggle into it, and she didn't have a spare chemise. But even her mother's exquisite planning couldn't cover all eventualities—such as the one where Grace had to hook up the back of her gown after being ravished in a coach.

Since she couldn't fasten her gown, she wrapped her cloak tightly enough around her to cover her bare back. Her maid would realize, of course. Looking at her discarded chemise and the gown, and particularly the blood staining her chemise, there would be no disguising anything from her maid. She bundled them back into the traveling bag, trying to think how she would explain it.

She would simply have to hold her head high.

Finally, she got up and went over to Colin. He was unexpectedly vulnerable, lying there with his eyes covered. Yet when she touched him, he stirred, and somewhat to her horror, his tool began to thicken and straighten, right before her eyes. She bundled him hastily into his breeches and did up the button placket, her own private parts sending her a twinge of dismay at the mere thought of how he had employed that—that *thing* of his.

When they reached the posting inn where the Duke of Ashbrook stabled his horses, she assumed the haughtiness of a duchess and swept through the door before the servants' coach had even entered into the yard. The innkeeper instantly escorted her to his largest bedchamber.

"My husband, Captain Barry, will require a room of his own," she told him. "And I should like a bath."

The innkeeper bowed. "Of course, Mrs. Barry."

Grace flinched at the title she didn't deserve, but kept speaking. "He has suffered an injury and, unless he has woken, he must be carried from the coach. He is temporarily blind."

The innkeeper's face twitched. "I'm so sorry to hear that, Mrs. Barry. We will take the best possible care of your husband."

She nodded and he left.

Grace sank into a chair, and then started straight back onto her feet. It hurt. Her most tender part felt . . . well . . . *hurt*. How did women put up with this sort of thing?

She went straight back to her first reaction to the act. She had been enjoying it until a certain point. She frowned, realizing what must be the truth. That first part was for her. And the second part was for him. Presumably the second part wouldn't hurt as much next time, though obviously it would never be as much fun as the preliminaries. She could probably live with that.

She took a pillow from the bed, put it on the chair, and then eased herself down while she waited for her bath to arrive. She would have to think about how often she would agree to have marital relations. Once a week at the outside. Perhaps once a fortnight.

No wonder young girls weren't informed about the details of such intimacies. They'd probably run off to Spain and join nunneries.

She looked up, caught a glimpse of herself in the glass, and actually gave a little shriek. Lord knew what that innkeeper had thought of her. Her hair was tumbled over her shoulders, and her lips looked swollen. There was—she turned down her collar to examine it more closely—yes, there was a bruise on her neck. As if he'd *marked* her. Like a savage.

Yes, it was no wonder that married women kept all these details to themselves.

Seventeen

Colin woke with an aching head. He rolled on his back and his elbow struck a wall; for a moment he thought he was on the ship again.

Then he froze. Where in the hell was he? This wasn't the townhouse of the most elegant woman in England.

There was a smell of roast beef in the air. He seemed to be lying on top of a bed, fully clothed. The pillow under his head was lumpy, and of a quality that the duchess would never allow on a guest's bed, and probably not even in the servants' quarters.

He sat up, bracing himself against the wall. What in the hell had happened to him? He had an indistinct memory of another laudanum dream. He couldn't remember all the details, but he knew it had ended satisfactorily, and that it was far more acceptable than those dreams that left him unmanned.

In fact, barring the headache, he felt better than he had in weeks. Since before the cannonball exploded just off the ship rail. Thinking of how he woke to total darkness, he reached up and patted the bandage around his head. It was still firmly tied.

The door opened and Ackerley entered. In the six weeks since he lost his sight, Colin had gained an extraordinary ability to judge people by how they walked: literally by how their feet struck the ground. Ackerley ambled. You could tell him there was a fire in the privy, and he would amble over to look. Hell, you could tell him that his own coattails were on fire, and he would think about it before he turned to peer at his arse.

"Where the devil am I?" Colin demanded, with no preliminaries.

"The Cow and Tulip, Captain, on the Bath Road."

He was half way to Arbor House, then. That made sense. But somehow, he had lost a day or two, because he had no memory of getting in the carriage. In fact, the last thing he remembered was telling a doctor that he didn't want laudanum . . .

Laudanum.

The old sod must have given him a dose anyway. Well, he could hardly curse the doctor for giving him the best dream of his life. The memory shot a little pulse of fever through his blood.

"How did I get here?"

"In the carriage," Ackerley said, without a trace

of irony in his voice. "Would you like me to order your bath?"

"Yes."

Colin brooded while Ackerley banged about the room. How the hell did he end up in a carriage? He must have had some sort of waking dream, because he managed to get out of the duchess's townhouse.

Ackerley removed his clothing and steered him into the large tin bathtub. "Your hair, Captain Barry?"

He hated this. He hated having to be bathed with every inch of his soul, but there was nothing to be done about it. "Yes," he said shortly. He closed his eyes as Ackerley pulled off the bandage and poured liquid soap on his head.

A moment later the man tied the bandage back around his wet head and handed him a toothbrush.

Colin used it and handed it back. "Put the towels and my clothing on the bed. You may leave." He was at the limit of his tolerance; he would not allow another man to wash his body.

Only once he was certain the door was shut did Colin reach out, finding the edges of the bathtub, searching for the small bottle of liquid soap.

He caught the bottle just as it toppled off the side, pouring some into his left hand and rubbing his right arm. There was an odd little purr of well-being in his body, something he hadn't felt in months.

Washing his other arm, he realized that he

might not have felt this good in a year. Even his headache had disappeared. It was that dream, of course.

He washed his chest, thinking about it. No wonder men became addicts who wasted into scarecrows in back alleys. The dream had offered him everything he wanted: Grace.

When he had walked into the duchess's townhouse, he had known instantly that Grace was in the entryway. He had *smelled* her; she favored soap that smelled like lemon verbena, and the scent hung on the air.

But just as he was about to greet her, there had been a shuffle of feet, and McIngle had stepped forward with his damnably pleasant voice. His words had been like a dose of ice water, but also a salutary reminder. Grace was betrothed to McIngle. She was going to marry the man.

So he hadn't thrown himself at her like a ravening beast. He had been polite and cool, even though he felt a tearing pain in his chest. It made him realize that in some dark corner of his soul he had been hoping that Lily was wrong, and Grace wasn't betrothed to McIngle.

But she was, and why shouldn't she be? He had asked for Lily's hand in marriage.

His hand slid farther down his stomach to his crotch—and froze. He was no mere stripling. He knew what his tool felt like when it had been in use.

Impossible.

But he couldn't deny the feeling. He must have

spent his seed in the carriage in the midst of that dream, which was a bloody embarrassing idea. He must be losing his mind. He couldn't remember ordering the carriage, getting into it, opening his placket, buttoning it back up, never mind doing himself a service in the grip of that dream . . .

Thank God Ackerley wasn't in the carriage. Or was he? A searing pulse of humiliation went through Colin.

He had put up with a great deal since the ship doctor ordered a bandage over his eyes. The man had said he would stay blind if even the slightest ray of light struck his eyes during the following six weeks. Hell, he might end up sightless anyway.

Ackerley had steered him to the water closet, taken his clothes off, handed him a toothbrush . . . This particular situation made those humiliations seem petty. Bloody hell, he hoped he hadn't made an utter fool of himself.

Then he thought about Ackerley's tone when he summoned the bath. The man wasn't the brightest, but if he had witnessed his employer thrusting away at the air, there would be signs of strain in his voice.

Ackerley had been as placid and uninterested as ever. So Colin must have been alone in the carriage. In fact, he'd bet the duchess had sent along a second carriage for Ackerley and his trunk. That would be like her.

He briskly finished washing, his body responding with a wave of good feeling that made him think he had done himself a disservice by staying away from women for months. Nor had he enabled himself in a private way.

But now he was almost happy.

He carefully climbed out of the tub, and groped his way to the length of towel Ackerley had left for him.

Five minutes later, he was clean and dressed. Ackerley hadn't returned, but he realized with a surge of energy that he didn't want to remain cooped up in the room. It must be the English air. He felt like venturing outside, and be damned if he lurched about like a drunken cow.

Perhaps he could find someone to take him to the stables. As a boy, he'd dreamed of impressing his adopted father with an illustrious career at sea, and never paid any attention to horseflesh. But in the last few years, he'd spent a surprising amount of his shore leave in the stables.

There was something in a horse's whiskery kiss, the peaceful way they cropped grass, and the comforting musky smell of a stable that helped put the terrible memories in their place.

In the past.

Eighteen

*C*olin descended the narrow wooden stairs of the inn with one hand on the wall and the other on the rail. Once at the bottom, he had a sense of empty space before him, perhaps a longish corridor leading outside, since a touch of wind came to his face. He heard a burst of noise, along with a potent smell of hops and ale. That must be the public room.

He was about to head toward the outside, when he heard a heavyset man enter the corridor. The feet paused and then bustled toward him, their owner smelling of horseradish and, faintly, of roast beef. "Captain Barry, welcome to my inn. I am Topper. You must be fair hungry."

"Good evening, Mr. Topper," Colin said. "Can you inform my man that I am up? As you can see, I have some trouble negotiating in my current state."

"I was coming to tell you myself," the innkeeper

said, his voice taking on a solemn tone. "Not more than twenty minutes ago, your wife's maid fell and broke her wrist. I had to send Mr. Ackerley along with the poor lass in a coach to Dr. Strickner in Andover; he's the only bonesetter in these parts. But it's a good distance and they'll have to stay the night there."

"My wife," Colin repeated.

"Your wife's maid," the innkeeper corrected. "Lawks-a-mercy, Captain Barry, if it had been your lady wife that had tripped, I would have told you immediately. No, it was your wife's maid, and as I said, I sent the two of them off together as I don't have a man to spare at the moment. Mrs. Topper can act as your wife's lady's maid this evening, and I'll do as much for you, Captain. Our own son is serving his country on the seas, and I'd be right honored to help a member of the Royal Navy." He stopped, seemingly out of breath after this flow of conversation.

Colin had a dizzy sensation, as if he were trapped in a laudanum dream that never ended. It was impossible.

He'd never heard of such a thing.

It was one thing to lose a day or two, to have no memory of giving orders regarding a remove to Arbor House. Hell, he meant to do that anyway. Perhaps he never woke, and the duchess, knowing his plans, bundled him in a carriage.

No, she would never do that. He must have been awake enough to extract himself from her care and demand his carriage.

But to find himself married was another question.

Who in the hell had he married?

"Did you say *my wife*?" he asked.

There was an infinitesimal pause, and the innkeeper's voice changed, taking on a dollop of sympathy. "I'm guessing that you suffered a fearsome blow to the head, Captain Barry, and you're experiencing some loss of your memory. That is entirely normal, I assure you. Why, after my neighbor's boy fell from the ridge top, he plumb forgot that he was left-handed and started using his right, like any Christian!"

"I assure you that I have not overlooked a wife," Colin said, barely stopping himself from reaching out and throttling the man's neck.

"Good, good!" Topper chuckled. "I think we can admit amongst ourselves that our better halves don't take well to being forgotten."

Colin ground his teeth. "I was not aware that my wife accompanied me."

That made the man much happier. "Of course, of course! You were deep asleep when you arrived and I had the men carry you up the stairs. Your lovely lady did come with you, Captain. She did indeed. She waits for you in my best private parlor. We'll have a meal served to the two of you within the quarter hour."

"No," Colin said. "I should like some time alone with my . . . wife."

He could hear the innkeeper rubbing his hands together. "Of course you do, of course you do!"

he all but shouted. "Young lovers separated by war are eager to be alone." Then he leaned closer, breathing roast beef onto Colin's cheek. "If you'll excuse the presumption, Captain, I could see from your wife's face when she entered the door that she'd given you a hero's welcome back to England!"

Colin hand shot out and unerringly caught the innkeeper around his fat neck. "If you ever speak of my wife in such an impudent fashion again, I shall knock you into the next county."

The innkeeper coughed and gabbled, "I'm sure I didn't mean the slightest presumption, sir, not in the slightest."

Colin let him go. "Lead me to the private parlor." The innkeeper took his arm and he suffered it, cursing Ackerley silently. What the devil was the man doing, trotting off with some maid to a bone-setter?

That would be the maid belonging to a wife he didn't remember. It made sense that he couldn't remember the maid, either.

And there was a woman waiting for him.

The innkeeper trundled down the corridor and turned left through an open door. Colin waited until the door closed behind Topper. Then he stood, back to the door, waiting.

He was greeted by silence.

This must be some sort of elaborate hoax, though to what end, he didn't know. There was a trace of roses in the air, the scent of the woman who walked into the chamber before him.

Roses? His heart plummeted into his boots. Could he have married Lily? Could the duke and duchess have remembered his long-ago request and paired him with Lily in an excess of patriotic zeal? Would he have gone through a marriage ceremony in a laudanum daze? Was that even possible?

There wasn't a sound in the room. Whoever she was, she was sitting still as a mouse. That didn't seem like Lily. She fluttered like a butterfly here and there, unable to sit quietly, as far as he remembered.

Still . . . Who else could he have married? He didn't want to have married Lily, with every ounce of being in his soul.

"Lily," he said, flatly. His life was over. He would have to sit opposite Grace at a hundred family dinners, watching her smile, watching her eyes light up at McIngle's jests, while he was paired with her silly sister.

There was a rustle of cloth across the room and a little gasp. Another drift of perfume reached him.

"Exactly when did we wed?" he asked. He might as well begin this marriage with honesty. "I have no memory of it." He would have walked forward, but he didn't want his wife to see him stumbling about like a fool.

Wife?

Impossible.

Suddenly rage flowed up his spine. He hadn't planned to marry, but damn it, if he chose to do so, he wanted the happiness of his parents, or of the duke and duchess. He had hoped for that soul-deep connection.

"Madam," he said, hearing nothing but quick breathing. "I must confess that I find this marriage not only unexpected, but questionable."

He heard a faint creak as she rose from her seat, and then the whisper of slippers against the carpet as she walked toward him. She was clearly young and lithe. Surely it was Lily, rather than an utter stranger. He crossed his arms over his chest, knowing that his face held the arrogant rage of a shipboard captain, but helpless to soften it.

He could not imagine the duchess party to such a wedding. He must have been married to a complete stranger, likely by the same lying bastard of a leech who drugged him. Her Grace would never be party to criminality.

Then memory of his discovery in the bath shot into his mind: the fraudulent marriage was consummated. He'd been taken, as neatly as any innocent maiden kidnapped by a rogue. The thought made him blind with rage—an oxymoron, in his situation.

"C-Colin," he heard, the voice just audible over the drumming of blood in his ears.

He located the woman by that whisper, took one step and caught her arm in a fierce grip. "Who are you?" His mind darted through possibilities. He'd been kidnapped, drugged, and married for his money . . . for his connections . . . "*Who are you?*" It came out in a bellow.

"Grace," came a faint voice, followed by a hiccup and another sob. "I'm Grace, Colin. Not Lily. I'm—I'm so sorry."

His mind reeled. "Grace? What in the hell are you—" He dropped her arm, fell back a step, and jumped to the obvious conclusion. "*You* were in my carriage. I—we—that was *you*."

There was another sob, and he surged forward again, gathering her into his arms. She folded against him, her body as fragile as that of a bird. He was holding Grace, just as he'd dreamed of doing. Every male instinct he had roared with triumph.

But her shoulders were shaking as she wept.

Slowly, it dawned on him. He hadn't been taken: he *had taken*. He'd ruined her. Worse, she likely hadn't even consented. Perhaps he lunged at her like a beast. Laudanum was no excuse if he had *raped* her. He had committed an evil for which he himself had cashiered sailors.

"I gather the duchess asked you to accompany me to the country," he said, swallowing hard. "Where's McIngle?"

"In London," she said against his waistcoat.

"We are not married, are we?"

"No." Her voice was a thread of sound.

He followed that truth to its logical conclusion. "You told the innkeeper that we were married because I took advantage of you in the carriage." He felt as if he had woken to find himself a stranger. "I was in the grip of a dream, Grace; I didn't know what I was doing. I would never have done such a thing if I had been in my right mind. I am deeply, *deeply* sorry."

It was a cry wrung from his heart. "It must have been terrible for you." His arms tightened around her. "Bloody hell," he whispered when she didn't respond, just cried harder. How could he have done such a thing, even in a dream?

"How—how awful was it?" he asked, needing to know, his conscience burning like glowing coals in his gut. "Grace, please. Tell me."

She said something against his waistcoat.

To hell with his eyesight. Whether he lost it or not, he had to see her eyes. He released her and raised his arms to his bandage.

"No!" She shrieked it, small hands grabbing his wrists with surprising strength. "What are you doing?"

"I need to see you," he said hoarsely. "I have to see in your eyes the pain I caused you."

She pulled, hard, so he allowed his arms to descend. "You didn't," she said, so quietly he could hardly hear it. Her hands slid down to hold his.

"What?" His heart beat in his throat, hard. The feeling of her hands in his . . . it made him crave more of her, all of her. "I didn't—in the carriage?" He thought back to the bath. "I know we did."

"This is so embarrassing."

But Colin was feeling a faint hope. Perhaps it wasn't quite as bad as he'd thought. "Did we make love, Grace, or did I take you forcibly?"

He heard her take a huge breath, and then she

said, "We made love but . . . but you were making love to Lily and I was making love to you!" Then she burst into tears again.

He scooped her up into his arms, holding her against his chest. She weighed nothing, this girl who had captured his heart. He waited until she sniffed, rather inelegantly, and then said, "Grace, I can't see which way to walk."

"Do let me down. This is silly." She began to struggle, so he tightened his arms.

"Which direction shall I walk?"

A little shudder went through her body. "There's a chair ahead of you," she replied, her voice thick with tears. "Just walk a few steps and I'll tell you when you can put me down."

Put her down? He walked forward until she said, "The chair is directly in front of you." He tested the distance with his knee, then turned about, and sat down.

"You could have fallen!" she gasped.

"I've been practicing for almost six weeks."

She moved again, as if to struggle free, but he didn't relax his arms. "Grace."

"Let me go," she whispered.

"No." A great, weary sense of peace was coming over him. He'd done something very wrong, and he would spend his entire life trying to make up for it. He'd taken Grace away from McIngle in the worst possible fashion. He'd ruined her, in the old-fashioned meaning of the word. But he hadn't broken his own sense of honor, and apparently, he hadn't raped her.

He didn't even like thinking about the word. Ravished her, perhaps, but not raped.

And she was *his* now. It satisfied a deeply primal side of him, which frankly didn't give a damn about McIngle. All he truly cared about was the fact that he had hurt Grace. He had made her cry.

He dropped a kiss on her hair, an entirely inadequate apology. "We'll have to be married as soon as we can."

She sniffled again. "I can't marry you, Colin."

"Yes, you can. And you will." There was no question in his mind about that.

"I cannot."

"Because of McIngle?" A hint of steel dropped into his voice. He should be sorry for the fellow. But in truth he wasn't sorry for him. He wanted to kill him for having the pretension to ask Grace for her hand.

"No."

His body relaxed. "Why, then?" His mind supplied a hundred reasons, and he added quickly, "I know you are probably deeply shocked by what happened in the carriage, Grace. We needn't . . . I'm so sorry."

She started crying again.

"We don't have to do it again," he added, feeling rather desperate. "Not until you feel differently about me."

"I'm sorry," she said, her voice cracking. "I thought . . . I hoped you knew who I was."

Colin frowned, trying to figure out what she meant.

"In the carriage, I mean. If I'd known you thought I was Lily, I would *never* have allowed you to touch me."

He had forgotten that she had said something about Lily. He adjusted Grace's curves into the crook of his arm, struggling to ignore the fact that her soft bottom had ignited an unruly and impolite passion in his loins. "I did not think you were Lily."

"But when you entered the room, you expected Lily."

"I was confused by your perfume."

"I'm not wearing perfume." He realized that now, of course. She smelled like lemon verbena and tears.

It was confession time.

"Are you in love with McIngle?" he asked instead.

She leaned her head against his chest. "If you're hoping that he might still marry me, you are wrong."

"You insult me. I would never allow another man to marry a woman whom I . . ." Loved? "Deflowered," he finished.

Grace sighed. "I apologize; I didn't mean that as it sounded. I was not in love with John. He deserved more from his wife, so I broke off our betrothal. It is not my feelings which will prevent this marriage, but yours. For—for Lily."

She hesitated, then repeated: "I made love to you, but you made love to Lily."

"I made love to *you*," he said, longing to rip off

the bandage and see her eyes. He dropped another kiss into her soft hair instead.

"What?"

"I thought I was dreaming of making love to you. But it was really happening." He grasped at the memory and it slid away from him, leaving tendrils of desire behind.

"You were?" she repeated, her tone dubious.

"Yes."

Nineteen

Grace was so bewildered that she didn't know
what to think. She had fallen into utter despair,
thinking that Colin made love to her while believing she was Lily. She was afraid to accept what he
said now. In fact, she wasn't sure she did believe it.

Colin had such a strong sense of honor that if he
learned he had deflowered a virgin, he would say
whatever he had to in order to marry her.

She tipped back her head and looked at his face.
It was a strong, almost harsh face that looked as if
it had been carved by sea winds.

The truth was that they probably meant different things by "making love." If she could see his
eyes, she would know for sure. She had learned to
read his eyes.

"It's very sweet of you to say so," she said.

"Not particularly." He was running his hands
up her arms, caressing her with a slow stroke that

made her feel like a cat. She shook off the feeling.

"Colin, you have no love for me, other than sisterly affection. You never . . ." She paused trying to figure out how to put it. "You looked at Lily in a way that you had never looked at me. You danced with her. You wrote Lily a long letter. You hardly wrote me back, ever." The memory made her heart wince, and with a quick motion she pushed free and leapt to her feet.

"Grace!" He roared it, stretching out his hands like a great wounded beast.

"I don't want dishonesty between us," she said, holding her ground, looking down at him. He was too strong and bold to need pity, this wounded lion of hers. He would be out of the bandages and glaring fearlessly at life again in no time.

His arms fell. "Neither do I."

"Well, then. I am the kind of person who greatly dislikes confusion," she said, sitting down in a chair opposite him.

He nodded.

There was a bleak look in his face that she hated to see, but she forced herself to continue. "You felt a sort of desire for Lily that you have never felt for me, and I recognize that. All the world knows that she is exquisite. You must have been in love with her, given the length of the letter you wrote her."

He opened his mouth, but she said, fiercely, "No. Let me finish." Then she swallowed hard and said, "I have always loved you, as I'm sure you surmised from all those foolish letters I sent you. So marrying you . . . marrying you is everything I dreamed of since I was a girl. But I will *not* be party to the pretense that you feel the same. I couldn't bear that."

"Grace—"

"You can say whatever you wish," she said, interrupting. "But we both know the truth: your actions speak for themselves. If you had loved me, you would have searched me out when you were on leave. You would have answered my letters. You would have kissed me by the river, or any other time when we were together since I turned sixteen. You would have shown signs of desire, if not love."

She was starting to sound pitiful, so she rallied her voice and straightened her back again. "You never have, and I accepted that long ago. But now we are going to be married, and I think we might learn to love each other in a different way, over time. I'm willing to try, *as long as you don't lie to me about it!*"

"But, Grace—"

She couldn't bear to hear him say anything, not just then, so she sprang to her feet and cut him off. "Please, Colin, could we not speak of this again?"

"I will not make that promise," he said flatly.

"I'm humiliated enough by the fact I wrote you those letters. Here we are. Almost married. Please, can we start afresh? I believe you when you say you are not in love with Lily."

"Your sister is a silly widgeon," Colin said bluntly. He looked very angry. There were white dents next to his mouth. "I care for her, but I am not in love with her."

"Then I'm sure we will get along together as well as we can. Just—just don't lie to me, Colin. I can't bear it." She ignored his characterization of her sister: he certainly hadn't thought Lily was a silly widgeon when he was waltzing with her.

He seemed to be frozen, his knuckles white where he gripped the chair arms. "Am I not allowed to say that I love you?"

"I know that you love me," Grace said impatiently. "I love everyone in your family, too. Don't be obtuse, Colin. I just don't want you to pretend to love me that way, like lovers. The way you might have loved Lily, if things were different."

"I do not like being told what to do."

"I'm not telling you. I'm begging you." Then she changed her mind. "Yes, I *am* telling you! And I think I have the right to that command. I wrote you for years, Colin. For years. You wrote me back perhaps a line or two, whenever it was convenient. I have earned the right to demand this one thing."

She could almost see his jaw grinding, but he kept his mouth shut.

"We'll just start over," she said, waving her arm even though he couldn't see her. "We can earn each other's love, the way people do who don't have our sort of past."

"You want me to *woo* you?"

He needn't sound so horrified.

"Of course not," Grace said, her voice a bit hurt, despite her bravado. "I know I'm not . . . I'm not the woman you planned to woo. There's no need to coddle me."

"You deserve to be wooed!"

"Yes, well, I've had that experience. John wooed me for almost a year."

His scowl was truly ferocious now. .

Grace was swept by an overwhelming sense of panic. This wasn't going the way she hoped. She didn't want Colin to think about how pitiful she was. The last thing she wanted to do was remind him of her pathetic infatuation with him.

Obviously the last thing *he* wanted was to woo her, a woman he'd— A thought struck her. He made love to her under the influence of laudanum. What if he didn't desire her without it? When she sat in his lap, he soothed her as if she were a little girl again, distressed by a bruised knee.

It was a stark contrast to the way he acted in the carriage.

She hadn't thought the question of marriage through properly. She couldn't bear a life of this humiliation. It was impossible. Her heart would break.

She simply couldn't do it.

The very thought of making love to him when he could actually *see* her, when he knew who she was, made her ill. Given the way he said she *deserved to be wooed*, he might even try to do that, to say sugary things that would never echo the delirious joy she saw in his face when he danced with Lily.

No.

She must have been mad to contemplate it.

"I have changed my mind," she stated, moving toward the door. He turned his head, following the sound of her slippers. "We will not marry. I'm sorry about the fuss I've caused."

He folded his arms over his chest. "Fuss?" His jaw set. "Why will we not marry?"

She might as well say it all. "You made love to me under the influence of laudanum," she pointed out, proud that her voice was steady. "I would much dislike to have to drug my husband before we could produce any children. I have changed my mind."

"You cannot change your mind. We have consummated our relationship, if not our marriage."

"We don't have a relationship! We never had one, except in my imagination. You needn't worry about me. I have to go," she cried, turning. "I just—I have to go."

And she fled, out the door and up the stairs, even though she heard him shout her name. He had the bellow of a sea captain who could be heard over hurricanes and squalls, but she didn't stop.

The inn's best bedchamber was at the top of the stairs. She slammed through the door as if the Furies were at her back, and looked about wildly. Her heart was thudding in her throat. She couldn't take the shame. No woman should have to bear this measure of humiliation.

Why had she admitted to loving him? She could have kept it to herself rather than voicing it.

Tears were coursing down her cheeks and she impatiently dashed them away, grabbing up her travel bag only to remember that it still contained her ripped garments. She flung them to the side, realizing she didn't even have another chemise until her trunk arrived tomorrow. All she had was her water paints and sketchbook.

That was enough. She was leaving . . . going somewhere. Anywhere.

If she were a more resolute type of woman, she would throw herself in a rushing river, the way heroines always did in two-penny plays.

No. She would never do such a thing for a man. Not even for Colin. Not for anyone.

But she *would* run away. She would go to a different inn and be alone for a day or two. Think. Try to decide what she wanted to do. She could send a groom to her family and they would rescue her.

She threw open the door of her bedchamber.

With This Kiss
Part Three

Twenty

Colin stood in the corridor, leaning against the opposite wall with his arms crossed. All his male beauty struck her like a blow in the face, and she cried, recklessly, "You can't stop me!"

His hands shot out and unerringly caught her shoulders. "Yes, I can."

She began to wiggle, and realized how stupid that was. "Colin, I must beg you to allow me to leave. I need some time alone. I have to think, to decide what to do next. If you would simply forget the events of the day, I would—"

"I would surmise this is your bedchamber?" he asked, cutting her off. Then he let go of her right shoulder and pushed the door open behind her.

She stumbled backward, dropping her traveling bag. "Let go of me!" At least she didn't feel like crying any longer. Instead, she found herself contemplating how hard she would have to shove a blind man in order to make an escape over his fallen body.

One glance at Colin's wide shoulders, and this idea fell by the wayside.

"Lead me to the bed," he said grimly, kicking the door shut and stepping forward again.

"I will not!"

He pushed, and she stepped back again. "If we're going to stumble into the chamber pot, you might want to warn me," he said, without a glimmer of humor in his voice.

There was something wild about Colin that she had never seen in the disciplined young officer who paid visits to her parents. He hadn't shaved that morning, and his face was dark with stubble. Even blindfolded, the set of his jaw expressed raw determination. He looked like a pirate, a man who would take what he wanted without regard for the consequences.

"No," she cried, trying to sound authoritative. Despite herself, her knees went weak at the sight of him. He looked like a hunter focused on his prey. She was stupid, *stupid*, to think that was attractive.

He crowded her again and she stepped backward once more, retreating before him until her knees struck the back of the large bed.

"Stop it!" Grace shouted, even as he picked her up and placed her on her back. "You have no right to try to do—whatever it is you are doing."

She twisted toward the far side of the bed, and for a moment she was escaping, but then he surged forward, pulled her back, and pinned her down. He was looming over her on his hands and knees, his hair falling over the bandage, his features so beautiful that her hand rose in the air toward his cheek before she snatched it back.

"Why have you changed your mind about marrying me?" he demanded.

"It is a lady's prerogative. This misadventure is over." She could feel a sob rising in her chest. How could she have allowed this to happen? His mouth . . . he was *beautiful*. He belonged with Lily, not with a quiet wallflower like herself.

"Please," she said, swallowing back the tears. "Let me go, Colin. Just let me go. For the sake of our friendship. Don't make me beg."

She could feel his glare even from behind his blindfold. But he didn't answer as she caught her breath, trying to stop herself from crying.

Then he grabbed one of her hands with that uncanny ability he had of knowing where her limbs were. Before she could stop him, he reared upright—and placed her hand directly on his crotch.

Grace squeaked and tried to pull away. "What are you doing?"

He held her hand firmly against his breeches. "You won't let me speak," he growled. "You refused to believe it when I said I desire *you*, not your sister."

Grace was so shocked she was sputtering. "Ladies don't— You can't do this!" He was pressing her hand firmly against him, and under her palm, that part of him pulsed. She felt a hot flush sweep up her chest, and her fingers instinctively curled slightly.

"That's it," he breathed, and thrust forward, into her palm. A sound escaped his mouth, something between a groan and a laugh.

Grace's mind was reeling. She was touching the part of Colin that she'd last seen in the carriage. It wasn't limp now. It felt large and strong as steel. He had responded instantly to her small caress, his breath hitching.

"I am not feeling any effects of laudanum now," he stated, his organ throbbing against her hand.

"What?" she asked, unable to think clearly, not when his voice took on that craving tone, a note of primitive sensuality that aroused her senses and made her dizzy with hunger. He was here, and everything in her body desired him. She even desired the strong organ under her fingers, the very thing she'd sworn to avoid.

"I knew it was you in the carriage, Grace. I want *you*. Not Lily."

Her traitorous body had forgotten the discomfort. All she could think of was the way pleasure had rippled through her body like sweet fire. The way he had shouted at the end, arching his throat back, completely taken by passion. Even though it had hurt, she had thrilled to that moment.

"I want you, Grace," he repeated. "*You*. I've dreamed about making love to you so many times."

"No, you haven't!" She pulled her hand away with a sharp jerk. "That's not a nice thing to say, not when we both know it isn't true."

He laughed, a savage pirate's laugh. "A gentleman always knows which lady he finds in his bed, even in his dreams."

"You have never looked at me in such a fashion," she stated, her voice shaky but firm. "You never wrote to me, you never wooed me. I know why you're doing this!"

"Why?"

"Because we did *that* in the carriage. You feel obligated to marry me. You needn't feel that way. And this isn't very nice of you. It's not kind of you to try to—to take advantage of my foolishness."

"I don't feel kind when I think about you. Did I rip your gown in the carriage?"

"Yes."

"I thought so." There was a distinct ring of male satisfaction in his voice. "I remember that. May I rip this gown as well?"

"What?" Somewhere deep inside her, she was reeling at the brutal way he said he didn't even feel kindness for her. This was like a nightmare. "Of course not!"

He bent toward her and thrust a hand into her hair. Pins scattered as he pulled the long sweep of it free of the simple knot she had shaped that morning. He muttered, "Your hair is like silk."

Grace was so confused and miserable that tears were welling up in her eyes again. "Please," she gasped. "Please let me go. Please let me—"

He cupped her head, bringing her mouth to his. At the mere touch of his lip, Grace's traitorous body melted. He was kissing her, just as she'd dreamed so many times, only better.

She was such a fool and yet she couldn't stop herself. She should fight back, but she surrendered instead.

His mouth was beautifully shaped, with a sensual lower lip that she had drawn in her sketchbook a million times. And now he was kissing her. She'd dreamed of that, too, though in her dreams, he was always gentle and reverent.

He wasn't gentle. He wasn't kind, either. His tongue was assaulting her, making all her objections and words and tears melt away under the force of a kiss that couldn't lie. It simply couldn't. He was claiming her.

She let that truth sink into her mind, kissing him back with the passion she had felt for years, with all the longing that drove her into the carriage in the first place.

Colin wasn't drugged.

Yet he was tasting her, playing with her tongue, marking her for all time as claimed. By him. By Colin.

Naïve as she was, she knew when a man's body was pulsing with lust. When his blood was pumping as hard as hers was. When that man had plans to take her, whether she would or no.

She would.

Oh, she would. She wound her arms around his neck and kissed him back.

Twenty-one

Colin had survived battles without feeling a surge of gratitude this profound. He had jumped from burning ships, felt bullets whistle past his temple, gone below just in time to miss a direct hit on deck. He had never felt a raw emotion so potent that he lost all common sense.

He had a hand at Grace's bodice before the feeling of fabric under his fingers triggered a memory. The cloth was thin, not made of sturdy worsted. He remembered that other fabric well enough— and then the memory of her body coming up from the seat came back to him as well.

He wrenched his lips from hers. "Did I hurt you when I ripped your gown in the coach?" He barked it, knowing that there would be a hundred questions like this, a thousand, if he didn't recover his memory.

"No," she said, her voice a husky song that made

him want to devour her. To feast on her until she pleaded for more, and then he would give her more, and more again.

"Good," he managed. It was the work of a moment to rip this light gown off her shoulders. She wasn't wearing a chemise, which was all to the better.

She squeaked something about having nothing to wear, but he pretended not to hear, just as he had in the carriage. That thought made his fingers still. "Did I hurt you the first time?" he whispered. "Was it terrible, Grace? You didn't tell me."

There was a second of silence. "Not all of it."

Not all of it. He could work with that. He made a silent vow to himself: he would never cause Grace even a whisper of pain from this moment forward.

Under his hand, her breast was round and unsteady. He brushed his fingers across her nipples and she squeaked.

"Are we making love again?" Her voice was breathless.

"Yes," he said, wondering why she was so hard to convince. "Again, and probably again after that. I don't know that I will ever have enough of you, Grace." There was silence in return, and he damned his loss of vision.

Was she frightened? Repulsed? Injured? "Are you too sore to make love again?" he whispered, thinking that he would probably embarrass himself by coming in his breeches, but better that than hurting her.

She was silent for another moment, and then she said, her voice shy and so Grace-like that his heart thumped in his chest, "I don't think so."

Grace had expressed so many emotions in the last hour that he felt exhausted by trying to keep up with her. It would be easier when he had the use of his eyes. She had screamed at him, and told him to leave, and told him she was leaving, and then kissed him so passionately that he felt as if his heart left his body.

Things were better when they weren't speaking. He felt the connection between them when they kissed, and no matter how she slashed at their bond with words, it was there. He simply had to make her understand that.

He shifted, lying down on his side next to her, his hand sliding from her breast to her waist, holding tight in case she tried to run away again. "I can't follow all the things you've said to me, Grace."

"Oh," she said. And then she took a deep breath. "What I said—"

"No." He was interrupting her again, but he had to. "You think I don't desire you. Do you still believe that?"

He heard the fabric of her ruined gown rustle as she shifted uneasily. He caught back a smile. Grace couldn't tell a lie. She never could, not even when she was a child.

"I suppose I do not entirely believe it," she whispered.

"It would be fair to say that I am mad with lust

for you." He tugged at her dress, pulling it down so that he could feel her soft, flat stomach. "You're so small."

She shifted, moving onto her side, which made her body form a lovely curve under his hand. He let his fingers wrap around her hip, telling her without words that he would never let her go.

"I don't see how we can make love again without further discussion," she said, her voice resolute.

Poor Grace. She made life harder for herself than it had to be. He shook his head, knowing she could see the gesture.

"Why not?"

"We can talk afterwards."

"But I am not going to marry you, even if we make love."

He wanted to roar like a lion and kiss her into silence. "I can't explain why I didn't write, Grace."

"You wrote to Lily."

The pain in her voice struck him to the heart, and he held her tighter. If she ran away, he would rip off the bandage and follow her. "I wrote to her because I wanted to know how you were."

She sniffed, a noise resonant with disbelief. "Colin, you danced with her, and you told my father you wanted to marry her. I don't even . . . You didn't write to me. And you didn't do more than ask for me when you were on leave, nothing more than politeness demanded."

He had a sense of panic, as if seawater were closing over his head. "I couldn't," he said, his voice hoarse. "You—you knew what it was like at sea. You knew how horrible it was. If I saw you, if I wrote to you, I was afraid that I couldn't keep it to myself. I didn't want that."

"You didn't want to see me?"

He hated himself, but it had to be said. "I was grateful when you didn't leave your room, and when I discovered that you were not at the ball."

"Oh." The word was so sad that he felt a stab of self-hatred that threatened to cleave his heart in two.

"I would have unmanned myself," he said doggedly, gripping her hip even tighter. She might have a bruise, but he didn't care. He couldn't let her escape. "You *knew*, Grace. I could tell in your letters. I felt as if we were having a conversation, even though we weren't." That was so stupid that he couldn't believe he had said it.

He should let her go to a decent man, a man who wasn't as mad as he was. What was he doing, taking her? Seducing her? Marrying a woman like her, given the kind of damaged man he was?

He forced his fingers to uncurl and pulled his hand away. "You're right," he said, the word burning his chest. "You deserve better than I."

"Mmmm," she said, and then he felt the light touch of her fingers on his neck. "I like the fact that you knew we were having a conversation, even if you didn't contribute very often."

"I was too much of a coward."

"You were in pain." Her fingers slipped up his neck to his cheek. "I have no idea how you survived the pain and guilt, Colin. You are so strong."

There was a sudden stinging in his eyes, and he spared a second to thank God for the bandage. "No," he said, his voice miraculously steady. "I am not strong. You need to understand that if we are to be married, even though I don't see how either of us can back out now, Grace. We made love in that carriage, and the fact won't disappear simply because you wish it would. I ruined you; I took your virginity. You had no choice in the matter."

"I meant to seduce you," she said, her voice barely a thread of sound. "Or announce that you had compromised me, if I didn't find the courage to actually *do* anything."

His mouth fell open. "You did?"

"You didn't wonder why we were alone in the carriage?"

He hadn't had time for that sort of logic; emotions had blown about them as wildly as a winter storm. But now she mentioned it . . . "The duchess allowed you to travel without a chaperone?"

"I forced her. If I changed my mind, we planned to announce that I had accompanied you as any family friend would have done, and that would be that."

"Her Grace agreed?"

"She did. I told her . . ." The words trailed away and her fingers left his cheeks, an unwelcome coolness following.

"That you wanted *me*." He shouldn't be astounded, and yet he was. "Even though you knew what a coward I am?"

She sat up abruptly, the bed shifting under her weight. "You are no coward, Colin."

"But I am." It had to be said. It all had to be said, if only to Grace, those things he had told her silently in the night, but never put on paper. "I was afraid, day and night. I still dream about it. Sometimes I think I hear a cannonball that doesn't exist, even though I'm merely walking down the street."

"And you felt guilty that you weren't injured, that you weren't killed," she added.

He was right. She had known. "Yes. And like an ass, like a coward, still afraid."

A small hand cupped his cheek. "Any man not afraid in the middle of battle would be mad."

"It's not manly," he muttered, thinking that he would never be able to explain how he felt, not to a woman.

Out of nowhere, soft lips descended on his, brushing a kiss. It was the first kiss *she'd* ever given *him*. He could feel the joy of that melting some of the self-hatred that consumed him.

"I think you're very manly," she whispered against his lips. "Your medals show how brave you are, Colin. You saved your men's lives, again and again."

His throat was too tight to answer.

"A man who was untouched by the violence and death around him would not be a man, but some sort of animal. An uncaring animal."

How did she know to say that? He had looked at his friend Philip sometimes, at the way he would tell a joke five minutes after a sailor died at his feet, see his blue eyes untroubled, clear . . . and think just that very thing. Philip was like a wolf, a predator who killed with impunity.

Grace's next question eliminated all his interest in that thought. "Are you going to take off your clothes this time?" Her voice was an enchanting mixture of timidity and curiosity.

"I didn't take my clothing off in the carriage?" Of course he hadn't. His voice rasping, he said, "I didn't treat you as you deserved, Grace. What an ass I was!"

"Because you didn't take your shirt off?" Laughter threaded through her words, making the pain in his chest ease. "*Or* your breeches," she added. "I had to button up your placket myself."

"Unprincipled," he muttered, one hand running down her back and pulling her ruined gown still lower, down around her hips. "Degenerate, repulsive, disgusting."

She giggled. Grace. His solemn, sweet Grace. He thought for a second about where they were situated in the bed, and then pulled her underneath him. It felt safer this way. She was protected from anything that could harm her.

"Oh!" she gasped.

"Since we have to marry, we might as well practice what married people do." He cupped a breast with his hand, found her nipple, and bent his head to it.

A moment later she wasn't giggling any longer. The joy was still there, but she was twisting up, trying to suck air into her lungs, crying out with pleasure.

Colin waited until he thought Grace had breath again. "One thing I can't remember," he growled, the words caressing her skin even as he stroked her breast. "Did you touch me in the carriage, or did I just touch you?"

"No, I didn't touch you." She whispered it, and he felt a surge of white-hot possessiveness.

"Would you like to?" He held his breath. It might take months for Grace to be demonstrative. Especially since she had these ridiculous ideas about him stuck in her head. Love her? Damn, did she think that he could make love to another woman as he had to her?

Actually, what did she know? Grace had never been with a man before him. Had never . . .

It occurred to him that she had never said that she had been a virgin. But his hands knew it. He could feel the surprised pleasure in her kiss, in her every shiver. She didn't love McIngle, so she would never have allowed him more than a kiss, not Grace.

"Yes," she breathed.

He sat up, swinging his legs over the bed. It was the work of a moment to pull his shirt over his head, wrench off his boots, and strip off his breeches and smalls. Grace stayed quiet as a church mouse, even when he pulled the remains of her dress down her long, slender legs and tossed it to the floor.

"What do you think?" he asked, hands on his hips.

There was a giggle from the bed that made him aware that he was suffused with delight.

"This isn't fair," he said as he stared down at the general place he knew she was. "You are able to see, and I am only able to touch." And taste, but he didn't think she was quite ready for that, yet.

A soft hand stroked his knee with sympathy that he didn't need. Luckily, he had an excellent memory, because he was able to swipe the remains of her gown back up from the floor.

"Are you enjoying the sight of me?"

"Yes." She surprised him. There was nothing less than pure desire in her voice. She'd probably keep surprising him for the next sixty years of their lives. Grace had so many complexities, so many layers and feelings, and thoughts . . . he would happily spend his life trying to unwrap her.

Thinking about it, he tore a strip off the hem of her gown.

"What on earth are you going to do with that?"

Without answering, he put a knee forward onto the bed, making certain he knew precisely where she was. The last thing he wanted was to land on her like a felled tree.

He let a hand run from her stomach up and over those luscious breasts, causing a little hitch to her breathing. He lingered on her collarbones. They were delicate and strong at the same time, exquisitely shaped, like the rest of her.

And yet her narrow frame held a heart so large

that it could encompass him. Even with his stupidity, with the way he never responded to her letters, with the way he danced with her sister . . . with his raw, unrelenting arse-hole qualities.

She loved him. He knew it. He could feel her love as a tenderness that fell on his skin like spring rain.

"You believe in fairness, don't you, Grace?"

"Of course," she said. But she was no fool: her voice was cautious.

Still, Grace was no match for hands used to tying sailors' slipknots. It was the work of a moment to wind the scrap of gown around her eyes and tie it, not too tight, but snugly.

Twenty-two

"*What* are you doing?" Grace shrieked, her hands going to her head.

Colin caught both of her wrists and pinned them over her head. "Putting us on equal footing," he said with satisfaction. He bent his head and caressed her lips with his own, letting a sharp ache of desire bubble up from his groin and fill his whole body. "I can't see you, and now you can't see me."

"I liked seeing you." She sounded a little sulky.

"This is our first time, Grace," he said, kissing the arch of her cheekbone. "In the carriage . . . that was something else, a dream, really. But this is our first time truly making love."

"Oh."

He couldn't tell what she was thinking, so he let his mouth drift down the angle of her jaw. "I want you to be with me," he murmured, stroking her soft skin with his tongue. She shivered under him, and he laid a trail of kisses to her ear, nipped the elegant shell with his teeth.

She didn't react, and he made a mental note, went back to her jaw and kissed his way to her neck. Then she sighed and arched her neck, giving him more flesh.

He made another mental note, and dropped farther down her body, allowing her hands to fall free. They dropped to his hair. "I want to see!" she wailed. "You didn't undress in the carriage and you're my first . . . You know that."

Colin smiled against the soft skin of her breast. "Do I?"

She clearly heard the laughter in his voice. "Yes, you do. I only got to look at you for a moment, whereas you had your eyesight when you were with other women."

He reared up, put a finger over her lips. "I will never be with another woman again. Not in the whole of my life, not if you die tomorrow and I live to be one hundred."

"Oh." She wasn't a woman to give up easily. "Still . . ."

"You and I will find each other in the dark, and I swear it will be all the sweeter, Grace. I've never made love to a woman without my sight, before you."

She made a little humming sound in the back of her throat that he loved. That he wanted to hear a hundred thousand times.

"We'll both be new to each other."

"All right," she whispered, her fingers still tight in his hair. "All right. But I feel terribly vulnerable. It's frightening."

"When you can't see, you have to trust your touch. My eyes would have told you everything you wanted to know in the parlor."

"The windows to the soul," she said, understanding.

"You would never have spouted that drivel about how I felt about Lily if you could have seen my eyes. Never."

She shifted onto her side, her body sliding under his hands like water. The feeling of her skin sent a rage of pure lust up his body.

"All right," she said. "All right. I'll . . . I'll touch you then."

His hands stroked down her bottom and she startled. "*I'll* touch you," she dictated. "Not both of us at the same time."

He sighed, rolled on his back, let his arms fall away. "I am here." Though he didn't like it. Lying on his back felt too exposed.

"Where?"

She sounded a bit tentative, but then her fingers descended on him like little flames. She started on his chest, her fingers tracing the muscles rippling under her touch as she stroked down his chest, across his stomach. Under her fingertips, he felt like a battering ram, a body honed into muscles for one reason, and one reason only: war.

He shook the feeling off. Somehow, it was easier in her presence. He hadn't felt the drowning weight of black memory all day, not even when in the grip of laudanum.

Instead, his body was tingling all over, his tool rigid against her hip, his stomach clenched with lust. Perhaps his body wasn't made for war, but for her. For her pleasure, for her amusement.

She had stopped caressing him; her fingers seemed to have stalled around his waist. "Here," he murmured, pushing her hand lower. At the mere brush of her fingers, his hips rose in the air and a groan burst from his lips.

"I wish I could see you," she breathed. Then she was silent for a moment, her fingers roaming from the curve of his inner thigh to an erection so pounding and fierce that he'd never experienced anything like it in his life. Her touch was close to causing him pain.

When her hand finally curled around him, he couldn't stop a surprised curse from erupting from his lips. He had the sheets clenched in his hands, forcing himself not to touch her. Not to throw her backward and bury himself inside her.

"You like that," she said, and the delight in her voice made the erotic hum filling his body more tight, more potent.

"I do," he managed. Her fingers tightened as she stroked him. If she kept that up, he would find himself begging. "Do you think that you've touched me enough, darling?"

Her grip froze. "*Darling?*"

He couldn't bear it another moment, not without losing all control and disgracing himself. He pulled her hands apart and then rolled her into what was quickly becoming his favorite position. He tucked her small body inside the shelter of his and kissed her, loving every touch of his fingers, the way her hands trembled as they caressed his shoulders.

"You're mine," he murmured, keeping his weight on his elbows. Then he kissed her forehead. "Mine. My darling. My Grace."

Her hands stroked down his back, but she made a stifled noise, almost like a little sob. He let a smile curl his mouth, knowing she was blind to it. "And I'm yours," he told her. "This body, such as it is, is yours, Lady Grace, soon to be Mrs. Barry."

"Mrs. Barry." Her voice was wondering, with an undercurrent of astonishment. But he knew her. Every word of her letters had taught him to love her and to know her. She was more joyful than surprised.

"My wife," he said, with satisfaction. "Are you all right?" He kissed her nose.

He caught her *yes* in her mouth, stifled it with a kiss that went on and on. When he finally surfaced from a pool of desire, he found that he had lowered all his weight on her, and he was grinding into the soft cradle of her body, his breath coming fast and hot in his chest.

"I want you." Grace's words came with a sigh and a sob that sounded hungry. He felt between her legs, realizing his hand was shaking. She was wet and warm, and she cried out at his touch.

"I want to kiss you there."

"No!" she cried, fierce as a warrior queen, pulling at him. "Just come inside me now. Do it!"

"Grace," he whispered against her lips. "Weren't you a bashful maiden all of five minutes ago?"

She was rubbing against him, as uninhibited as a lady of the night. "It's this blindfold," she breathed. "I feel as if my skin is alive. The feeling of you is making me mad." Her hands stroked down his hips and then across his arse. "You are so . . . I love touching you."

He loved it, too. The very feeling of her hands shaping his rear made the blood roar in his ears.

"I want you," she sobbed.

He was her knight. He could not say no. "I'm afraid this will hurt," he said.

"I know all about that. I understand. Just . . . just please come to me, Colin. I feel so"—she twisted up against him again—"strange. Like when you were kissing me, in the carriage."

Kissing her? Thank God, it sounded as if he had done that, at least. He wanted to lick her now, but at the same time, if he didn't plunge inside her, he felt as if he would die.

So he rubbed himself against her soft, wet folds and then slowly began to work his way inside. "Gods," he gasped after a second. "You're so tight, Grace. I've never felt anything like this. Is it painful?"

"No," she replied, but her voice was a bit odd, so he paused.

"Really all right, or just telling me so?"

"It doesn't hurt like last time. In fact, it feels quite good."

He was spending every ounce of control he had going slow, desperate not to hurt her. "Just tell me," he said through clenched teeth. "If it hurts, we'll try again some other time." When she didn't answer immediately, he started to withdraw.

Grace's hands tightened on his shoulders; she arched her hips and pushed back at him. "It's not enough, it's not enough. I feel . . . I feel empty and *wanting.*"

Her words were like a dam breaking during a storm. Colin heard the tone in her voice over the thudding of his heart. He felt her fingernails on his shoulders—gentle Grace, beside herself with passion, wanting him as much as he did her. He thrust inside her, seating himself where he most wanted to be.

She cried out, from pleasure, not pain.

He pulled back, felt her tighten as he escaped, heard a thread of sound. "Nooo."

Captain Colin Barry hadn't laughed in a year, perhaps longer. He had smiled now and then, with genuine amusement, sometimes. But laughter . . . laughter comes from joy, and joy comes from the heart, and his had turned to stone at some point.

Now, in Grace's arms, hearing her cry out as he sheathed himself deep inside, then whimper again as he withdrew . . .

This laughter came from true joy, that of heart's delight.

He only stopped laughing because Grace pulled

his mouth down to hers. She was kissing him wildly, pulling his body closer as if she could stop him from leaving her body.

But he insisted on withdrawing, even though she sobbed every time until he thrust back again, and again, until the fire spread up his legs and through his body. He slipped a hand between their bodies and touched her . . . just the faintest pressure.

She tightened on him until it almost hurt, except it was the kind of pain he wanted to feel every day. Then she cried out again with a kind of guttural, raw pleasure, wrenched from her chest, followed by a pulsing that coursed through her body and gave wings to his desire.

He wrapped her in his arms and pumped into her, mad with lust, loving the fact she was tucked under him, safe, warm, *his*.

"I love you," he gasped, at the moment when everything he had in his body and heart coursed out of him. "Oh God, I love you, Grace."

She arched into him, caught by a second wave of pleasure. He caught her scream with his kiss, saying it again, and again, silently, without words.

It didn't matter.

She had heard him.

"I love you. I love you, too," she whispered.

Twenty-three

$\mathcal{G}$race woke early the next morning, just as a cool, pinkish light came over the windowsill. At some point in the night she had pulled off her blindfold. Colin, *her* Colin, lay beside her, tousled hair falling over his face, an arm thrown above his head.

She was so happy that her heart hurt. Colin loved her; he had said so again and again. He wasn't pretending. She knew him better than anyone else in the world, so she knew that.

He was hers.

Just then he made a small noise and she saw his hand clench into a fist. His jaw tightened and he made a noise so pained that her entire body froze.

"Colin," she whispered, putting a hand on his shoulder.

"The blood," he said, turning his blindfolded eyes toward her. "It's running over my boots again. Send my boots to be cleaned."

"I will," she said, but his face remained anguished. So she moved and lay down on top of him, naked body to naked body. "Your boots are clean now," she whispered into his ear.

She could feel little shudders running through his body. "Did you wash off all the blood?" he rasped.

"I did," she told him. "I washed it all off."

His hand touched her back. A small smile curved his lips. She held her breath. If he didn't know who she was . . .

"Grace," he breathed. "My Grace."

She waited a long time, but his breathing became regular and he never woke up. Finally she slipped off his body, thinking hard. It seemed that war didn't go away once a man walked off a ship.

She finally eased from the bed and crept to the bathing alcove. She used the chamber pot hidden in a small chair, and then washed at the basin. It was interesting to discover a jumble of little red marks on her body, as if his kisses had burned a pattern into her skin.

She washed herself between her legs and her touch caused a tingle, but not of pain. Her nipples seemed a darker rose, perhaps from all those kisses. She frowned at that, and then pulled on a nightgown: it was literally the only thing she had left to wear, given that Colin had destroyed two gowns.

The gown was a muted pear color, sewn from a silk that shifted color constantly, going from milk to faint pink. The problem was that she had never thought of wearing it in front of a man, though, of course, it was designed for just that.

Now a look at the glass showed her that the gown was more like a scrap of cloth with pretensions to being a garment. It didn't even reach her ankles, and the fabric was far too sheer. She crossed her arms over her chest. That was not acceptable.

It wasn't really a sound that warned her; it was more like a change in the very quality of the air. She turned and there he was, wearing nothing more than a twist of sheet around his hips. He was smiling at her, his eyes heavy-lidded and gleaming with an emotion she'd never seen in them before.

"Where is your bandage?" she gasped. "Colin!"

"Six weeks today," he replied, holding up a black swatch of cloth with one finger. "But I am not throwing this out, Grace."

"Because your eyesight is hazy?" she asked, anxiety streaking through her body. "The doctor said it might be. You should put it back on."

"My vision seems absolutely normal." He emphasized the words. The look on his face was akin to the giddy joy that lit his eyes on seeing Lily at the ball. But it was a deeper, more intoxicating joy that bound love and desire together.

Grace smiled back, as delighted as he was. "Oh, Colin, I don't have the words to say how happy I am!"

"But perhaps I should test my eyesight. May I say how much I love that gown you're wearing?"

He slowly looked over her entire body, starting at her toes, taking his time, enjoying it. When he reached her breasts, she folded her arms in front of her chest again.

He shook his head.

"What?"

"Drop your arms, darling."

She frowned at him. "I won't. In fact, you shouldn't have looked behind the bathing screen. I'm certain that's not what married couples do."

"Who knows what married couples do? We're both new at this."

"And not even married," she said, remembering that.

"We will marry tomorrow morning. I'm guessing your mother will send a special license by messenger this afternoon."

She laughed. He was right.

"I've known the duchess almost as long as you have," he remarked. Then: "Drop your arms, Grace." His voice was quiet, but his eyes burned into hers. There was a moment between them that weighed the years she had known him, the trust she had in him, her love.

She dropped her arms. And then, just to make him happy, she arched her back the slightest amount because her nipples . . . well, she knew he could see them.

She saw his throat ripple, and that was a victory of sorts. But he held up the black cloth again. "I'm not throwing this away, because last night was a revelation."

A flush swept up her cheeks. It was true that after he blindfolded her, she seemed to lose all dignity, all claim to being a lady.

Colin stepped forward and dropped a kiss on her nose. "You are the most beautiful woman in the world, Grace."

She bit her lip. His head bent and he brushed a kiss across her lips. His eyes closed, and thick lashes lay on his cheekbones.

"I am not," she said, wrapping her arms around his neck. "I am nice-looking rather than beautiful, and I don't like fibs." She gave him a kiss to make up.

He opened his eyes and looked down at her face. "Can you read my eyes?"

"I think so," she said cautiously. She had certainly spent enough years watching his face.

"I love you. I want to marry you. I think you are the most beautiful woman in the world." His eyes were the color of the ocean at twilight: deep and tranquil, yet shining with a luminescence lent by the last rays of the sun.

"Oh," she said, rather foolishly. "I see."

"We both see," he whispered, rubbing her nose with his. "Your love kept me alive, all those years at sea."

She buried her head against his shoulder and held on tight. "Don't say that. I hate to think that you were in danger."

"I think my heart would have withered entirely, but for your letters. Will you come to Arbor House with me?"

She nodded, her cheek rubbing against his warm chest.

"We'll leave immediately. After eating."

"No."

"Why?"

Grace pulled away and walked a few steps, to the edge of the screen. Then she turned and looked over her shoulder. Who would have thought she had such a coquette inside her? Not she. But she didn't like the idea that Colin thought she was brave only when her eyes were bandaged.

His jaw looked tight. He wasn't a man who liked to be countered. Which meant it should be on her daily list of activities.

"Colin," she said, rather amused to find that her voice was throaty and soft.

"Yes?" He raised an eyebrow at her.

"Do you remember how you ordered me to lower my arms?"

"Yes." His voice deepened.

She let her hips swing as she walked from the bathing alcove. The gown helped, rippling against her skin.

Then she turned around and pointed at the bed. "On the bed."

"*What?*" His voice was quiet but with a dangerous undertone. Captain Barry was clearly not accustomed to being given a direct command, except perhaps from an admiral.

The bashful side of her was anxious, but Grace ignored her own burning cheeks. "I *order* you to lie down on the bed."

There was a moment of dangerous silence in the bedchamber. But she raised her chin and met his eyes. She didn't want to be forced to obey a man, even a man whom she loved as much as Colin. He was used to captaining a ship, and she understood that he had been the leader onboard. But not on shore.

Instead of obeying her, he walked over, tipped up her chin, and stared down into her eyes. To her extreme annoyance, he was smiling. "Grace," he said quietly, "are you making a point?"

She just stopped herself from chewing her lip. "Perhaps . . . Yes."

"You don't like being told what to do, any more than I do?"

She nodded. "You were a captain, Colin. But I am not a member of your crew. We're to be *married*. I don't want to be ordered about as if I were no better than a midshipman."

The spark in his eyes was positively wicked. "What if I promised that I wouldn't order you about . . . most of the time?"

"Never," she said firmly. She'd had years to examine the relationships of men and women from the edge of the ballroom and the quiet side of a dinner table. Some men felt free to command their wives to do as they wished. She'd even seen one particularly horrid fellow order his wife not to eat another sweet, because he didn't care for her hips.

A man would *never* behave like that to her.

Colin nodded. "May I order you to leave a house in case of fire?"

"Yes."

"And will you do the same for me?"

"Of course."

He grinned. "I am looking forward to being saved by you."

She smiled back, rather uncertainly.

Then, with no warning, Colin scooped her up into his arms. Grace blinked and wound her arms around his neck. He smelled so good, with just a hint of the sea still hanging about him. "I only want to order you about in the bedchamber," he said, growling it.

"Oh," she breathed, her whole body jolting into sensual awareness.

He bent his head and nipped her lip. "I don't need to be the captain on land, Grace. I don't even want to be."

He smelled so good. One whiff of potent, sweaty man, and her legs turned liquid. "I suppose I could allow it sometimes," she said, her voice coming out a throaty moan. "If you want it that much."

"I *do* want it, Grace," he stated. His eyes burned into hers. The question wasn't even a question; one look from him like that, the look that told her that he found her more desirable than anyone in the world, that he loved her so deeply, that he wanted to . . .

"All right," she whispered giving in.

He carried her over to the bed, and then put her on her feet. "But first, was there something you wanted, Grace?"

Morning light was pouring in the window now, emphasizing that broad chest. His sheet had fallen, and he was so masculine, so *perfect*. No wonder she had never managed to paint him. The thought made her feel painfully shy.

"I'd like to paint you," she said, offering it up because she couldn't shape those other words he wanted.

He grinned at her and threw himself on the bed. As she watched, he rolled on his back, just as he had the last night, and spread his arms wide. "I'm on the bed, Grace. As you ordered."

It sent a bolt of pleasure through Grace just to see him there, his eyes glinting. He would do whatever she wanted; she knew it instinctively.

But at the same time, just as clearly, she could see that the position didn't come naturally to him. Maybe it would years from now. Just at the moment his muscles were rigid, for all he was smiling. He needed to be in control. There had been too many rivers of blood over his boots, too much danger coming from all directions.

"Just a moment," she said, running back into the bathing chamber and returning with a basin full of fresh water, and a clean cloth. Then she climbed onto the bed and knelt beside him.

"What are you doing?" he asked.

"Caring for you," she said. She wrung out the cloth and began washing his shoulders. She drew the cloth over the wide shape of his chest, stroking him softly down the rippled muscles of his stomach.

He didn't make a sound and neither did she, even when she reached his groin and his body involuntarily shook and arched into her hands. She kept going, washing every inch of him, loving him as she did it.

When she reached his legs, she washed his thighs, learning the shape of a man's leg . . . so different from the slender shape of her own. His hair was rough under her fingertips, the contained power in his thighs unbearably erotic. She kept going, letting her hair fall over her face so that she didn't embarrass herself.

But without a word he reached out and tucked her hair behind her ear. She knew that he could see raw lust on her face, even as she washed his feet.

When she finished, she dried him off with a soft towel, touching every part again with a softer stroke, a sweeter kind of torture. Her breath came fast by the time she reached his shoulders.

Neither of them had said one word. She hadn't met his eyes. She had no idea whether he remembered asking her to wash off the blood.

By the time she had finished drying the strong column of his neck, Grace didn't know what to do next. Her body felt wrung with desire. Every time she touched him she felt a stab of heat in her body. And yet, she didn't know what to do.

"Would you order me to do something else?" Colin asked. His voice was low and inviting. "I'm at your service, Grace."

She shook her head, feeling desperately embarrassed. It was different, making love when the sun was streaming in the windows. She was overwhelmed by a feeling of impropriety.

Colin made a stifled noise and then surged up, hauling her into his arms. A moment later she found herself tucked under his body, and all the anxiety and embarrassment drained out of her.

Her legs were spread, pressed to the bed by his weight, and her silk gown was up around her thighs. "I want you," he growled.

Grace's heart thumped at the wildness that entered his face. This was the Colin only she saw: the one who existed only for her. "I'm yours," she breathed, reaching up to give his ear a little bite.

In response, he pushed down the bodice of her nightgown. His mouth at her breast drew a cry from her. When he added in a hand, kneaded and suckled and caressed her, she bent her knees and began to plead . . . Instead, he moved back and lowered his head between her legs.

Grace stared at the ceiling, hardly seeing the boards over her head while Colin licked and petted her, making her writhe and cry out, over and over.

Finally, he said, voice dark and lust-filled, "Fair warning. I'm going to give you an order, Grace. I want you to come."

So she did.

And then he put her on her hands and knees and tucked her under his big chest, and touched her again until she was whimpering, and finally, finally slid into her.

It was wild and fierce and a bit out of control. By the end, they were both panting and covered with sweat and altogether improper.

After bathing, they ate breakfast in their room. Thankfully, the carriage sent by the duchess arrived, along with some clothing. Grace's maid reappeared, broken wrist in a sling. They sent her and Ackerley back to London, and continued on to Arbor House by themselves, with no more escort than the coachman and a groom.

"We'll send him to the village, and we can be alone in the house. I'm sure the servants have all been sent home; that's what my mother always does when they are not in residence."

Grace laughed. "And what shall we eat, Captain Barry?"

"*Mr.* Barry now," Colin said. "I will find someone to cook. I will provide for you always, Grace." She gave him a kiss. "And I will be your maid," he added.

In the carriage, he decided to practice unlacing her gown. But one thing led to another . . . "Maids never rip their mistress's clothing," Grace informed her almost-husband. "You'll be lucky if I don't terminate your service."

He laughed, but his eyes were still hungry, and then he reached up and banged on the roof of the carriage, and shouted, "Find an inn, Grimble!"

"We're only six or seven hours from home," Grace pointed out.

"We're stopping for the night. I want you again,

Grace. And I'll be damned if I take my wife on these bloody carriage seats one more time."

"I'm not your wife yet!"

"You will be tomorrow morning." He hauled her onto his lap and tucked her against his chest. "We're stopping in the next village, and in the morning we'll be married by the vicar."

"Colin!" Grace said, laughing, and trying to ward him off. It wasn't fair that he merely looked at her, and a melting heat swept down her body.

"Grace."

His eyes were dark with fierce passion, and she couldn't resist him. Any more than she could later that night, when they were ensconced in the bedchamber at the Rose and Thorn in the village of Piddlepenny, and Colin took out the blindfold again, and she found herself face down over his lap while he . . .

And then she found herself doing things that would make an experienced courtesan blush.

They both loved it when she begged him for more, her voice husky, imploring him with broken whimpers and throaty moans.

But toward the end he pulled off her blindfold, so he could look into her eyes while he stroked into her. Colin had never felt more grateful for his recovered vision than when he met Grace's eyes and saw the trust and abiding love that would be his for all the days of his life.

"I love you." His words came out in a husky whisper. "I love you so much that I wouldn't want to live if you leave me, or die before me, Grace. The earth would be dark without you. You are everything to me. Everything."

She cupped his face in her small hands and kissed him so sensually—and so lovingly—that he finally understood that he had been given the greatest gift that any man could possibly receive.

Yes, he'd lost years to warships and battle . . .

But none of that mattered because Grace was his.

Henry Dobson, vicar of St. James Church in Piddlepenny, raised an eyebrow at the two people who had just handed him a special license, signed by no lesser personage than the Archbishop of Canterbury.

Piddlepenny might be a small town, but Reverend Dobson did not consider that the size of his flock meant that the archbishop should infringe upon his ecclesiastical authority. He did not approve of hasty marriages.

"This is most irregular," he stated. He was suffering from a bad cold and wanted nothing to do with something that looked very much like an elopement.

In fact, he was growing a bit cynical about weddings in general, having seen too many in the last years that were (in his opinion) entered into for the wrong reasons. So he ushered the couple into his study with the firm intention to turn them down, archbishop or no archbishop.

Clearly, they were gently born, and of comfortable means. They could travel down the road to someone else's parish. He was not the man to put together couples who married without the approval of their family or without due attention to the gravity of the ceremony.

"Lady Grace," he said now, repeating it. He'd never met the daughter of a duke before, but he was pleasantly surprised. She didn't seem terribly high in the instep. In fact, she was holding hands with her beau, quite as if they were the butcher and his beloved.

"My father is the Duke of Ashbrook," she said, nodding.

"And Mr. Barry," he said, turning to her fiancé.

"Yes." No title. That was interesting.

"Lady Grace, is your family aware of your intention to marry?"

She smiled at him, her eyes clear. "Yes, they are, Reverend. My mother obtained the special license you have before you."

Against his better judgment, he actually believed her. He would have thought a daughter of the Duke of Ashbrook would be married by a bishop, rather than by special license. But what did he know of polite society?

Very little.

"Mr. Barry, do you have the means to support a wife in the manner to which she is accustomed by birth?"

Barry met his eyes straight on. "I am unworthy of Lady Grace in every way possible. My birth is humble in comparison, my patrimony minimal. However, I was recently discharged from the Royal Navy. As captain of the *Daedalus*, I was lucky enough to be awarded three purses. I will be able to support my wife without aid from her family."

Dobson had no doubt the man had been a fierce officer. He had the look of a warrior. And again, his eye was caught by the way the two held hands, so tightly . . . almost desperately . . . certainly tenderly.

Lady Grace beamed at him. "Mr. Barry was the youngest officer ever to be made captain in the Royal Navy. He is the adopted son of Sir Griffin Barry, and far too humble in recounting his station."

"So you are Captain Barry and Lady Grace Ryburn?"

Barry shook his head. "I have been granted an honorable discharge. It's Mr. Barry now."

Again Dobson's eyes were drawn to the hands so tightly clasped before him. Barry must have been injured, some disability that didn't show. Dobson began to feel a bit more sympathetic. "Marriage," he observed, "is one of the most weighty ceremonies in a man's life."

"Nothing will ever be more important to me," Mr. Barry said quietly.

Dobson cleared his throat. He wasn't accustomed to this sort of emotion. "As it says in the Lord's book, to everything there is a season, a time for every purpose under heaven." He paused, organizing his thoughts. This pair, charming though they were, ought to return to their own parish and post banns. A ceremony without friends or family was no way to start a life together.

Lady Grace spoke before he could continue. "Mr. Barry has received His Majesty's highest commendations for bravery. But now the time has come when he need not defend our shores. Finally, I have him home with me."

There was nothing Dobson could say to that. She'd voided his argument. And honestly, even in the midst of a wretched cold, he no longer cared to refuse their request. The eyes of these two made him remember why he became a priest in the first place.

He rose without another word, and escorted them into the church.

After he donned his tippet and cross, he called them to the altar, summoning his churchwarden and housekeeper to act as witnesses. The couple came before him still holding hands.

For a reason he hardly understood, he chose a different Bible verse from that which he generally read in the performance of the sacrament.

"And Ruth said, 'Entreat me not to leave thee, or to return from following after thee: for whither thou goest, I will go; and where thou lodgest, I will lodge: thy people shall be my people, and thy God my God: Where thou diest, will I die, and there will I be buried.'"

Reverend Dobson never forgot this particular wedding. It restored some deep part of his soul that had grown hungry, and small, and come near to being cynical.

When he finally pronounced the words, "I declare thee man and wife," the joy in Mr. and Mrs. Barry's faces was enough to bring tears to his eyes.

He kept the memory of that marriage in his mind. It wasn't often that he saw two people whom he considered to be blessed by their love for each other. It was a salutary reminder of God's gifts on earth. In his more fanciful moments, he even thought that the name of the bride was a message in itself.

"God resisteth the proud," he would tell himself, thinking of the soldier's dark, haunted eyes, "but giveth grace unto the humble."

Twenty-four

$\mathcal{A}$rbor House was completely empty, since the Barrys were still abroad, and the servants had been sent home for a holiday. Colin told his coachman to put the horses snug in the stables and then find lodging in the village and be back in the morning.

They woke in the big, silent house and ate porridge for breakfast—ably cooked by Colin, who had learned such things at sea—after which Grace retreated to the summerhouse to paint, and Colin walked to the village to find help.

Winkle was small, with only a few streets, graced by names such as Dew Street and the unforgettable Cockermouth Lane. Colin strolled down High Street, enjoying the sunshine warm on his shoulders. *This* was what he missed by being at sea . . . that sense of lasting peace one found in an English village, where life moved slowly and at a—

"Dang blast it!" a voice screeched from a narrow street that ran to the left of the baker's shop. "If you ain't the nastiest beast I ever saw, then I'm not fit to be a— You blasted whoreson, don't you kick me again, or I'll slice off your berries with a rusty knife!"

At the first harsh syllable, Colin's entire body slammed into alert and he flung himself into the shelter of a wall. His heart was pounding and he was flooded with a feeling of rage and fear.

Bloody hell.

The street remained quiet, but a stream of vitriol continued to pour from the darkish alley. Slowly Colin forced himself to relax, toe by toe and then finger by finger. He wasn't at sea. There was no danger here, merely a foul mouthed, abusive Englishman.

Finally he took a deep breath. He felt nauseated, and his forehead was covered with beads of sweat. Still, the man raged on.

When his heartbeat was more or less back to normal, Colin straightened and moved away toward the street. He felt like a damned fool, but thankfully, no one had seen him hurtling himself against the wall like a five-year-old frightened by a clap of thunder.

He made himself walk toward the shouting. He could hear the sound of blows now, along with curses. He pulled himself together: he didn't care what sort of man or beast was being visited with this abuse, he wouldn't stand for it.

It was a horse, a huge, gaunt chestnut.

As Colin entered the alley, the horse tried to wheel and kick the man holding his reins, undaunted by the blows landing on his back. With utter disgust, Colin realized that the man was wielding a thick wooden club, striking the horse on the shoulders when he could, dragging the reins back to the ground by hanging on them, so he could hit the animal again.

In a moment, Colin had skirted the horse and jerked the reins away while he simultaneously leveled a kick at the man's crotch.

Direct hit.

The man dropped in mid-curse, his eyes rolling into his head as he clutched his genitals and curled into a ball.

Then Colin looked up the horse, which had taken advantage of the situation to rear again, his hooves flailing the air as he tried to escape.

But Colin's arm was pure muscle after years at sea. He gave the reins a hard jerk and the horse landed back on the cobblestones with a jarring thump. Then he gave the animal one stern look. "No."

The horse's face was wet with sweat and froth; his eyes were filled with terror and rage. The idiot at his feet had managed some solid blows to the shoulder, because Colin saw a streak of blood along with wood chips and dark sweat.

Colin wound the reins around his hand, keeping the horse's head close to him. "No more," he said quietly. The beast made a huffing noise and tried to back away, shaking his head violently.

Just then the fool on the ground managed to stagger to his feet, hand still cupped over his privates. "Who the devil are you?" he screamed, his voice rising higher into the air.

Colin noticed that some villagers had finally noticed the noise; a baker in a white apron was walking from the far end of the alley, followed by a few others. He ignored the man's question. "What in the devil were you doing to this animal." He made it a statement, not a question; they both knew the answer.

"Beating what is mine," the man cried, staggering forward and trying to snatch the reins. "That limb of Satan is mine, and if I want to strike it dead in front of the church, I'll do it. You give me back my horse!"

The baker stopped, hands on his hips. "Joshua Bunbutt, you are no more than a drunken rogue, beating that horse in such an unprincipled manner. You ought to be ashamed of yourself."

"Well, I ain't," Bunbutt said, with a snarl that raised his top lip in a remarkably unattractive fashion. "You can throw me in the jug when you decide I've drunk a bit more than you fools consider necessary, but you can't stop me from dealing with a problem that I *own*. So just take your sanctimonious arse back into the bakery, Wadd."

He swung back to Colin. "Give me back my reins, you son of a—"

"I wouldn't," Colin said softly.

Bunbutt obviously caught the likelihood of violent engagement in Colin's eyes; he fell back a step. "Look here," he said with a bit of a whine, "just give me the damned horse and I'll take him home with me."

"Home!" the baker snorted. "You haven't got a home, you old scoundrel. Your missus told everyone in the church the other day that she's kicked you out. She's a decent woman, and you've worn her to a nub."

"My wife is none of your business!" Bunbutt said, his voice rising again. "She's another limb of Satan. I've got nothing but betrayal on all sides."

"How much?" Colin asked.

He could hear the horse breathing harshly behind him but he had settled, and was merely moving from hoof to hoof. It sounded as if he wore only three shoes.

"I ain't selling him," Bunbutt shouted. His cheeks were turning red again. "I know your game! You're trying to take away my livelihood, and then you'll let me starve by the side of the road. An' my *Christian* wife will walk by and spit on my head. I'll take my horse!"

He charged forward again, so Colin gave him a stiff uppercut to the jaw.

"I'll have the parish constable on you!" Bunbutt cried, reeling backward, a dribble of blood coming from his mouth.

Colin took out a gold sovereign and tossed it, deliberately, so that it fell on the ground between them.

Bunbutt's eyes followed the flash of gold to where it lay on the cobblestones. "Yer trying to buy me horse for a measly—"

Another followed.

"That animal isn't worth more than two," the baker said, stepping forward. "The poor thing has been abused by this fool here for the past three years." He turned and poked Bunbutt in the chest. "And no saying where you got him from. He's too fine an animal for you to own, and we all said so from the first. You stole him!"

"I did not!" Bunbutt screamed.

Colin threw a third sovereign.

"That's too much," the baker said.

"I'll take another!" Bunbutt said greedily. "You want this horse, you have to pay for him. And pay good. He's a fine animal, of a championship pedigree."

Colin didn't give a damn what pedigree the horse had. What he saw was a dumb beast, beaten and abused by a drunken, uncaring bastard. In fact, the world would be a better place without Bunbutt.

The man must have seen that thought in his eyes because he suddenly dropped to his knees and scrabbled for the sovereigns.

"He's yours, then!" he said shrilly, backing away so sharply that he struck the baker.

"Faugh, you smell!" the baker said, thrusting him aside.

"I hope that limb of Satan kicks you just as you kicked me. God will make sure of it."

"God!" the baker scoffed. "As if he'd know the difference between you and a common stone on the ground."

"Leave," Colin stated. "You no longer belong in Winkle."

Bunbutt leaned forward and spat. "That's what I think of you." Then he turned around and ran, with an odd stumbling gait, from the alley.

"You paid too much for that horse," the baker said. "Though it was an earthly kindness of you to rescue it. I doubt it's good for more than the rag-and-bones man."

"We'll see," Colin said. He unwound the reins from his hand. "I'm Sir Griffin Barry's son, and I just came to Arbor House last night with my wife. I need a woman to cook and clean, since there are no servants in residence at the moment."

"Mrs. Busbee does for Sir Griffin," the baker said immediately. "I'll send a boy and she'll be there in an hour or so."

Colin walked the horse back to Arbor House. When he arrived, he took it around to the stables, discovering that Grimble had already come back from the village to care for the carriage horses.

"I'll wash him down," Grimble said, eyeing the animal with a dubious expression. "He does have nice flanks for all he's too thin, and an excellent fetlock. It might be that you can sell him for a pretty penny once he's cleaned up, and those wounds have healed." He carefully felt the horse's shoulder while Colin held the reins tight. "Nothing broken. He's a lucky fellow."

"I'll groom him," Colin said, backing the horse into a stall. "You deal with the other horses, Grimble."

Then Colin leaned against the half door and

waited. Long minutes passed before the horse looked up.

"You're a mess," Colin said conversationally, making no move to touch him. "You're covered with sweat and dirt, there's dried blood on your right shoulder, your mane looks as if a bird shat in it, and even your eyelashes are tangled."

The horse lowered his head again, his head hanging so low that his nose touched the straw. Colin fetched a bucket of oats, but the moment he put an arm over the door to pour it in his trough, the horse's head whipped up and he reared straight into the air.

Colin ignored him and poured the oats. "You look as if you're trying to fly," he told the animal. "I believe I'll name you after my former ship, the *Daedalus*. The ship was named after a Greek man who flew too close to the sun for comfort, but made it back to earth."

The horse ignored him. He had all four hooves on the floor again, his sides heaving, a fresh coating of dark sweat on his neck. After a good four minutes, Daedalus lowered his head and began to eat.

"Grimble!" Colin called. "I've given him a name: Daedalus."

"That's a fancy one, sir," Grimble said, coming to stand at his side. "Foreign-like, isn't it? Shall we tie him close and I'll wash him down?"

Colin shook his head. "I don't think there's much chance of infection since the wound closed so quickly. We'll leave him for the night, Grimble."

"It don't seat right with me," the coachman said, staring at the horse. "Leaving a good horse in that condition."

"He doesn't care about dirt as much as he cares about not being struck again. Perhaps tomorrow. For now, let's just let him get used to us. Bring him some hay and mash, will you?"

He stood at the door for a few more minutes before telling Daedalus that he had to find his wife. The horse's ears twitched, although he didn't look up. "I'll be back tomorrow morning. And the morning after that. And no one will hit you ever again."

The horse lipped his oats, weary with fear and pain.

Colin walked back to the house, thinking about parallels that were too obvious to be ignored.

Mrs. Busbee was already in the house. She had made tea and was scrubbing the kitchen. She was disturbed by Colin's refusal to allow servants to stay in the house at night. But finally she laid out supper in the kitchen, and promised to return the following morning with some women to help her do a thorough cleaning.

"Though how you'll get along by yourselves, I don't know," she told him. "It isn't natural having Quality doing as such by themselves."

Colin just smiled. Once she left, he brought a silver tray down to the lakeshore and served tea.

And then he seduced his wife under the shade of the willow.

Afterward, Grace lay on the grass, her head on

Colin's leg, and watched the late afternoon sun cast shadows of thin spears over his dark limbs and her pale ones. In her opinion, it wasn't possible to be any happier than this.

That was before supper.

Colin put aside his plate after they finished Mrs. Busbee's pie. Then he took out a sheaf of paper.

"What is that?" Grace asked, made tipsy by the combination of an excellent wine and too much sun.

"A letter," he said. He looked up at her, his eyes glittering over the sheet. "Years ago, I received just such a letter."

She took a closer look and burst into laughter. "That's the one I sent you after Lily cut the fingers off my gloves."

"Your very first," he said, smoothing it on the table. "As you can probably see, it's been read two or three hundred times, Grace."

The laughter died in her throat.

"I never had the time or the courage to write you a proper response, though I might have jotted down a line or two. This afternoon I wrote you the letter I should have sent, had I been braver and you a bit older. God help me, I remember that week far too clearly."

He began to read.

Dearest Grace,

I'm sorry about your gloves. I would love to buy you some more, but as a lowly midshipman, I'm not al-

lowed to leave the ship when it docks. This last week was rather horrible for me, too, but for different reasons. We encountered a ship full of slavers. I think that we probably could have avoided an actual battle by boarding it in an orderly manner, but Captain Persticle is eager to sink ships. You see, the navy gives you a prize if you defeat an enemy ship. We did sink it, after a battle that seemed hours long, but turned out only to take forty minutes. Unfortunately, the quartermaster, Mr. Heath, who has two little boys at home, was caught by a bullet fired by one of our own sailors. And the slaves . . . the slavers threw them all overboard.

He took a drink of wine. Grace took a deep breath and held out her glass; he refilled it for her. She sipped wine that smelled like flowers, while Colin's steady voice told the story of how Mr. Heath died, and what he had said about his children the day before.

He paused, looked at her. "Are you all right?"

"Yes." Grace was holding his left hand tightly. "I am so glad to know of Mr. Heath, Colin. And to hear of his children. And those poor African people. It is *important*."

He didn't say anything, just nodded, but his voice lost a bit of its impassiveness. Her letter had been one sheet; his was five sheets.

The next day he worked with Daedalus all morning and then, in the afternoon, he wrote a letter to Mr. Heath's wife and children. After that, he found Grace's next letter, and answered it. His was more than eight pages long, and much of it was difficult to hear. Grace cried, because Colin did not (but should, in her opinion).

The next night he did, though. Just a tear, but she thought it was a priceless tear. He told her, in that letter, what it was like to kill someone. The man had jerked upward as the bullet hit him, and then collapsed, falling to the ground, one leg twisted underneath him, staring at the sky. He had written about what it was like to know that someone—some mother's son, no matter how despicable—was dead by your own hand.

And he wrote about the ordinary moments when he would think he saw the man walking across the deck, shoulders hunched, walking somewhere fast, as if he had a place to be. A person to meet.

That night Colin didn't dream of blood.

A fortnight or so later, Grace woke in the night and propped herself on an elbow, looking at Colin's face by moonlight. It was shadowed and hollowed by all that had happened to him.

As she watched, a smile shaped his lips. "Come here," he murmured, pulling her down onto his chest.

The letters were helping, and so was she; she knew that truth deep in her bones. Death stood on one side, and she on the other. Every time they made love, every morning he spent taming Daedalus, every afternoon he spent writing, every evening when he read aloud another letter, every time he teased her or asked her a question about one of her paintings, she dragged him farther onto her side.

The side with life in it, not death.

She came out of that kiss a little breathless. Sometimes they just looked at each other and that was all it took. He would roll on top of her.

This night they didn't say a word, and yet he didn't tuck her underneath him. Instead, he lifted her so that she was poised above him. She fumbled, learning this new way of making love, thinking about the fact that he was not protecting her. Not afraid for her.

Colin thought about the same thing, though neither felt the need to say it aloud. He felt free to allow the person he loved most in the world to sit on him, pale, lovely breasts glazed by moonlight, her head thrown back.

He wasn't afraid.

Grace was his, and life was good.

And he wasn't afraid.

Epilogue

Ten years later
Arbor House

*B*y late summer, Portia was almost nine and the rest of them were a little or a lot younger. There were many children, a whole tribe of them. That's what their mamas called them. A pack of wolves, their papas said.

That August they rocketed about Arbor House, all the children whose grandfathers had been pirates, though Portia felt that *she* was the most important. Both of her grandfathers had been pirates, and her papa had also been a fierce sea captain. What's more, she was the oldest of all of them.

She had the sea in her blood, and sometimes, if she lay very still at night, with one ear pressed into her mattress, she could even hear the sound of waves.

If that wasn't the sign that the sea was in her blood, what could it be?

But now August was coming to an end, and pretty soon everyone would have to go back to their homes because no one lived at Arbor House, except in the summer. Mama said (and Grandmother agreed) that the house had grown old from being battered by too many children.

Portia loved Arbor House with a passion, and she meant to live there when she grew older. The back garden was full of half-wild barn cats, and there were nettles in the fields that smelled like black currants. Her mother spent her days painting by the lake instead of tucked away in her studio.

And her papa was always there, too. This summer he had taught her how to shoot a bow and arrow, and how to tie a slipknot. She didn't really want to live on a boat, but those skills would be useful in case she ever capsized at sea and landed on a desert island. Portia liked to plan ahead. Her mother said that she inherited that from her grandmother, the duchess.

This particular afternoon Portia had organized her troupe of eight—all the children who had learned to speak—to put on a play she had written herself. It was a very patriotic play, in which the queen (played by Portia) would quell the rascally pirates (played by the boys), with the help of her sister, who happened to be her twin. Twin or not, Portia was eleven minutes older than Emily, and liked to think that those eleven minutes were very important.

All the parents had gathered in the courtyard, ready to watch the play. Four mamas sat together, laughing, wearing gowns of strawberry pink and pale green. Portia's papa was leaning against the wall, talking to his father, who used to be a pirate, but was now an earl. There was a lot of champagne being poured.

She clapped her hands, but she couldn't get her audience to settle down until her father finally barked at them.

The play opened with Edmond, who, at two and a half years old, was as fat as a pigeon, and had rather a waddle. Portia knew it was just his nappy, but even so, she was glad that he was her cousin and not her brother. Edmond was supposed to start the rebellion by shooting an arrow at the queen, but of course they couldn't give him a real weapon. So he ended up throwing a twig in the air, then picking it up and giving it to his mother.

Portia had to explain what had just happened— an assassination attempt followed an attack on Her Majesty's Royal Navy (the entire fleet ably represented by Emily). It wasn't easy to be a playwright when her actors couldn't remember their lines or shoot arrows properly. She had grown used to narrating the story, because her audience was often unable to follow.

By the time she got around to explaining the middle of the play, her father had moved from where he was leaning against the wall and scooped up her mother. She was sitting on his lap now, leaning against his shoulder.

Her mother and father were mad for each other, which meant they kissed when they thought no one was looking. And if someone caught them, her father would laugh and tell them that his wife had saved his life. Sometimes he was talking about a pitcher of water she threw over his head, and sometimes it had to do with the time Papa was in the navy. The facts were unimportant.

It was just one of those things that papas said.

"Go on," she told the band of pirates, who were all armed with wooden daggers clenched in their teeth, or at least what teeth they had. Her cousin Cedric was missing almost all of his in front. "It's your turn. Yell and run about, but don't forget that when Emily points her rifle at you, you have to fall over and play dead."

It was a little irritating how long they each took to die, especially Cedric. Finally, she hissed at him until he stopped twitching and she was able to straighten her crown, put her foot on his stomach, and shout, "Huzzah!" while Emily pranced about with her sword in the air.

Everyone clapped in a very satisfactory fashion, even though Emily had forgotten a couple of lines of her victory speech, which made Portia cross. She had written the whole piece in iambic pentameter, which they learned all about in the spring by studying Shakespeare, and that wasn't easy.

Since she meant to be a writer someday, she knew it was important to master these things. Later that night, in the nursery, she pointed out that Emily could have tried harder.

"You're a despot," Emily said, looking up from her book and scowling at her.

"I'm an enlightened despot," Portia retorted. She had just learned that term, and she rather liked it. "Why do you think that all the fathers fell about laughing when Cedric said he was a warrior?" she asked. "I didn't think it was so funny."

"They were drunk, that's what Nanny said."

"Papa was not drunk!"

"Not Papa," Emily said with a shrug. "But the other uncles. And maybe Grandpa, too."

"Which one?"

"The duke," Emily said. "He was laughing very hard, and then he gave the duchess a kiss on her ear—I saw him. That's not the way that dukes are supposed to behave."

"He never behaves like a duke," Portia said, dismissing that as evidence. "Look at that portrait Mama made of him—the one in the National Gallery. He looks more like a robber baron than a duke."

"Do you suppose," Emily asked, "that they still do . . . *that*?" She waved her hand.

Portia frowned at her. They had just learned about *that* from the laundry maid, and while it was rather fascinating to contemplate, obviously no one as old as their grandparents did anything of that nature. "Of course not!" she whispered. "Be careful Nanny doesn't hear you, or we'll be in trouble."

"Grandpa looked as if he liked kissing Grandma," Emily said.

Portia thought about it. The laundry maid had explained about how a husband and wife fit together like puzzle pieces and then kissed, which resulted in children. It seemed rather undignified, and she was pretty sure that their parents had done it only a very few times.

She couldn't imagine the duke and duchess doing such a thing, though one had to suppose they had when they were young. "Perhaps Grandmama and Grandpa on the other side," she decided. "Grandpa the earl. They . . ." She hesitated, not sure how to explain what she meant.

"They like each other quite a lot," Emily said. "Do you suppose that we'll do that when we're as old as they are? Grandpa the duke must be, oh, one hundred years old or even more. Parts of his hair are quite silver."

"Don't be silly," Portia replied. "He told me once that Grandmother *stupefied* him."

"What does that mean?"

"Makes him go to sleep," she explained. "You can't be kissing and so on, if you're asleep."

Portia often knew the answers to questions like that, which was proper given that she was oldest. Just now she didn't want to talk any longer, so she pushed the window in the nursery open and hung over the sill, smelling the country air. Bats were darting about as if they were weaving lace in the sky.

Her father's favorite horse, Daedalus, had escaped from the stables again and was munching on the grass under the shelter of a willow; he would probably end up sleeping there all night. No one worried about Daedalus running away, because he was old and fat and very sweet. All the children had taken their first ride on his back.

Down by the lake Portia saw the pale green of her mother's gown. She was with Papa, of course, and as Portia watched, he pulled her into his arms. They must be kissing, though she couldn't see that far in the hazy light. Their bodies were so close together that they looked like one person. There was something about the way Papa held their mother tightly, as if she were very precious, that made Portia happy down to the bottom of her stomach.

"What's out there?" Emily said, coming up behind her.

Portia pointed, even though ladies don't point.

"Ridiculous," Emily said with a huff of disgust. "That'll end in another baby, mark my words, Portia."

And it did.

Want more Eloisa James?
Continue reading for a sneak peek
at her next fantastic fairy-tale romance

Once Upon a Tower

Coming Soon
from Avon Books

$\mathcal{G}$owan Stoughton of Craigievar, Duke of Kinross, not to mention chieftain of Clan MacAulay, loathed rooms crowded with Englishmen. He had a fixed conviction that they were all babbling gossips with more earwax than brains. As his father would have said.

Though Shakespeare said it first.

Yet here he was, entering a ballroom in the middle of London, rather than at home in the Highlands, as he preferred. The moment he was announced, a cluster of women swiveled toward him, each face flaunting a gleaming array of teeth. To his mind they all looked constipated, though more likely the smiles were a knee-jerk response to his title. He was, after all, an unmarried nobleman in possession of all his teeth. Hair, too. He had more hair than most Englishmen. And a castle.

He managed to avoid meeting any particular lady's eyes by looking resolutely over their heads. That wasn't hard since he was a giant by comparison with most of them, not only taller than the average Englishman, but broader in the shoulder and thigh. He'd always found his height and breadth useful in abetting the requisite attitude of ducal indifference.

The Earl of Gilchrist was waiting at the bottom of the steps, so the rapacious ladies did not instantly pounce. Gowan liked Gilchrist: he was stern but fair, with a brooding gaze that was almost Scottish. They were both interested in financial markets, unlike most gentlemen, and the earl was a damned fine investor. Since Gowan was a governor of the Bank of Scotland and Gilchrist held a similar post in the Bank of England, they'd exchanged a good deal of correspondence over the last couple of years or so, though they'd rarely met.

"Your Grace, may I introduce my countess?" Gilchrist asked, drawing his lady forward. Rather surprisingly, the countess appeared to be in her mid-twenties, significantly younger than her husband. What's more, she had sensual, full lips, and lush breasts framed by a bodice made of a twist of rosy silk—by all appearances, one of those aristocratic women who emulated the attire and manner of an opera dancer.

Whereas Gilchrist resembled nothing so much

as a Puritan preacher from the 1600s. Surely that could not be a harmonious pairing.

The countess was talking about her stepdaughter, so he bowed and expressed his ineffable pleasure at the idea of dancing with Lady Edith.

Edith. What an awful name.

A long-tongued person would have that name. A fusty nut, a flap-eared . . . *Englishwoman*.

Without warning, Lady Gilchrist slid her arm through his so he might accompany her to the adjacent reception chamber; he just stopped himself from flinching. When he was young, servants were always hovering about him, adjusting his clothing, touching his neck, wiping his mouth. But after the age of fourteen or so, he had suffered no such intimacies unless absolutely required.

Since he had very little time alone, he preferred to maintain a small barrier between himself and the world. He wasn't lamenting his lack of privacy; he felt it would be a waste of time to dress, for example, without hearing his secretary's report at the same time. If there was anything that Gowan hated, it was wasting time.

Time wasted itself, in his opinion. All too soon, and out of the blue, you toppled over and died, and your moments were all gone.

It would be rank foolishness to pretend that those moments were infinite and endless, which—in his opinion—was precisely what people were doing when they dawdled about in a bath or spent hours lazing about reading a piece of fiction.

This ball was a case in point. He wanted to ask

Gilchrist's opinion as regards a knotty point about the fate of the one-pound note before returning to Scotland on the morrow; Gilchrist was giving a ball, which young ladies would attend; it was time to embark on the marital part of his life.

Ergo, two birds with one stone. He preferred four birds with the same stone, but sometimes one had to settle for less.

The only problem was that the room was filled with Englishwomen, and he wasn't sure it would be a good idea to marry one of those. A Scottish nobleman always had good reason to tie himself to one of the great houses of England.

But an English lass was, perforce, *English*.

Theirs was an indolent race, as everyone knew. Their gentlewomen sat about doing naught but drinking tea, while their Scottish counterparts thought nothing of running an estate with a thousand sheep at the same time they raised four children—and without the help of five nannies, either.

His grandmother hadn't been of that lazy frame of mind, and neither was he. If reading was to be done, she had always said that it should be for improvement of the mind. The Bible or Shakespeare, with a dusting of the classics.

Gowan rather thought a good work ethic was his sole requirement in a bride (other than the obvious—that she be beautiful, maidenly, and well-bred). The future Duchess of Kinross could not be a time waster.

The thought brought with it a faint prickle of

unease. Wooing was not an activity at which he considered himself likely to excel. Shakespeare would be no help, unless he discovered that one of his grooms was in reality a young lady in breeches. His grooms leaned toward hairy, burly clansmen, so he was probably out of luck there.

Still, strictly speaking, he needn't waste time courting his chosen wife. Lady Gilchrist had towed him through the ballroom and now entered a large chamber crowded with people uninterested in dancing. One quick glance told him that there was no unmarried man present—and likely only three in all London, other than royalty—who matched him in wealth or title.

Marriage was merely a market like any other; when he found the right lady, he would simply bid higher than his rivals.

The countess's hand slipped from his arm, and she introduced her stepdaughter in a low, rather sultry voice. He was thinking about the countess's sensuality and her lord's brusque lack of it as he focused on the woman who stood before him.

It was the sort of moment that cleaves the past from the present, changing the future forever.

Lady Edith didn't belong in an overheated English ballroom. There was something magical about her, as if she was fairy-born and dreaming of her home under a hill. Her eyes were deep pools of dark green, the color of the loch below his castle on a stormy day.

He stood frozen, like a great lummox, drinking her in. She was delightfully curved, with hair that glimmered like the golden apples of the sun. It was pulled up on her head, and all he wanted was to unwrap that hair and make love to her on a bed of Scottish heather.

But it was her eyes that caught him: they met his with a kind of curious disinterest, a dreamy peacefulness that showed none of the feverish interest with which unmarried young ladies generally looked at him.

Gowan did not consider himself a man who was carnally given. A duke, to his mind, had no right to play the fool with women.

He had watched with amusement as men of his acquaintance fell at the feet of a woman with a saucy smile and a round bottom. He had felt pity, as he did for the earl with his lush wife.

But all of a sudden, love and its attendant poetry made sense. Looking down at Gilchrist's daughter, a line came to him as if it had been written for that moment: *I ne'er saw true beauty till this night . . .*

Maybe Shakespeare was useful for something after all.

Lady Edith's rosy mouth curved into a smile. She dropped into a deep curtsy, bending her head. "Your Grace, it is a pleasure to meet you."

To Gowan, it was as if the earl and his wife had ceased to exist; indeed, a room full of people faded to pale wallpaper. "The pleasure is all mine," he said, meaning every word. "May I have the honor of your hand in this dance?" He held out his hand.

His gesture was not met by rippling excitement, but by a composure that drew him as surely as excitement repelled him. He wanted nothing more than to make those serene eyes light for *him*, to see admiration, even adoration, in her gaze.

She inclined her head, and took his hand. Her touch actually burned through their gloves, as if it warmed some part of his chest that had been cold until this moment. Rather than flinch away, he had the impulse to pull her closer.

He drew her fingers into the crook of his arm, and met Gilchrist's eyes, registering her father's approval. When they reached the ballroom, the dance kept separating him from Edith and then bringing them back together. They had reached the bottom of the ballroom before Gowan realized that they hadn't exchanged a word.

He had been taught to make polite conversation. A whole drawing room full of people unsettled by the presence of a duke could be put at ease with a few well-chosen words.

But young ladies did not usually need his input. Generally, they smiled feverishly, their eyes sending sparkling messages, words tumbling from their lips.

Not so Lady Edith.

She danced in his arms as lightly as the wave of the sea. And she was *quiet*. He couldn't remember the last person who'd been quiet in his presence, yet she seemed to feel no need—or inclination—to speak to him.

He was aware of a feeling of profound surprise.

They turned and began to proceed up the room again. He tried to think of what to say, but nothing came to mind. On the other hand, it occurred to him that it was the most comfortable silence of his entire life.

Gowan was no fool. He knew when life had just presented him with a fait accompli. Everything about Lady Edith Gilchrist was exquisite: her easy silence, her peacefulness, her enchanting face, the light way she danced, as if her toes hardly touched the ground.

She would make a perfect Duchess of Kinross. Already he could envision the portraits he would commission: one of the duchess alone, and then another of the four of them—or five? he would leave the number of children to his wife—to hang over the mantelpiece in the great drawing room.

The dance ended, and the strains of a waltz began.

Lady Edith was curtsying before him, preparing to return to her stepmother.

"Will you dance again?" His voice tumbled out without its usual measured tones.

She looked up at him, and then she said, "I'm afraid that this dance is promised to Viscount Standish—"

"No," he stated, though he'd never done such an impolite thing in this life.

"No?" Her eyes widened slightly.

"Waltz with me."

He held out his hand. She paused for a second, and then put her hand into his again. Carefully, as if he were taming a bird, he placed his hand on her waistline.

Who would have thought that all the romantic tripe about being burned by a lover's touch was true?

As they danced, Gowan was vaguely aware that the whole room was watching them. The Duke of Kinross was dancing twice in a row with Gilchrist's daughter. It would be all over London by the next morning.

He didn't care. His heart was thudding in his chest in tune with the music as he studied her slowly, feature by feature. She was utterly delicious, from the watery gold of her hair to the apple blossom flush in her cheeks.

Her feet and his moved in perfect harmony with the music. Gowan had never danced better in his life. They swept through the waltz like sparks thrown from a fire, neither of them uttering a word.

It occurred to him that they didn't need to. They were speaking through the dance itself.

Another thought came to him: He had never realized that he was lonely. Not until now.

The music drew to a halt, and he looked up to find Viscount Standish waiting at the side of the room.

"Duke," Standish said, a distinct chill in his voice. "I believe you mistook my dance for yours." He jutted his elbow toward Lady Edith with the air of a man ill-used.

She turned to Gowan with a polite smile of farewell, and slipped her hand into Standish's elbow.

Gowan found himself burning with the desire to wipe that smile from her face. He was a Scotsman: he didn't trade in that sort of politeness, not between a man and a woman. He wanted to tell her what he felt, snatch her behind a pillar, wind her in his arms and kiss her. Roughly. No, tenderly.

But she wasn't a Scotswoman . . . *yet*. He had to follow the rules until she was. He watched his future wife move into the dance on the viscount's arm.

Gowan had more money than Standish. What's more, Lady Edith's father had obviously asked him to the ball for reasons that had nothing to do with whether the English government reimbursed its banknotes with gold sovereigns or not.

And he was better-looking than the viscount. Unless Edith liked that slender, twiglike look. He frowned, thinking about her feelings on the matter.

He couldn't say that she had looked at him with desire.

Of course, one wouldn't want a lustful duchess. His father had met his mother at a formal dinner and had known instantly that she would be the next duchess, even though she was only fifteen and shy for her age. One didn't want one's future duchess to be gazing at strange men through a glaze of lust.

He would return to the house in the morning to pay a call. That was part of the marriage rituals in England. Go to the house three or four times, take her for a drive, and then ask Gilchrist for her hand in marriage.

Once that was settled in his mind, he searched out the earl and broached the subject of pound notes. Their work concluded, he said, "I'll stop by on the morrow to pay a call on your daughter before I return to Scotland."

Again he saw approval in the earl's eyes, and thanked God for the title he didn't really give a damn about. For the first time in his life, he felt blessed to have it, and the money, and the castle.

He did not dance with any other women. He didn't have any inclination to do that, and he certainly didn't want to lean at the side of the room and watch Edith dance with other men. The very thought made his jaw set.

Jealousy was the downfall of his nation. But it was the flip side of their greatest virtue—loyalty. A Scotsman is loyal until death: unlike fickle English husbands, he would never turn from his chosen bride and seek other beds.

Still, Gowan knew he was a damned possessive bastard, who put loyalty above all else. It would eat him alive to watch Edith moving from man to man before he had a ring on her finger that told the world she was his.

And if not a ring, his imprint on her soul.

Instead of spending the evening snarling at Edith's suitors, he went home and composed a message to his London solicitor, Jelves, to be sent directly to the man's house. The note stated he planned to marry in the immediate future, and directed Jelves to draw up a suggested settlement and bring it to his door in the early morning.

The task would probably keep the solicitor up

all night; Gowan made a mental note to send him a bonus.

The next morning he rose at dawn and spent several hours working. A night's sleep hadn't changed his mind about Lady Edith—not that he could recall ever changing his mind about something important. So he gave a concentrated hour to the question of marital settlements. He and the solicitor drew up a settlement that Jelves rather nervously suggested might be overly generous.

"Lady Edith will be my duchess," Gowan told the man, knowing his eyes had gone wintry. "She will be my better half. Why would I stint what she will own after my death, or enjoy during my life? We don't treat our women with the disdain you do in this country. Even if she and I have only one daughter, that daughter will inherit my title."

He must have come close to baring his teeth, because Jelves swallowed and bobbed his head.

Gowan was running late, damn it. He had to be on the coach road out of London in a matter of two hours at the very least. Instructing his retinue to follow in the second coach and wait for him, he directed his coachman to return to Curzon Street.

The Gilchrist butler took his cloak and informed him that the countess and Lady Edith would shortly join their guests. Then he opened the door to a large and gracious drawing room that currently resembled nothing so much as a gentlemen's club.

Men were everywhere, posies and bouquets of

flowers by their side, laughing among themselves. There was even a game of cards going on in one corner. He only recognized half of them. What's more, it hadn't occurred to him to send someone to buy roses or anything of that nature.

"If you would join the morning callers, Your Grace," the butler said, "I will serve refreshments very shortly."

Standish was there, decked out in an orange coat with garish buttons. Lord Pimrose-Finsbury was there as well. Pimrose-Finsbury wasn't in the nobility, but he owned most of the East End. He held a delicate little nosegay made of violets.

Gowan turned on his heel and walked back into the entry.

"Would Your Grace prefer to leave a card?" the butler asked, following him.

"I would prefer to speak to Lord Gilchrist. When did Lady Edith debut?" he asked bluntly.

The butler gaped in a very undignified fashion. "Last night," he said. "She debuted last night."

He wasn't the only man who had taken one look at Edith and pictured her in his bed.

But Gowan now knew precisely why Gilchrist had asked him to attend his ball: the invitation had included the gift of his daughter's hand. There would be no competition if he chose to take up the earl's silent offer.

"If you would inform His Lordship that I would like to speak to him." He didn't ask. Gowan never asked; he stated. He found it didn't make any difference, since he always got what he wanted. And there was something lowering about *asking*.

Dukes, in his opinion, didn't ask.

They stated.

He had a shrewd feeling that there would be no *asking* with regard to Lady Edith's hand, either.

Give in to your Impulses!

These unforgettable stories only take a second to buy and give you hours of reading pleasure!

Go to *www.AvonImpulse.com* and see what we have to offer.

Available wherever e-books are sold.

AVON**IMPULSE**